THE YEW
and
THE ROSE

A 17th Century Life

by
Lizzie Jones

**Grosvenor House
Publishing Limited**

All rights reserved
Copyright © Lizzie Jones, Prince Rupert hys Vangarde 2016

The right of Lizzie Jones to be identified as the author of this
work has been asserted in accordance with Section 78
of the Copyright, Designs and Patents Act 1988

The book cover picture is copyright to Neil Howlett,
Prince Rupert hys Vangarde 2016

This book is published by
Grosvenor House Publishing Ltd
28-30 High Street, Guildford, Surrey, GU1 3EL.
www.grosvenorhousepublishing.co.uk

This book is sold subject to the conditions that it shall not, by way of
trade or otherwise, be lent, resold, hired out or otherwise circulated
without the author's or publisher's prior consent in any form of binding or
cover other than that in which it is published and
without a similar condition including this condition being imposed
on the subsequent purchaser.

A CIP record for this book
is available from the British Library

ISBN 978-1-78623-036-2

Also by Lizzie Jones

Mr. Shakespeare's Whore
the story of Aemilia Bassano

The Tangled Knot
a novel of the English Civil War

On Wings of Eagles
the story of Ferdinando Stanley and Alice Spencer

The Minstrel's Girl
a novel of the 15th century

The yew is associated with grief,
hence its location often in churchyards.

❃

The rose is a universal symbol of love.

For Caroline, Patrick and Gavin,
Catherine and Stephanie,
Kate and Jessica,
Caitlin, Bethany and Kyle.

With the hope that they may realise
how fortunate they are

"I think that the poorest he that is in England has a life to live as much as the greatest he."

Thomas Rainsborough 1610–48

(Colonel in the army of Parliament)

Chapter 1

Summer 1678

He pulled the rough blanket up as far as it would go. It was thin but scratchy. His nightshirt wasn't long enough. Mama said James could have it and she would make him another one but she had been too busy. He tried to cover his ears because he didn't want to hear Mama and Papa arguing. In this last week they had argued a lot and now he could hear their angry raised voices soaring up the loft ladder to the low room beneath the thatch that was their bedchamber. The others were undisturbed, James curled up beside him and on the adjoining pallet little Eddy was wrapped in Mary's arms. But Richard couldn't sleep, not only because of the unaccustomed shouting but because he was anxious, his stomach cramped in a painful ball of fear. He wished he could talk about it to James but he was fast asleep and besides he was only five years old whereas Richard was seven.

Until these past few weeks they had all been happy together, as happy as they could be when they were poor. It was summertime so there was more food to be had and they didn't need such warm clothes, and his father had mended the hole in the thatch so the rain had stopped dripping into the loft. They had a good father. He didn't beat them as some fathers did, he whittled playthings for them – whistles, a poppet for Mary which Mama had dressed with some scraps of material, fishing rods for them to play in the river Douglas. At Yuletide he had made Richard a bow and some arrows. James had been jealous but their father said he wasn't old enough to shoot a bow safely so he had made him a wooden sword. Now that Richard was seven he sometimes accompanied his father when he worked in the fields in fine weather where he would help by picking out weeds and stones and sometimes be set to scare the birds. On Sundays when his father didn't have to work he would take them to the river and they would skim stones or sail reed boats. He had promised to hollow out some pieces of wood so they could have more permanent boats and race them. When the weather kept them indoors he taught Richard to play dice and knucklebones. And at night when they were abed Richard would be able to hear his parents talking and laughing together, especially as his father was teaching his mother to read and write, and sometimes she would sing softly as he played his pipe.

"Who's to blame for this madness, John Turner or your brother John?" his mother cried angrily.

There was silence for a time then his father began to speak again quietly. Richard climbed out of bed and went to sit on the top step of the loft ladder. The room below was in shadow though the summer evening light was still struggling through the tiny small-paned window so there was no need to burn a candle yet. Richard knew his mother didn't like to waste candles and besides the tallow ones, they couldn't afford wax, gave off an unpleasant smell. They saved money by using rush lights and Richard would help his mother make them, gathering the rushes which she then dipped in hot fat, but they didn't burn for long and only gave out a dim light.

"What is there in life for me here? Either sitting at a loom all day weaving cloth for others or eking out a wage by working dawn till dusk in the fields in summer for a pittance. Even the house we live in is dependent on my work, it will never be ours and if I lose my job I lose our house. I can't even move for a better job or more money, not even to the next village or I will be sent back and humiliated, as we have seen all too often. And Catholics are not supposed to move more than five miles anyway. What does life offer me, offer us."

"No Edward, the 'us' is an afterthought. You said it, twice, what does life offer *you*, that is all that matters, *you*. You have always been selfish, always thought mainly of yourself, though I didn't see it at first. You were thinking of yourself when you persuaded me to sleep with you when I was only sixteen and then we had to get married before Dickie was born even though you weren't quite of an age."

"No that isn't true, Marie, I loved you. I still love you and I thought you loved me."

"I did love you, passionately, and I still love you which is why I can't bear the thought of being without you. But you can't love me, or our children, or you wouldn't be thinking of leaving us now to fend for ourselves, God knows how."

"I would take you all with me if I could but it isn't possible you know that. It wouldn't be part of an agreement but more than that how could we subject the children to such a long perilous voyage, Eddy is still a baby, and even if it were possible to take *you* with me I know you would never leave the children behind. I will send for you all as soon as I am settled and have made some money. They say that when you have finished your contract you are given land of your own and it is easy to make money then."

"But you said a contract is usually for four years and how can we manage on our own till then?"

"You could live with our relatives for a time. The children would be old enough to join me then and in four years you would still only be twenty-seven, all our lives in front of us."

"But suppose I don't want to leave here to go and live in Maryland," Marie said.

"It's a Catholic county and we wouldn't be persecuted there. You heard what Master Nelson was saying at the Hall last Sunday that ill-feeling to us is building up now that the Duke of York has become a Catholic. Most people, especially those in positions of power, fear a Catholic king as King Charles has no children and his brother is his heir. They are spreading rumours that a Catholic revolution is being planned and there is talk about an army being raised." Richard Nelson, the owner of nearby Fairhurst Hall, had actually read part of a speech which the Jesuit Provincial, Thomas Whitbread, had given on his tour of the Jesuit training colleges in Flanders and which had been printed and circulated to Catholics in England. He had warned *"Can you undergo a harsh persecution? Are you content to be falsely betrayed and injured, and hurried away to prison? Can you be brought to the bar and hear yourself falsely sworn against?"*

"It might be a false alarm," Marie said hopefully.

"I don't think Master Nelson would have mentioned it if there hadn't been some substance. If there is anything going on then it will reflect seriously on us here in these parts because so many of our gentry are Catholics with mass centres in many of the Halls. And suppose the authorities begin to pry too closely and discover that Scarisbrick Hall is a secret training college for priests."

Richard didn't understand some of the words but he knew they were Catholics. They didn't go to the parish churches of Eccleston or Ormskirk on Sundays and feast days as many of the children in Parbold did. Instead they walked the hilly country lane from Parbold towards Wrightington to the big Hall on the top, called Fairhurst Hall, where Master Nelson and his family lived. They usually went when it was dark and they always went in at the back and down stairs to a little room below ground. All their relatives were there – Websters, Aspinwalls, Swifts, Masons – as well as some of their friends like the Turners, the Crosses, the Bartons, the Blundells. They said prayers together though Richard couldn't understand the words because they were in the Latin language but he had to learn them by heart. Then Master Nelson would speak about how important it was to hold onto their Catholic faith at all cost and would give out news about what was happening in these parts and sometimes even in London. Occasionally a priest would come. Then it was different. Candles were lit and incense burned, an altar brought out covered with a white cloth on which stood a large gold crucifix and the priest in his robes would say the mass and the people would take communion. Richard felt uneasy at these times and he didn't know why, perhaps it was the strange smell of the incense. But everything was done in a rush and people seemed anxious and Master Nelson whispered often to a man who stood at the door. It was at times like this when people were married and babies were baptised, as little Eddy had been a short time ago.

"So if the authorities are going to increase our penalties you will be away and our families and friends left to suffer," Marie said.

"We don't know that for sure." Edward sighed. "Anyway I'm not going yet, only thinking about it. But John says planters will pay the whole cost of the voyage if you sign a contract to work for them for four years afterwards, as you know from his letter, and several of the planters have trading connections with Sir William Blundell."

"And John Turner is already making enquiries, yes?"

"Yes," Edward admitted reluctantly.

"But John Turner is sixteen years old, not married with a large family." Marie sighed and said, "I'm tired and I have a headache, I can't argue any more tonight. I'm going to bed."

The chair scraped on the flagged floor as she rose and Richard quickly scampered back into his bed and pulled the blanket over his head as her footsteps sounded on the wooden rungs of the ladder. He didn't know what it all meant but it seemed as if father was going away somewhere. In any case it was making his parents angry and both these facts frightened him. His father followed his mother to their bed at the other side of the loft a short time later but instead of hearing them laughing together as he sometimes did there was silence. Eventually he fell asleep.

Because the next day was Sunday his father did not have to work and he lay late in bed though his mother was up at her usual time to feed Eddy and make their breakfasts. Instead of their usual bread and dripping Sunday meant eggs. There were a few hens in the back garden where Marie grew some vegetables and herbs and Edward kept a pig for the winter, but the eggs were often exchanged for milk from Goody Atherton who kept some cows. Sundays however she saved some for them to have one each for breakfast. Young James and Richard gulped theirs down but Mary at four years old had hers chopped up and spent an age eating it and James usually managed to sneak some on his spoon. They all had a wooden spoon and their father had carved their initial on the handle so they knew which was which. Richard was now old enough to have a knife like his parents. Marie finished feeding the baby and laid him on the woven mat in front of the empty hearth, telling Mary to keep an eye on him while she supervised the boys' daily wash. Because it was summer the water didn't have to be heated and they squealed protestingly.

"We don't need a wash, Pa will take us swimming in the river," James cried.

"Not today," his mother said, "He's going to visit Grandma Webster and Uncle Thomas in Wrightington."

"Can we go too? I like Gran Webster, she gives us apples and we can play with Uncle Thomas's children."

"I don't know, you must ask your father. Can you walk so far?"

"Yes, yes, I can walk for miles. And when I get tired I can ride in the cart."

Edward had entered the room and took his place at the table where Marie had his breakfast ready.

"You won't be able to ride in the cart, Jamie, that will be for Eddy and Mary. If you come you will have to walk with Dickie."

"You could carry Eddy when I get tired then I can ride in the cart," James protested and Edward was forced to laugh. "What do you think I am, a giant?"

"Yes, yes a giant, like the giants in the stories you tell us."

"I'll keep Eddy here with me," Marie interrupted, "but I won't be able to come to the Hall tonight, I can't carry him so far. I suppose you'll go straight to the Hall."

"I was thinking of it, it's a long way back."

"I don't want to come. I want to stay here with Mama," Richard said.

"It's too far for him to walk," his brother said mockingly. "Why can't we have a donkey like Uncle Thomas then we could go everywhere together."

Edward's brother Thomas was a weaver and needed to fetch and carry linen to and from the markets at Eccleston and sometimes at Ormskirk or Wigan so he shared a donkey with two of his fellow-weavers.

Edward said nothing but studied his eldest son carefully. Richard never minded walking. He was above average height for his age with a sturdy build. He had thick fair hair that reached his shoulders and blue-grey eyes, a legacy of their Viking ancestors, and though temperamentally serious he had a quick smile that lit his face and touched his eyes. Although Edward would never admit it, his eldest child was his favourite and it troubled him that he didn't want to share his company that day but he said, "So be it. I'll take Eddy as well then, my mother would like to see him and it will give you some free time, Marie."

Marie and Richard watched the little party set off. She had brushed the children's hair, tying Mary's straight fair hair from her face with a length of plaited wool, and they were wearing their best clothes. They only possessed two sets of clothes each and their Sunday best were shabby, especially James's which were hand-downs from Richard. When they had money for material Marie would make their clothes but otherwise she bought from one of the second-hand shops in Ormskirk. She watched Edward's figure disappear up the road, pushing the two youngest in the little wooden cart he had made with Jamie striding purposefully beside him. He was neither very tall nor sturdily built but he was strong and though he spent many days indoors working with bent shoulders at a loom weaving linen there was not enough money to be had by only weaving so he also spent much time working in the fields, using a hoe and a scythe and pushing a plough. She could only see his back, sturdy boots not quite reaching his woollen trousers, his blue wool jacket slack behind him, a shapeless felt hat almost covering his light brown shoulder-length hair. She imagined his face, sun-browned now with working outside, his handsome clear-cut features, the mouth that was always ready to laugh or jest and the audacious grey eyes that had first attracted her to him. Her heart contracted with love and pain as she watched him go. He was twenty-seven years old with four children, a house tied to the farmer for whom he worked and to whom they paid rent, two jobs—one tedious, one strenuous – both without prospects. He could read and write, had a quick mind and an easy tongue. He was amiable, inventive and prone to mischief, popular with his companions (and the girls) and made them laugh in the taverns at the tales he made up. Perhaps if he hadn't have married her when they were both so young he could have done better for himself. She had been poor, her father only a farm labourer, the cottage shared with two brothers and a sister. She had been sixteen, eager to get away from her work in the fields and the household chores and she had fallen passionately in love with Edward Webster the first time she had seen him when everyone in the area worked together to bring in the harvest. He was twenty years old and she found him handsome, amusing, daring, and a Catholic like herself. But she had brought him nothing and given him nothing except four children. If he had waited he could perhaps have found a girl from a farmer's or craftsman's family with prospects for him to inherit a better life. Now he was planning to go in search of one.

"What shall we do Mama now it's Sunday and you don't have a lot of work to do," Richard asked eagerly, glad to have her to himself for once.

"I still have some chores to do," she laughingly reminded him. "But what would you like to do?"

"Can we walk to the river and I can paddle? And afterwards you can tell me a story."

"Yes of course. And for our dinner we can share what's left of yesterday's rabbit stew, which we couldn't have done if Papa had been here." Richard cried his glee and smacked his lips in anticipation. "But we shall have to eat it cold because there's no fire," she warned.

They walked together to the river and to the ancient stone chapel, named Douglas chapel after the river, which was now disused because a minister couldn't be found to service it. Other village children were also playing by the river but Richard seemed disinclined to join them and stayed close to his mother. Marie intuited that all was not right with her eldest child but decided to say nothing until she was aware of what was troubling him. On the way back they played guessing games and tried to guess the time by blowing dandelion clocks as there was no horn or whistles for the farm workers it being Sunday.

When they had eaten their dinner Marie said, "I want to go and visit the Turners, Nicholas and Anne I mean, I don't want to go all the way up Stony Lane to see Jane and Thomas. Do you want to come with me or do you want to go and play until I come back?" The Turners were neighbours of theirs, weavers and Catholics like their own family. Marie was surprised when the little boy said he would accompany her for he didn't usually do so when his mother went to gossip.

Nicholas Turner and his wife lived in a cottage in the village of Parbold itself, part of a row of small weavers' houses built of stone with low thatched roofs and where the loom took up one of the two downstairs rooms. It was similar to where Edward's brother Thomas lived in Wrightington and where Edward sometimes worked in the house of another weaver in Parbold, dividing his time between weaving and working on the land. Nicholas's wife Anne opened the door to them and took them into the back room which was the living room and kitchen combined. Nicholas looked up from where he was repairing a worn leather bag, laying down the bodkin and twine with relief at the sight of a visitor and standing up to welcome them. He was about thirty years old, a thin young man with a pale face and a slight stoop from working all day at a loom. He offered Marie his chair and took a stool for himself, pulling the boy onto his knee, and they exchanged pleasantries for a time on the fine summer weather. His wife sat at the kitchen table sewing a piece of linen that looked like a baby's cap and making the odd comment. Suddenly Marie said, "What do you think about this idea of John going to Maryland?"

There was silence for a time then Nicholas said, "He was here this morning, you could have asked him yourself. He's gone up Stony Lane now to talk to our parents."

"So has Edward," said Marie grimly.

Anne rose from the table and said to Richard, "Would you like to look at our new baby? She's lying in her crib in the garden."

Richard was not interested in babies, he had a baby brother of his own and girls were even less interesting, but Anne was taking his hand and leading him out of the back door adding, "Hunter is out there too and he always likes to play," so he had no option, but at least a dog sounded more promising.

Nicholas looked embarrassed. "I know you must be upset about John and yes our parents feel the same. They are worried and distressed about him embarking on such a long dangerous voyage into the unknown and my father is not well as you know." He paused then said, "However my feelings are a little different. I can understand his reasoning. John is the youngest of us and at seventeen years of age he wants something more than his family has – working at looms or in the fields for six days a week with barely enough to make a decent living, then on Sundays being persecuted for worshipping in the way we feel is right, always in danger of being fined or at worst imprisoned. He is sure he can find work with an English planter, there are many who have made their fortunes in the new world, in a land where Catholics worship freely and are welcomed there. He believes he too can make his fortune but irrespective of this hope the chance of an adventure such as this, at no cost to himself, is too tempting for him to refuse." He was expecting Marie to speak but she just kept looking at him and he knew she was waiting for him to add more. He threw up his hands helplessly and continued, "But I know it is different for Edward and if John is trying to persuade him to go too then I am sorry."

Marie spoke now. "As you say John is a single man, only seventeen years old. I see enough of our sort dissatisfied with their lives, longing for something better and I too can understand his willingness to take such a risk. But he has filled Edward's head with these dreams and is encouraging him and Edward is not a single man with nothing to lose. He is married with four small children. His responsibility is to us. He married me and sired our children, he just can't leave us. He would never have thought about it but for John explaining how he could go about it, giving him the information about planters seeking workers and paying their passage, telling him about William Blundell's ships taking people from Liverpool."

"I'm sorry Marie if my brother has been responsible for Edward's intentions. I don't think it right for Edward to go, his circumstances are different, and I know the rest of my family think the same. I'll have a word with John and tell him to try and undo the damage. But although he has been responsible for giving Edward information and telling him about his own plans he can't be held entirely to blame. After all Edward's brother John went last year."

Marie pursed her lips. "John Webster had no responsibilities. He married Susanna Mason just before he left but he took her with him and they had no children. And he wasn't a weaver with a skilled trade, merely a labourer. If Edward had been influenced by his brother he would have gone with him and besides he went off to some place called the Barbados whereas Edward is planning to go to Maryland with your brother."

"I believe Barbados is the first step to Maryland," Nicholas said. "That is where William Blundell's ships sail to."

Richard had returned and was standing by the door leading from the kitchen into the garden. "We should go now," Marie said, not wanting the little boy to hear more.

"Please stay for something to drink," Anne suggested, following Richard with the baby in her arms. "I have some barley water and some elderflower cordial that is ready now."

Marie thanked her but declined then after admiring the baby and planting a kiss on her forehead asked, "When do you think you will be able to have her baptised?"

Anne shook her head, "I don't know when we shall get a priest here. At least she looks healthy enough for us to be able to wait. But as you know, we can't always get news of a priest in time and he has passed on before we are aware of it."

Marie thought fleetingly of how she and Edward had not been able to marry until just before Richard was born because there had been no priest to perform the sacrament earlier. If infants were weak and sickly the parents sometimes felt they couldn't wait for the unpredictable arrival of a priest and had to take them to the parish church, a practice condoned by the Catholic church under special circumstances. She asked Anne to let her know when a baptism was arranged and promised also to make a visit to Nicholas's parents whom she knew must be troubled by their son's plans to undertake such a dangerous voyage. Then she made her farewells and they began the walk home.

She was deep in thought on the way back to their house. She wondered how Edward was faring with his visit to his mother. She was hoping that her mother-in-law would be able to dissuade him from his mad notion. Mary Webster would certainly not be too happy to lose another of her sons to the new world across the ocean.

"Why did Uncle John go to this strange place with a funny name?" Richard asked.

Marie sighed. "He didn't have a very happy life," she replied.

"Father has a happy life with us doesn't he?"

Marie almost said *I thought so* but replied instead, "Your uncle John never wanted to take the trouble to learn the skill of a weaver like your grandparents so he never had any permanent work. He was always moving about, living with different people as work on the land became available." She recalled the year she had married Edward when John Webster, his elder brother, had been ignominiously thrown out of Lathom by a powerful farmer Robert Crane. John had been lodging with a relative and trying to find work in Lathom but he had been an unauthorised lodger in contravention of the law which forbade people to take in strangers from another parish when they had not been given an official permit of residence. Robert Crane reported him to the magistrates and he was publicly and humiliatingly deported from Lathom and forced to return to his previous employer at Dalton even though he hadn't been paying him enough. Marie's youngest brother Thomas who was just ten years old at the time had tried to escape from his work on the same Ashcrofts farm but the magistrates had compelled him to go back also. Her young brother's association with John Webster had given Marie the opportunity to further her acquaintance with Edward. "John didn't have enough money to marry but then last year he fell in love with Susanna Mason, one of the daughters of the blacksmith at Wrightington. Some friends of the Masons were planning to leave the country because they were being persecuted for their religion," she went on to explain.

"Were they Catholics like us?" Richard interrupted.

His mother looked fondly at him, not knowing how much he really understood about the difficulties of their life although she knew he was aware they had to worship in secret and the fact that they did not attend the parish church set them aside from many of their neighbours and the children's playmates in Parbold. "No they weren't Catholics but because they also refused to attend the parish church they were fined and often imprisoned as we sometimes are." Marie herself was not sure about the details of these people of which there were several in Wrightington, Langtee and Croston. They called themselves 'friends' and their group 'the society of friends.' Like Catholics they refused to attend the parish church or use the prayer book and met in each other's houses to pray and read the Bible, but openly not in secret like Catholics. It was also said that they refused to show respect to the authorities, not giving their superiors their titles and believing that all men were equal, a viewpoint that would have appealed to John Webster. "They decided to leave the country and make a new life for themselves in what is called the new world and Uncle John and Susanna went with them. I don't think they knew exactly where they were going when they went to find a ship from Liverpool. The new world is a very big place. But we heard afterwards that they were living in a place called Barbados, I think it is an island."

Richard remained thoughtful for a time then asked tremulously, "And is father going to go away too? What will happen to us without him?"

"Enough questions, Dickie. I don't want to hear anything more from you." His mother's voice was sharp and loud and he was chastened. She rarely got angry, especially with him. Neither of them spoke again until they reached home. She still didn't speak as she busied herself with the supper and he sat miserably by the empty hearth. He knew there wouldn't be much of interest to eat because the fire wasn't lit. Some bread and cheese and some chopped greens from the garden plot.

"See if you can read some of the book your father was reading to you now that he is teaching you your letters," she said at last, wiping her hands on the rough brown apron and reaching a worn book without a cover from a shelf above the low window. He took 'Aesop's Fables' obediently but he couldn't decipher the strange shapes to make sense. "Who will teach me to read if father goes away?" he asked but he was saved from his mother's response by the arrival of the rest of the family. Both James and Mary were asleep in the cart and Edward was carrying the baby who was crying fretfully.

"He's hungry and soiled," Edward said irritably and looking at his face Marie guessed there had been no amicable outcome from the day's outing though she also knew he was desperately tired.

She took the infant from him to see to his needs while ordering Richard to wake his brother and sister. "You can all sit at the table, the supper's ready," she said.

The children ate listlessly, James and Mary still not properly awake but when Marie had finally settled the baby in his crib and returned to the table for her own meal she surprised them by bringing a dish of thin custard, the milk watered down and flavoured with tansy instead of the expensive ginger, into which they all excitedly plunged their spoons until Edward had to call for order and insist each took a share as they squealed excitedly at this unexpected luxury.

Afterwards the children played together by the hearth, rolling smooth-polished pebbles down the shovel in a competition they had invented, while Marie washed up the wooden plates in a bowl of cold water and Edward wiped them with a linen cloth before stacking them neatly on the shelf above the stone sink.

They shared the task of putting the children to bed in the loft then as it was still a light summer evening they went to sit outside under the pear tree on a seat Edward had made from a tree trunk. He put his arm around her and she leant against him. She took off her linen coif and her hair tumbled around her shoulders, darker than it used to be but still more fair than brown when the light caught it.

"You're beautiful Marie," he murmured, "but too thin," as he felt the bones of her shoulders above the low neckline of her shift.

"Most women grow fat after four children," she smiled.

Her face turned towards him showed her blue eyes large in her thin face with its defined cheek bones and pointed chin and he knew she gave most of the food to him and the children.

"I didn't go to the Hall," he said. "I didn't feel like it and I thought it hardly fair to leave my mother with all the children."

She nodded. She wanted to ask him if they had talked about him going away and what his mother had said but she didn't want to spoil this moment of closeness. They were together in their own house, only rented and without luxury but it sufficed, the children of their union sleeping peacefully in their beds. The evening was warm and balmy, the silence around them broken only by the bark of a dog and the hoot of an owl. Above them stars began to appear in the velvety curtain of a cloudless sky. Edward tightened his hold on her and she turned up her face for his kiss. For tonight it was as it used to be and it seemed as if nothing could change it.

The summer wore on. Like many poor people they loved the summer. It didn't cost so much to live–the fire often wasn't lit as they ate cold meals and only needed to be kept low when it was necessary to cook; the long light evenings saved candles; warm clothes weren't necessary; beds weren't cold and damp; and food was plentiful with lots of fresh fruit from the orchards. Visits could be exchanged with relatives and friends in Lathom, Dalton, Wrightington, Langtree, practically impossible in winter when early darkness enveloped everything in pitch blackness and miry roads with floods, especially near the river and in the surrounding mosses and marshes, were often impassable. Marie occasionally took the children to the market at Eccleston, a long walk but worth it for the excitement that ensued and the opportunity for the children to see crowds of people. Sometimes there would be travelling minstrels there. Edward spent evenings in the taverns when work was done, drinking outside with his friends and neighbours while they told tales and played music, he could play the flageolet. Work in the fields was pleasant and the women could earn extra money, especially as harvest approached when all available labour was necessary and there was the reward of harvest festivities to follow. The children played by the river, swimming or paddling, catching newts and frogs and other water-life. The summer of 1678 remained long in the memories of Marie and Edward and their eldest sons. But it was always tinged by a perceptible uneasiness, a heaviness in the air as if a storm threatened though the skies remained free from such alarms. Catholics grew increasingly worried as rumours filtered through their secret channels of information about a threat posing graver dangers than had been known for some time and the fact that the precise nature was not known increased their anxiety as it hovered over them like an amorphous many-headed hydra ready to strike. Although he said little to her, Marie knew that Edward was making plans, keeping in contact with John Turner and concluding small items of business – paying off debts, finishing work on the loom. One day he said to her, "If I am going to Maryland it will have to be soon, before the summer ends because boats will not be leaving

Liverpool when the weather worsens. Crossing the ocean is dangerous at any time but in the winter it is too risky for merchants to trust their cargoes."

"You say *if* but you have already decided haven't you," Marie said, her voice trembling. "How are you going to get there? The journey must be expensive and we have no money."

"I go to Liverpool. At this time of year there are many ships leaving for the new world and the islands in the Caribbean ocean, like the Barbados. If they have room on their ships the captains are willing to take travellers free who will work their passage, or they have mandates from planters who pay the captains the passage fare on the agreement of the travellers to work for them for a fixed time, usually four years, to pay off the debt. It might mean hanging about for a few days but they say there is no difficulty in finding such a ship. You know that Sir William Blundell has been exporting Ormskirk linen to Barbados in his own ships and bringing back sugar and tobacco for more than ten years now and being a fervent Catholic he is always willing to help his fellow-religionists." His face became animated as he spoke then he sobered as he repeated, "But you see how impossible it would be to take you and the children."

"If the voyage is as dangerous as they say, you might not even get there," Marie said tremulously as she knew the argument was lost.

"If I go now I'm sure all will be well and I will survive," he said and she recognised his habitual tendency to act spontaneously without due consideration of the consequences, as with their unpremeditated marriage.

"But what will happen to us? How can we manage without you?" she repeated the words she had said so many times in her heart.

"Just hang on, love, it will be worth it. One of our relatives will take you, when the children are a little older you can find some work, so can Dickie in a year or two. The time will pass quickly and as soon as I have made some money I will send for you all and our life will be so much better than here. It will be worth it, trust me."

Marie sighed. It sounded easy when he said it. But how many of their relatives would be willing to take her with four young children, burdened as they were with children and family responsibilities of their own. If she were single she could have gone with him, as Susanna did with John. She had to acknowledge that he was determined to go. He was leaving her and the children and she had to force her mind to accept the fact and concentrate on how she was going to manage without him. And she must make herself believe that what he said was true – that he would make his fortune and send for them to share a new life so much better than the old one.

Towards the middle of August they said farewell. Edward had made his preparations swiftly and largely furtively. He made last-minute visits to his mother and brother Thomas, ignoring everyone else. The day before departing he packed up his belongings, which were few – all the clothes he had, his flageolet, his knife and spoon, his razor, his battered copy of 'Don Quixote'.

"I'll leave you 'Aesop's Fables'," he said to Richard, "You must learn to read, it's important and the woodcuts in the book will help you understand." He had nothing to leave to Marie.

He said little to any of them and Marie judged he was partly embarrassed and partly trying to control his emotions. She tried to busy herself with her normal chores and the younger children were happily ignorant of what was happening but Richard sat silently watching him.

He left in the early morning of the following day. It was nearly twenty miles to Liverpool, about six hours walking. Marie had packed up food in a linen cloth. He hugged the children and finally kissed Marie, holding her close.

"I will come back with a lot of money or I will send for you to come and join me. I promise. I'm going to try and get a better life for us. Don't lose faith. Just wait and do your best. There will be someone to get a message to you." Then he added, "If I can't get a ship from Liverpool then I'll come back anyway."

They followed him to the door and watched him set off up the lane where he was going to pick up John Turner. After a few yards he turned to wave to them, hitching his pack higher onto his shoulder. As his figure got smaller in the distance Marie wondered if she would ever see him again. She was convulsed with a wave of loss and longing – how much she loved him, how much she needed him. And lying beneath was a hard rock of terror as she wondered how she was going to manage without him. She felt like falling down on the ground and weeping inconsolably but the children were looking lost and bemused and she went to gather them in her arms.

"You will have to be the man of the family until your father comes back," she said to Richard. "I know you are only seven but you are the oldest, Dickie."

"If I am to be the man of the family then you must call me Richard," he said. "Dickie is a childish name. I want to be Richard like my grandfather."

Marie wanted to weep at the sight of his serious childish face.

Consumed by her own troubles the general unease felt by Catholics at worrying news filtering through from London passed her by. Reports told of growing antagonism in government circles to what was considered an increase in Papist activity supported by the Catholic Duke of York. Nonetheless local people were blissfully ignorant at this time of the machinations of a shabby figure prowling the halls of power with proof of a Catholic plot to kill the King and replace him with his brother.

Chapter 2

Autumn 1678

It was the knock at the door she had been expecting. Master Lathom was standing on the threshold, looking uneasy and though he accepted her invitation to enter he refused a seat. "I'm sorry Marie but you are going to have to leave the cottage," he said unhappily, after clearing his throat a couple of times. "I haven't had any rent for four weeks and I know you have no money to pay." He looked around the bare room, seeing the absence of food on the table and the empty cauldron swinging on a chain over the hearth. "Also your husband was one of my workers, I shall have to replace him and they will need somewhere to live."

"I could do some work for you," Marie offered.

"You can't do the work of a man and how can you work anyway with four small children, one just a babe." Marie bit her lip and he continued, "You do have someone who will take you in, one of your many relatives?"

Marie said nothing. All their relatives were overburdened with their own affairs, poor farm labourers or weavers earning only enough to support themselves, all with large families or elderly dependants to care for.

How could they possibly take on another five people, four of them small children.

Farmer Richard Lathom was a Catholic himself and as compassionate as his occupation could allow him to be. "I won't ask you to leave immediately," he said. "I will give you another two weeks to prepare an alternative but I'm afraid that after that date I shall need the house to be vacant for a new tenant, unless something untoward happens and your husband returns."

For the first week after his departure Marie had half-expected Edward to return saying he could not secure a passage from Liverpool. Every day she had stood looking up the lane, all the time knowing it was a fruitless hope. Then Nicholas Turner had come to inform her that John and Edward had sailed on one of William Blundell's ships taking linen to the Barbados in return for Caribbean sugar. "But the Barbados is only the first step on their journey to Maryland. Most ships from Liverpool sail there first because of the currents and trade winds," he explained. "They also need to revictual at this time. Apparently John has been given an indenture of service to a planter called Galloway and Edward sworn to work for a French tobacco planter called Mark Cordea, both in Maryland, and who have paid their passages."

All the hope seeped from Marie's heart. He was somewhere in the middle of the turbulent ocean on a small ship and she doubted she would ever see him again.

Now he had been gone for five weeks. The little money she possessed had been all used up. She had sold the mat Edward had woven and also the pig but there was nothing else of value. She couldn't pay the rent and although she saved the few pennies for food they were dependent on the generosity of neighbours to eke it out. Everyone knew now that Edward had left and she didn't like to go about, hating the pitying glances and the whispers. She feared that older people suspected she hadn't done her duty as a wife while the young unmarried girls took a secret delight in the fact that Marie Swift who had snared a handsome young man at only sixteen had now been left bereft. She had tried to find some work for herself but there was little work on the land now that the harvest was past and it wasn't possible to seek service in one of the large houses nearby because of the children. They had been sickly lately, especially the baby Eddy who was worrying her. She sold most of the eggs from the hens so that she could buy milk and cheese which she considered essential for them. The older children came in from their play and sat expectantly at the table.

"I'm hungry," Jamie said,

"So am I," said Mary.

"It will have to be bread and dripping again," Marie said, aware that she had already given them this for their breakfast and their lunch. "I'll chop up an egg and you can divide it between you."

"We always used to have an egg each," Jamie complained, pulling a face.

"You can have my share," Richard said.

Marie was going to disagree but was saved by a knock on the door and Margaret Crosse, one of their Catholic weaver neighbours came bustling in with a basket. "I thought you might like these, as usual I made too many for us," she said placing a dish of cheese pancakes on the table and unfolding a linen cloth with some thin slices of ham.

As Marie thanked her profusely and the children clapped their hands with glee, she said to Marie, "And make sure you take your share, don't leave it all to the children. You must keep your strength up, you've been looking really peaky and it won't help if you get ill." Then turning to Richard she said, "Go to the river tomorrow with your fishing rod, they say salmon have been seen. You can fry or grill them," she added to Marie, "have you enough wood?"

"The boys do go and pick up fallen sticks for the fire," Marie replied.

"You really must ask for some help," Margaret Crosse said. "I know you are proud and don't want to live off the parish but when my Richard hurt his leg three years ago and couldn't work for a time we had to ask for charity. Now it seems that Edward is not coming back, not in the foreseeable future, and you can't manage alone."

Marie winced at her words, she never let herself believe that he wouldn't come back and said, "I don't want us to be classed as paupers. I don't want the children to have this stigma. Our families, the Swifts and the Websters, have never had much money but we have always worked, always paid our way, even paid our fines as Catholics, never had to ask for help from the parish. I want to find work for myself, on the land or as a servant."

"You may be able to do that in the future, when the children are older. But that isn't possible at the moment is it? You are thinking of the children but the best way to do that is to get some financial help for them. It might only be temporary. Later when they are older you can be independent again. But you must go to the overseers of the poor here in the parish and state your circumstances. If you won't go, Marie, I'll go for you." Marie remained silent and Margaret said briskly, "I'm off now so you can enjoy your dinner. But I shall have a word with my husband to talk to Jeremiah Stopford on the board of overseers and get him to come and see you."

When she had gone, with the gratitude of the family ringing in her ears, they ate the unexpected meal as a banquet to be savoured.

"We are the poor, aren't we Mama," James said.

"We've always been poor," his mother snapped.

"We weren't poor when father was here," he persisted. "Is he not going to come back? I want him to come back."

"So do I," Mary wailed.

Marie was thinking of how to answer them when Richard interrupted by asking, "Who are these overseers?"

She was relieved not to have to talk to them about their father. "They are people elected by the parish to look after those who are poor because they are old or ill or genuinely can't find work. Those of the parish who can afford contribute a small sum of money every week and this is divided by the overseers amongst those who they think really need it, not beggars or idlers or those who don't belong to the parish," she explained.

"Will they help us? Then we can have eggs and pancakes and ham," Jamie asked, licking his fingers.

"I doubt they would give us so much," his mother said grimly.

A few days later they received a visit from Jeremiah Stopford, a tailor in Parbold and one of the overseers of the poor. Marie had come to the conclusion that she must shed her pride and accept what help was offered. After the generous meal given to them by Margaret Crosse the children had been crying with hunger as Marie tried to stretch out another offering of bread and cold bacon from the Haughtons, making it last for two days. Jeremiah Stopford was a gaunt gruffly-spoken man of middle years with bushy eyebrows and piercing eyes in a long bony face but with a kindly disposition disguised by a stern demeanour. He weighed up the circumstances of the family before Marie stammered her apologetic request.

"We don't have a lot of money to hand here in Parbold because we are a small community," he said. "However I'm going to draw up a petition to the Justices of the Peace at Wigan asking them to give you some financial help in view of your husband going as far away as Maryland and you having four small children. Fortunately we shall be in time for the Michaelmas quarter sessions which start in just over a week. It will mean you going to Wigan to present this petition in person. I will draw it up for you and bring it to you."

He was as good as his word and a few days later returned again with a neatly-written sheet of parchment. He read it to her : *"The humble petition of Mary Webster wife of Edward Webster of Parbold and her four children I humbly present. That your petitioner's husband Edward Webster having left her and her four children and gone to Maryland not leaving your petitioner and her children anything to maintain them and are ready to starve for want of relief. May therefore your good Worships tender your petitioner and her four children some speedy relief and your petitioner as in duty bound will ever pray for."* She nodded her agreement.

"If you wish to make a cross I will write your name beside it," he said kindly but she said, "I am able to write, sir, my husband taught me in case it should ever be of use to me." She had never thought that such an occasion would arise.

He took from a wooden travelling case a sharpened quill and small pot of ink and she slowly and laboriously signed her name while he waited patiently.

"How will you get to Wigan?" he asked.

"I suppose I shall have to walk. I've never been to Wigan, how far is it?"

"Some eight miles or so. Perhaps someone might be travelling there with a cart, going to buy or sell merchandise," he suggested.

"I could walk there in two or three hours, I'm used to walking," she said.

"But then you have to walk back and you will be tired," he reminded her and she promised to see if anyone might be going that way in a few days time, he had stipulated the fourteenth day of October.

However before Marie could make the journey startling news was being passed around, relayed from information that had reached Fairhurst Hall, and Marie's personal misfortunes were submerged in a general catastrophe. Newsletters were coming from London to the provinces with reports that a man called Titus Oates had given evidence to King Charles and the Privy Council that he had proof of a plot by Catholics to kill the King. Repercussions had been immediate–all Catholics in the royal household had been dismissed, especially the lowly servants; the Council ordered that all Papists should be disarmed and carts were being daily taken to the Tower loaded with weapons said to have been found in the houses of London Catholics; no Catholics were allowed to come within twenty miles of London. The informer of the plot, Titus Oates, was a previous student at the Jesuit college of St. Omer in northern France where he claimed the assassination plot had been instigated. All would-be novitiates for the priesthood had to be trained abroad because no priests were allowed in England. He said he had proof that the chief conspirator was the president of the college, a Jesuit called Father Edward Neville. The news sent shock waves of fear into the Catholics of west Lancashire for they were well acquainted with Father Neville, although this wasn't his real name for priests never used their own names but went under cover of aliases for security reasons. They knew him under his real name of Edward Scarisbrick for he was a local man whose family lived at nearby Scarisbrick Hall. The Scarisbrick family were all ardent Catholics and not only was their Hall used as a mass centre where they entertained priests but was also a secret college for the training of priests. Local young men went there to be trained secretly for the priesthood and many of them afterwards proceeded to the college at St. Omer. By naming Edward Neville as chief perpetrator of the plot Titus Oates had focussed the attention on west Lancashire. Another local Hall and mass centre, Burscough Hall, was the home of Dr. Henry Long who was a member of the Jesuit English college in Rome. As Marie worried about her appointment with the Justices at Wigan it was in an atmosphere of general anxiety as Catholics wondered how soon this thunderbolt would fall in their midst.

The appointed day dawned cloudy but rainless with a chill breeze that would be good for walking. She hadn't made enquiries about anyone travelling to Wigan because she felt ashamed of having to beg and had told few people apart from close Catholic friends like Margaret Crosse and Anne Barton as well as Edward's mother Mary and his older brother Thomas with whom she lived. It was Thomas who said, "If you can get to Standish there will be plenty folk going to Wigan from there. But you would be better following the Douglas, the road is easier and a bit shorter. Once past Appley Bridge you might find a carter. And there's bound to be people coming *back* from Wigan in the afternoon, at least part of the way."

She set off soon after daybreak because Jeremiah Stopford said she must be there before noon. "I have to go a long way to Wigan," she told the children. "I am going to try and get some money for us. I will be back as soon as I can but it will perhaps be supper time. You must be good. Richard you must look after them but Betty Mason says she will come and help you and Goodwife Margaret is going to make you some dinner so you must take them there at noon, you will hear the horn blow for the workers in the fields."

"Can we not come with you? Jamie never does what I tell him and I would like to see Wigan," Richard said. "It's a big town isn't it, bigger than Ormskirk."

"I couldn't push the cart all that way and even you couldn't walk so far. I've never been to Wigan but I think it is a big place. I'll tell you all about it when I get back."

She waved them farewell and set off towards the river. It was quite an easy walk and she enjoyed being out in the fresh air alone, a novelty for her, though she felt guilty at the pleasure she felt in being released from the children for a long period. The leaves were turning brown and gold and red, the fields had been newly ploughed and the gentle flow of the river was soothing, meandering through dells and copses flanked by low hills. But there was little to occupy her mind as she walked and inevitably she began to think of Edward, wondering if his sea voyage had ended, if he were still alive and if he ever thought of her. She relived their early days of happiness together when they only had one child and their resources were not so stretched, when they still hungered for each other's touch and hated the time they spent apart. Then her fond recollections turned to anger at the thought of his desertion and of how she was being forced to go and beg in order to keep his children. Trying not to let bitterness overcome her she turned her attention to the matter in hand but that brought anxiety about what was going to happen in Wigan and she began to worry about having left the children alone and the responsibility she had placed upon seven year old Richard. The path began to swing away from the river as she reached the outskirts of the town and along the lane were wooden houses that had been built to house the victims of the plague brought by the Scots during the civil war. She was soon able to see the square tower of the church rising above the cluster of buildings in the near distance and as the road began to dip it became well paved and lined with substantial houses built of stone. As she reached the market place the clock on the church tower was striking nine. She didn't feel tired, being braced with apprehension and curiosity at the novelty of her surroundings. The market place was thronged with people buying and selling and gossiping, there were many shops and inns along each side and down the narrow streets and alleys leading from the cross. Horses and carts were clattering on the cobbles, bringing in produce from the countryside, and the conduit had a queue of women waiting to fill their jugs and buckets. In front of the imposing stone church stood the Moot Hall and the Guildhall as had been described to her, people coming and going up and down the steps of both buildings. Taking a deep breath she mounted the steps and entered the Guildhall.

There was a clerk seated at the door inspecting the petitions of people. Marie took the document from the linen bag she carried on her shoulder and nervously offered it to him but after glancing briefly at it he told her to proceed to an inner chamber and wait there until it was her turn.

Following his direction she found herself in a crowded hall raucous with loud talk and noisy arguments. It was easy to see that most of the people were of the rougher sort and some of the men were in the custody of constables. The hall was set with benches but they were all occupied, old women wrapped in shawls showed toothless gums as they chatted to each other, a lot of the younger women were unkempt with dirty clothes and no hair covering, accompanied by ill-mannered children and wailing babies. People were arguing and shouting and every so often an official would appear and roar at them to keep order. Marie stood to one side but as near the front as she could so as not to miss her name but while she waited she took the opportunity to study her surroundings. The hall was lofty with a ceiling of wooden beams interspersed with tiles and the walls were covered with linenfold panelling. She had never before been in such a splendid building. She managed eventually to find a seat on one of the benches but was feeling more apprehensive by the minute and she reckoned two hours must have passed before her name was called and she was led into a further chamber. This room was smaller but with painted panels on the walls, a floor of black and white tiles and a long oak table behind which were set shields and coats of arms and over which hung a huge brass candleabrum. Three high-backed chairs of carved oak were set behind the table and occupied by the Justices in their crimson robes, grey-haired men of middle age with stern faces and rigid composure, while a clerk sat at a separate table with his writing materials laid out before him. Marie offered her paper and stood hesitantly while they perused it in turn. The justices were as stern as they looked when faced with criminals, trouble-makers, idlers and those of loose morals, but they were not bereft of compassion when faced by genuine need. They saw a young woman in her early twenties, painfully thin and whose face with its pointed chin, prominent cheekbones and troubled blue eyes was already showing signs of hardship, in worn but clean brown skirt and bodice of green wool with a neat coif covering her hair, left alone with four very small children. The sight affected them all and they showed no hesitation in awarding her a shilling a week to be given in her hand every Saturday by Parbold's overseers of the poor. The clerk made a note of the fact and she was asked again to make a cross to signify her assent. Once again she replied with a sense of pride, "I can write," and once again she made them wait as she laboriously formed the letters as Edward had taught her. She might be classed as a pauper, being forced to beg, but she was determined to keep some dignity.

She left the Guildhall trembling with relief and stood in the market place for a time trying to regain her equilibrium. A young man passing edged close to her saying, "How about a drink in the Old Dog Inn, it's just over the road there." She was desperately thirsty with no money to buy a drink but moved hastily away from him, excusing herself. There was a conduit in the market place and she cupped her hands to drink before making her way through the churchyard to take the road she had come. She was turning left past the demesne of the rector when a cart came through the arch leading to the church house, driven by a young man who whistled cheekily at her and on impulse she cried, "Are you going out of the town?"

"I certainly am. I'm ready for my dinner," he laughed.

"Which direction are you taking?" she asked, encouraged by his friendly manner.

"Why, do you want a lift? I'm going to Standish."

It was the opposite direction to the road she was planning to take but she remembered Thomas's words so said, "I would be very glad if you could take me with you to Standish."

"Then climb on," he said, "I shall be glad of some company."

She climbed up onto the seat beside him and enjoyed the different route they took from the town. The lad liked to chat and as they left the town and climbed up the slope towards Standish he told her about the great battle that had taken place in the civil war nearly thirty years before and where Lord Derby was wounded.

Then he pointed out to her the old thatched inn called the Boar's Head which he said might even date from the time of the Crusaders. He liked talking so Marie did not have to say much apart from telling him her name and saying she lived in Parbold. He assumed she had been shopping in the town and she didn't enlighten him about her business. For the first time in months she felt temporarily young and carefree and treacherously wished she could respond to a young man's friendliness. But all too soon they arrived in the market place of the little town of Standish and reality intervened as he set her down pointing out his house near the church with its pointed steeple. Now she must face the long walk home though at least she would be going down the steep slope of Parbold hill and not up it. However she had only just begun the descent when a cheery voice hailed her as a cart passed. It stopped and she recognised George Hulme, a farmer from nearby Newburgh. He didn't even bother to ask if she wanted a ride but called, "Climb up and I'll take you down the hill. I've been delivering some skins to the tanners in Standish so you'll have to abide the stink."

Consequently when they parted company at the bottom of the hill near the river she hadn't far to go and she was home much earlier than she had expected.

She walked into the house to find the boys fighting together and four year old Mary trying to amuse the crying baby with a ball made from patches of cloth.

"Dickie's been hitting me," Jamie said, then "Have you got some money?"

"Yes," she said shortly, "but we shall have to wait until next week, I haven't got it with me. And it won't be much, not as much as your father used to earn but at least we won't starve."

"What was Wigan like?" Richard asked.

"Let me see to the baby and get myself a piece of bread then I'll tell you," she said, feeling suddenly weary and hungry.

"Goodwife Margaret sent you a piece of cheese and we had broth for our dinner," he informed her. Tears sprang to her eyes. People were so kind but there was a limit to how much they could spare from their own modest resources and large families. But she felt revived when she had eaten and drank and gathered them around her to describe the thriving town of Wigan and her journeying there, her morning walk by the river then her two rides in carts.

"So you see how kind Our Lady has been to me and how she cares for us, letting no harm come to us. She will always keep you safe and give you her protection and you must always remember to thank her and pray to her. Let us get our beads and say the rosary together."

Their voices rose and fell in the familiar litany, four year old Mary trying to remember the words. Marie thought again about Edward and wondered where he was. After two months he might now have reached some land unless the ship had foundered in storms which reports said were all too common in the perilous Atlantic sea. She shuddered and said a hasty prayer for him though she never omitted to pray for him every night. How she missed him, she missed his lively conversation and tall stories, his constant activity around the house, she missed him in bed as she lay cold and lonely and longing for love. She didn't think she could ever stop loving him even though she was angry with him. She was determined never to give up hope that he would come back to them. But winter was on its way, the nights were already turning cold and she wondered how they could manage on their shilling a week.

She had only been returned a few days when more serious news was relayed from London. On the seventeenth of October the magistrate appointed to judge the evidence of Titus Oates, Judge Sir Berry Godfrey, had been found murdered in a London ditch by unknown assailants. The general opinion was that he had been removed by Catholics who feared what truths might be revealed by his investigation. Fury against Catholics intensified and the Government was pressed into increasing the penalties against them. The inhabitants of Parbold and the surrounding villages wondered anxiously how it would affect them.

Chapter 3

Winter 1678

"I'm cold," Mary wailed and started to cry.

"So am I, and I'm hungry too," James joined her.

"I don't know why, there is a little fire," their mother snapped, almost at breaking point as the baby cried and fretted, coughing and snuffling. She sighed as she looked at the rain running down the window panes obscuring what little light they gave and heard the wind plucking at the thatch and roaring down the chimney bringing splatters of rain that almost extinguished the fire. It was poor wood that wouldn't burn properly and there was only choking smoke not flames.

Richard was cold and hungry too but he was determined not to say so and add to his mother's distress. He was the man of the family now and he had to set an example to his brother and sister. He had seen her cutting up her cloak to make a jacket for him because his old one could hardly fasten and didn't cover his wrists, ("You're growing so fast," she had sighed,) so it had been passed onto James even though it was well worn. Now he had a longer jacket of green wool but his mother had to manage with her shawl when she went out. They all slept in one bed now, the bed their parents had shared, so that they could huddle together and use all the blankets they had and they went to bed early to keep warm. But it wasn't warm enough in the cold attic because although the heat rose the thatch was draughty. Now it was getting near Yuletide and the weather was worsening. The shilling a week brought regularly to them by one of the parish overseers bought them enough food so they wouldn't starve but it wasn't enough to fill hungry little bellies even though Richard noticed that his mother often gave them her share. And it didn't allow for any extras like clothes or enough wood to make a blazing fire. People were kind enough but they had their own problems and large families to see to on meagre resources, especially at this time when work was always scarce, there being little to do on the land. They sometimes received small helpings of food from their neighbours but clothes had to be passed on amongst their own growing children. Occasionally one of the husbandmen would bring them some wood but usually it was Richard who went to look for fallen sticks. "I could earn a penny by picking stones in the fields," he had volunteered but his mother said the weather was too bad at this time and he could do that when the weather improved in the spring. *If we ever get to the spring,* Marie sometimes thought to herself. She thought it highly unlikely that the baby Edward would survive. He had always been weaker than the others and she was worried about his cough. Alice Yate had brought her some goose grease for his chest which had eased it a little but she had still thought it necessary to send Richard to the apothecary in Lathom for a herbal syrup. She knew three miles was a long way for a seven year old but Parbold village did not warrant an apothecary and she couldn't go herself.

"You should be able to get a lift for at least part of the way," she assured him, giving him a penny. "Tell him that's all I can afford but if it is more I will give him the rest later."

A cart had stopped for the boy just past Newburgh and the apothecary had refused to take the penny saying his journey had paid for it, while on the way home a rider on horseback had let him ride pillion to his great delight.

As well as having to cope with hardship Marie was caught up in the general anxiety consuming Catholics, about which they received the latest news from Master Richard Nelson, a gentleman yeoman farmer, when they went to Catholic meetings at his home Fairhurst Hall. They couldn't have masses for it was not safe for any priests to attempt a visit at this time but they met together sometimes for solidarity, support, and news. The latest news was that the constables had been ordered to draw up lists of suspected Papists in each parish and forward them to the Justices of the Peace. These magistrates would send for them and if they refused to take the Oath of Allegiance and could not provide bail for their appearance at the next Quarter Sessions which were due at Epiphany they were to be imprisoned. People listening to Master Nelson were justifiably worried but they had been accustomed to evading the authorities for many years. They kept quiet about their religion to all but their associates, they attended masses secretly in different houses and at different times and some of them even made occasional visits to the parish churches, often under the obligation of having a child baptised (negligence to have a record put in the parish records could impose a fine), even though they would have it re-baptised when a priest could come. They were used to subterfuge so it was difficult for the authorities to have absolute proof of Catholics and the church wardens could not always remember how long it had been since individuals had attended church, if they said they had been there then it was almost impossible to refute. However now it was enough to be a *suspected* not a proven Papist. There had always been informers, some of them called pursuivants paid by the authorities, though generally neighbours and local officials preferred to turn a blind eye. But now with the alarming prospect of violence and rebellion planned by Catholics they might very well let fear overcome their neighbourhood loyalties. Suspected Catholics were also to have their houses searched and be deprived of any arms in their possession. To most of Marie's friends and relatives this was not a problem although the farmers and husbandmen usually possessed fowling pieces, but the gentry were very resentful about having to surrender their pistols and their swords, the mark of a gentleman. All priests and Jesuits were to be arrested and instead of the usual deportation they were to be immediately imprisoned to await trial. Unfortunately not all Catholics were peace-loving and law-abiding and in December some Wigan Catholics had gathered in the streets to make bonfires, proclaim seditious speeches and show their contempt of the government, an action which did nothing to help the present situation.

One afternoon Marie was surprised by a visit from a man she didn't know but who announced himself as Walter Brighouse, a constable from Ormskirk.

"Are you the wife of Edward Webster?" he demanded and when she answered that she was he continued,

"We are looking for him on the information that he is a Catholic."

"Well you aren't going to find him because he has gone to Maryland," she replied, showing more satisfaction than she intended to do.

"So you aren't denying that he is a Catholic?" the man pounced on her.

Marie remained silent, thinking that it couldn't do any harm to him now and knowing that they could not touch her, a pauper with young children.

"So how do we know this is true. You say he has gone to Maryland but that's rather a long way isn't it. He could be merely hiding somewhere," Walter Brighouse continued. He pushed past her and climbed the stairs then clattering back down the wooden ladder he opened the back door and went to look outside while the children watched wide-eyed.

When he returned Marie said wearily, pointing around the bare room, "Do you think we would be living in such poverty if he were here."

"So you say he has gone to Maryland which is a nest of Papists in itself. Why should he flee there if not guilty of something?"

Marie felt too tired to explain that he had gone to seek a better life, realising also that it was not the right thing to say in the circumstances. Instead she said, "What can he be guilty of, a poor weaver?"

The constable looked at her sternly, his eyes boring into her. "Don't play the innocent with me. We have information that not only did he regularly attend prohibited masses but that he has acted as a guide to lead traitor priests from one secret mass house to another, all of which houses are being investigated at this time.

I'm a local man and I know it is impossible for any stranger to find his way in the dark across the marshes and swamps without a guide and priests only travel under cover of darkness."

"I agree but Edward certainly did no such thing and surely your argument speaks against there being travelling priests in this area, it just would not be practical."

The constable scowled but turned to leave saying, "If he does come back he will be found so if you have any contact with him give him a warning."

When he had gone she felt faint and sat down on the only chair, which had been Edward's chair, the children clustered around her. Was there any truth in this? Had Edward sometimes accompanied priests from Fairhurst Hall to Park Hall, Burscough, Rufford? She doubted it. But he often stayed out late in the taverns and she was in bed when he returned. He wouldn't have said anything to her because he wouldn't have wanted her to be implicated nor worried. She knew he was reckless and bored and always eager for diversion. Without in any way doubting his religious convictions she knew the dangers and subterfuge of being a Catholic added spice to his mundane existence. Was there another reason why he had fled to Maryland? Several of the Catholic gentry were now leaving the country and making for the safety of the New World, some of the Blundells amongst them. She wondered what would have happened if he had still been here. He certainly wouldn't have sworn the oath of allegiance.

"Why did that bad man come looking for Papa?" Mary asked.

"Did he think he had done something wrong? If he comes back will they send him to prison?" James cried.

"He hasn't done anything wrong. If he had, wouldn't our own Parbold constable have known about it?" Marie answered. (Their own constable, although not a Catholic for Catholics weren't allowed to hold official positions, was sympathetic and never bothered them so long as no trouble was caused.) "It's because times are hard for Catholics just now. It's too difficult for me to explain the reasons until you are older but it has happened before and we just have to pray and stick together and hope that it will pass as it has done before."

"What is the oath of allegiance?" asked Richard who listened carefully to all that Richard Nelson told them at the Hall.

"It's a law that everyone must swear to saying that they believe the King is our rightful king and we will obey and serve him and all his laws. But that includes the law that he is head of the church which in England is called the Anglican church and they do not accept the Pope. This is why Catholics will not swear to it. They accept King Charles II but not as head of the church. The true church, the old faith, is the Catholic church whose head is the Lord Jesus and in whose name the Pope rules. The trouble at this moment is that all those who do not sign the oath are to be put in prison."

"Would Papa not have signed the oath?"

"No he wouldn't," Marie admitted.

"Then it is good he isn't here, even though we miss him," Richard said.

Marie had to admit that he was right. There were many who would not be found and who would be able to avoid the penalties but it seemed that Edward had already been noted. If he had still been here he would have suffered.

"Will you sign it, Mama? Will they put you in prison?" Richard asked fearfully.

"No my dear children, I shall not leave you," Marie assured their frightened faces. "I would not sign the oath but it will not be asked of me. They don't bother about women generally because we don't have any rights, only those of our husbands, unless women are independent."

"Will I have to sign the oath when I am older?" Richard asked.

"You will probably be ordered to but I hope you will refuse. Hopefully things might have changed by then," said his mother. "Let's say the rosary together again and pray that our family and all our friends will be safe"

But by Christmas things had only got worse and many of their friends and neighbours had been summoned to the Epiphany Quarter Sessions knowing that, at the very least, fines would be imposed on them and in anticipation they would have to economise on their Christmas feasts. Marie knew it was going to be a poor festive season. She had warned the children that she couldn't afford any presents though the boys had been out and collected holly and laurel to put around the window and the hearth and the red berries gave some cheer. There was to be a Christmas morning mass at Fairhurst Hall under the pretence of feative hospitality and they had been surprised by a visit from Edward's brother Thomas inviting them all to dinner at their house in Wrightington afterwards. Despite a lack of presents this would be an exciting event.

Christmas Eve was the beginning of a period of holiday for most people. Although the twelve days of Christmas were not kept as their grandparents described them before the civil war when every day was celebrated with a different event culminating in the final jollities of Twelfth Night, nonetheless it was a period when work was slack and people took advantage to visit friends and relatives and entertain in their homes with music and song. The big houses would invite their neighbours in for food and a Yuletide drink of spiced ale and a group of mummers could usually be formed from the surrounding countryside to black their faces and perform a version of the Saint George play. However this year celebrations were noticeably muted. There was usually a midnight mass at the secret chapels on this most special of days but this year no-one dared. Many of the Catholics of Parbold, Mawdesley, Burscough, Lathom, Dalton and Wrightington had been summoned to appear before the Justices at the Ephiphany Quarter Sessions.

Christmas Day brought a light covering of snow but Marie and her children walked along the hilly road to High Moor to Fairhurst Hall. The children held hands to keep them warm but their pale faces were pinched with the cold as flakes of snow stung their cheeks and eyes while Marie hugged the baby close in the shawl deriving some warmth from his body. Richard was very conscious that his jacket had been made from her cloak. She had pulled an old wool cap of Edward's over her coif, not very flattering but it kept her ears warm and she had put on both her petticoats beneath her better skirt of brown wool. When they arrived at the Hall they didn't go in at the back door to the secret chapel as they usually did but into the main hall which was thronged with people. As they entered a gush of warmth engulfed them and made their hands and faces tingle for a huge Yule log was blazing in the wide stone hearth and the rising heat made the air aromatic with the scent from the evergreens, holly, rosemary and laurel, hanging from the beams. It was the first time the children had been in the Hall itself and they gazed around in wonder, amazed by the unaccustomed warmth, the oak-panelled walls, the rugs on the brick-tiled floor and the candles burning in the wall sconces to offset the gloom of the wintry skies visible through the leaded panes of a row of small windows. Their father had sometimes told them stories of princes and princesses who lived in great castles and it seemed to them that this was such a place, even though in reality Fairhurst Hall was a glorified farmhouse. Cecily, wife of gentleman Richard Nelson, was handing out cups of mulled wine that warmed stomachs and cold hands, helped by her daughters while her husband, his two brothers, neighbouring farmers, and their son Maximilian greeted people.

Richard Nelson, a well-built man in his early fifties with greying hair and observant eyes in an intelligent face, then called for silence and after welcoming everyone to the Hall and offering a Christmas blessing said, "This is a seasonal gathering to wish all our tenants, friends, neighbours and those in need the traditional hospitality at this time. If anyone disturbs us then this is the truth. Father Julian, who is here at great risk to himself and to whom we offer our deepest gratitude, will say a mass that will be brief, covering only what is necessary for our communion. As you can see he will dispense with his vestments and the table will be our altar. Someone will be on guard outside and if we are interrupted then we will continue with our merrymaking. Now let us pray together."

Father Julian was a young man of no more than thirty years with fine-boned features and black shoulder-length hair. In his rough wool jacket, boots pulled over his cloak-bag breeches, he looked no different from any of the other countrymen until he began to softly intone the familiar words of the communion ritual. Marie felt the tears starting to her eyes and she fingered the wooden cross tied on a ribbon around her neck, Edward's present to her for last year's Christmas when neither his departure nor this new persecution had been dreamt of. James and Mary at four and five years old let their gaze wander around the unaccustomed comfort of their surroundings, the fire with its crackling log, the evergreens and a wicker kissing bough hanging from the beams. But Richard felt as if he were in the midst of some enchantment, engulfed in spice-scented warmth, the soothing rhythm of familiar words "Hoc est enim corpus meum," "Hic est enim calix sanguinis mei," the expression on the young priest's face, the tangible emotion of the communicants yet shot through with an undefinable sense of unease. He felt the tension but did not comprehend as did Father Julian who likened the shafts of fear piercing their devotions to the wounds of Christ. Richard was always to remember this moment as he watched his mother, baby Edward in her arms, go forward to receive the Sacrament with tears in her eyes and an expression of exquisite joy on her face.

Afterwards there was much rejoicing as co-religionists greeted each other, trying not to let the happiness of Christmas be overshadowed by the fact that many of them had been summoned to the Quarter Sessions at the end of Yuletide. Cecily Nelson, helped by her two daughters, now served trays of mince pies though without the traditional Catholic decoration of the baby Jesus in his manger. Marie's children greedily savoured the delicious mixture of minced meat and spiced fruit after their meagre breakfast of bread and ale and Mistress Nelson ensured that they helped themselves to more than one.

All too soon they were to leave the comfort of Fairhurst Hall and brave the cold to walk further on to Wrightington to Edward's brother Thomas's house, but the light snowfall had now stopped and it was with the encouraging expectation that dinner awaited them. They were tired and cold when they arrived but there was a log fire burning in the grate and a delicious aroma pervaded the small space. It was a weaver's cottage with the front room largely taken up by the loom and the back room was crowded with a bevy of excited children into whose midst Marie's children were soon absorbed. Thomas led Marie to one of the two rush-bottomed chairs beside the fire and she took off her shawl. A large cauldron of winter vegetables was simmering over the fire and from the oven emanated an appetising smell.

"Roast goose," Thomas said proudly.

"Did you catch it on the mere?" Marie asked mischievously. Illegally catching geese on the thousand acre marshlands near Burscough was a known activity for adventurous young men in the area.

"No I didn't. We Catholics are in enough trouble at the moment. As a matter of fact I bought it at Eccleston market though they were going fairly cheap," he laughed. She thought how like Edward he was, though considerably older, and her heart hurt. Edward should have been here joining in the traditional family celebrations and she wondered what he was doing on this day and whether they kept Christmas in the New World. Was he thinking of them?

Her mother-in-law, Mary, had stopped her culinary preparations to greet her younger son's family but then returned to the table where she was busy cutting up bread and laying out wooden plates while Thomas's wife Anne was making a sauce.

"I thought you might have been at the mass," Marie said.

"I'm afraid I've been a coward, Marie," her brother-in-law said. "You see, I haven't been arraigned, I've slipped the net. I've been being careful, what else can I be with a wife and large family and a job that doesn't pay much, I can't afford to pay big fines. So they haven't been able to find any proof against me and I didn't want to upset the applecart but I know I've been a coward." He paused then said, "My mother's been caught."

"No!" Marie cried. Her mother-in-law came towards her, wiping the flour from her hands on her brown linen apron, and Marie stood to let her take her seat, putting the baby on her knee.

"I don't mind," Mary Webster said with her customary calm acceptance of whatever life dispensed. Her face was prematurely lined and her hair grey beneath her coif but she still retained her warm smile that was reflected in her eyes. "It's better that I take the blame for the family, as a widow they can't ask me to pay what they would have asked of Thomas and he will pay it for me anyway. And to be put on the recusants list is of little importance to me at my age, in fact I consider it an honour. The reason I wasn't at the mass this morning is because I can't walk so far now I'm past sixty and it was too cold for me to come on the donkey, in fact that would have meant Thomas coming with me." She then went on to ask all the details of the gathering, what happened and who was there and Marie was glad to oblige her.

It was a good day. The meal was plentiful even though there were many to share it, the roast goose eked out by tasty vegetables followed by plum porridge, a little short of fruit but filling, and Marie knew it would have to last them for a long time. The children had playmates in their cousins and Marie enjoyed the companionship of Edward's family, distance and young children making it a rare occasion.

Just before they were due to depart Thomas said apologetically, "I'm sincerely sorry we can't help you more, Marie, but you see how crowded our household is and since father died and Mary and Margaret married we have been looking after mother. It takes everything I have to keep us all together and quite frankly I have absolutely nothing to spare."

"I know that, Thomas, don't think I expect anything of you."

"Ned was very wrong to do what he did and I'm ashamed of him," her brother-in-law said.

Marie hesitated then asked, "Did he do anything that he shouldn't have done before he left?"

"Ned was always doing what he shouldn't have done. If he ever does come back then he'll be in trouble with me," Thomas said grimly.

"He always did ride too close to the wind," Mary Webster said, a shadow crossing her face at the thought of how her two younger sons had disappointed her. "I'm sorry too my dear that I cannot do more for you and the children but age and circumstances are not in my favour. I have been greatly distressed to lose two of my sons but Ned's desertion has upset me most and I know his father would have been very angry. However one thing I am determined of and that is to find work for your boys with my family when they are of age. They will learn the skills of a weaver not be labourers." Mary's family, the Aspinwalls, was extensive with a long tradition of weaving in different places – Parbold, Wrightington and Dalton.

Marie was loath to leave the warmth of their cottage and take the long walk home but Thomas said he would get the donkey and cart that he shared with two fellow-weavers. "You ride the donkey, Marie, I will walk and the children can ride in the cart."

Anne Webster supplied them with blankets to wrap around them but said, "I'm terribly sorry but I must ask Tom to bring them back because they are needed for the children's beds."

However Richard, James and Mary were excited at the prospect. It was a clear moonlit night and though there was no snow a sharp frost sparkled the trees and hedgerows and made the country lanes glassy in places. The donkey was slow and stumbled sometimes on the slippery patches and although it wasn't much faster than walking it saved Marie's feet though she was cold with only the shawl wrapped around her. The children however snuggled together in the cart wrapped in the blankets their Aunt Anne had lent them. James, Mary and the baby fell asleep but Richard stayed awake, gazing at the stars in the cloudless black sky that stretched unendingly above them and thinking how big the world was. He wondered if his father could see the same stars and if he was thinking about them. The events of the day swam in his mind – the warmth and the good food in Uncle Thomas's cottage and most of all the warmth, the scent and the strange unearthly atmosphere at the Hall when the priest was saying mass. He didn't completely understand what it was to be a Catholic but he felt that it was a part of his life that held him fast and he wanted it always to be so.

Chapter 4

Winter and Spring 1679

The Epiphany Quarter Sessions drew up lists of all those Catholics who refused to swear the oath of allegiance so that they could easily be identified when needed and included Edward's mother and all the families the Websters were acquainted with–the Nelsons, Aspinwalls, Fairhursts, Turners, Crosses, Yates, Bartons, Taylors, Haughtons, Blundells and many more. They were all fined, some more than they were able to pay and had to borrow from friends, sometimes Protestants who were sympathetic to their plight. Landowners like the Nelsons also had to sign recognizances for at least £200 as a surety for their good behaviour until they were willing to sign the Act. Those who couldn't pay or who were suspected of being militant Catholics, holding masses in their houses and entertaining or helping priests were imprisoned. Marie could not understand how Richard Nelson managed to escape except that no proof was forthcoming. In this part of the county some of the constables and even Justices were of necessity Catholics and unwilling to pry too closely. Catholics were not supposed to hold official positions but often shortage of suitable candidates forced the ruling to be neglected. In fact a complaint came from the Government that the officials of Lancashire were not imposing the sanctions rigorously enough. However the gentry were not very wealthy here and unable to contribute a fortune to the government's treasure chest as richer nobles were often compelled to do, therefore it was enough to make public note of them and to threaten them with punishment so that there was a continual sword hanging over their heads. Some people however were imprisoned for provable offences and some landowners and gentry were leaving the country afraid of increased penalties, some to France and the Low Countries but others as far away as Maryland. Marie thought about Edward and wondered what would have happened to him had he still been here. Part of her was glad he was away though her problems had increased.

She had received two visits after Christmas. One was from Richard Lathom who said apologetically that she must definitely leave the cottage within the next week as he had some paying tenants who were eager to take on the lease. The other was from her mother. Marie rarely saw her mother for she lived on the far side of Dalton bordering on the little hamlet of Skelmersdale in the cottage where Marie had grown up and it was too far for her to get to Parbold on foot now that she was getting older and transport was not generally available. Marie was surprised to find her on the doorstep when she answered the knock, accompanied by her youngest brother Tom holding the reins of an old nag.

"I heard all the news but I couldn't come before," she announced, giving Marie her shawl and going to sit on the one chair beside the hearth with its smoky fire.

"Saint Peter, it's cold, that wood's wet," she said.

Marie said nothing but embraced her brother when he had tethered the horse to the fence. A lanky lad of seventeen he had Marie's thin features and light brown hair hanging limply to his shoulders with a fringe straggling over his grey eyes.

"Tom managed to borrow a horse from old Ashcroft but it's on its last legs, I had doubts we were going to make it here," Ellen Swift said. "God's light, you look bad, Marie, when did you last eat, you're thin as a lath."

"I can't give you anything, Ma, the bit of bread and milk is for the children's supper."

"Well I'm not surprised he's left you if you looked like that. Were you not a proper wife to him?" her mother said, looking her up and down.

"If you mean did I not fulfil my marital obligations to him then surely four children in seven years is proof enough," Marie said bitterly.

"Well I'll say no more at this time," Ellen said in a tone that implied there was much more to be said at a later date. "You'd better all come and live with us, I can't leave you here like this. I'm not happy about it, there's little enough room and not much money. You'll have to share a bed with me and the boys can go in with Tom. You'll have to find some work, I can look after the children, it will save me having to go out and work myself, I've worked long enough."

Marie did not like the suggestion either but realised there was no alternative. "Thank you, Ma," she said humbly. "It will only be temporary. I'll find some work and get on my feet again and Edward will be back soon."

Her mother merely snorted but Tom said, "It will be good to see you again, Marie, and I will help you with the boys," and she gave him a grateful smile.

"Bring what you can with you," Ellen said, looking around the sparsely furnished room. "I'll need some bedding and some more stools for the children. Someone will surely lend you a cart. Now I suppose we'd better get back before that horse dies on us."

Mary appeared on the ladder from the loft carrying the baby who was crying and Marie went to take him from her.

Ellen kissed them half-heartedly and said, "The boys are out I suppose."

The door burst open and Richard and James ran in both crying excitedly, "Whose is the horse? Can we ride him?"

They stopped shyly when they saw their grandmother and their Uncle Tom but greeted them politely when Marie prompted them.

"I'll let you ride him if I ever borrow him again," Tom said, holding out his hand to both his nephews.

Ellen made talk about how they had grown and hoped they had been making themselves useful then hastened Tom about leaving so they wouldn't have to ride back in the dark.

When they had departed Marie told the children the latest news. There was silence as they pondered the implication then Richard asked, "Do we have to go? I don't want to go and live there, I like it here in Parbold."

"Our friends are here, we won't know anyone," said James.

Mary started to cry, joining with the wails of the baby. Marie felt herself sinking into the depths of despair. She didn't want to go back and live with her mother, back to the house from which she was so eager to escape when she was sixteen, seven years ago. Her father, James Swift, had recently died and she had never been close to her mother who had a sharp tongue. The small cottage had no privacy with one downstairs room and one partitioned bedchamber upstairs which had to accommodate her mother, her elder sister Margaret and her younger brother Thomas, her older brother James being already married. She had hated working in the fields which was back-breaking work and preferred the times she was called to help out at the big house where the other Swifts lived. Her father was only a farm labourer and both James and Tom had followed him as soon as they were old enough but there were several families in the area with the same name and some of them were wealthy and respected. One family of Swifts lived in a place named after them, Swifthouses, they were Protestants, church wardens, and when any of the family died they were buried inside Ormskirk church, a special honour. Sometimes she had gone to help out at their houses when they were entertaining or when it was time for the big wash in summer. When she had met Edward Webster who lived a distance away in Parbold it had provided her with an opportunity to escape and marriage had promised her freedom, her own house, independence to do what she liked. Now she was back where she started but burdened as well by four small children. She missed Edward more than ever. Sometimes at night she would wake from sleep thinking it was all a bad dream and he would be sleeping beside her. However much as she hated the idea of returning to her childhood home she knew she had to be optimistic for the children's sake.

"It will be better for us," she said to them. "We cannot stay here any longer because there is not enough money to pay the rent. At Grandma Swift's there will be enough to eat and a warm fire. You like Uncle Tom and there are cats and a dog. And you will find other children to play with."

"Will be able to come back here sometime to see our friends and visit Grandma Webster and our other Uncle Thomas?" Richard asked.

"Yes of course," Marie answered, while not at all sure. "And it won't be for long, just until things improve."

"Will father come back?" James asked.

"Yes of course. Or we shall go and join him. We just have to wait," she said, more confidently than she felt.

The move to Dalton was accomplished quickly in the next two days. Richard and James helped Marie to collect together their few belongings – bedding, kitchen stuff, a few items of clothing. She had asked John Standanought, a Catholic husbandman from Wrightington whose wife Ellen was well-known to Marie and who were distantly related to the Websters, if he could possibly take them to Dalton with his horse and cart and he had kindly obliged, waving away any offers of payment which he knew she wouldn't have been able to make. When he arrived at the cottage he helped her with the few pieces of furniture – a chair and three stools, an old chest filled with their clothes and all the bedding they possessed, and the baby's crib. Before she shut the door she took a last look around the house where for a few years she had been happy with Edward, the drooping evergreens with their withered red berries draped around the window and the hearth mocking her with their promise of hope. It seemed that by leaving their house she was leaving Edward too, leaving behind any hope that he would return here and they could be together again.

John Standanought informed her that his neighbour Thomas Turner had recently died, his end hastened by his youngest son's departure to an unknown destination, another family affected by the lure of the New World.

She sat on the bench seat beside John Standanought and the children climbed into the crowded cart, Mary holding the baby. They were clutching their precious possessions – Mary her poppet and the boys the fishing rods their father had made them. James had his wooden sword and a pocket of shiny pebbles and dice they played with while Richard had his bow and arrows with a canvas bag around his neck in which were the missal, their rosaries and a wooden crucifix together with the book of Aesop's Fables. The journey seemed to take for ever, even though it wasn't much more than three miles, due to the load the horse had to pull and the wintry weather that made the road miry and slippery. They were cold as odd flakes of snow began to fall. Everything then had to be unloaded at Ellen Swift's house, a small lath and daub cottage with a thatched roof, which was on Beacon Lane at the juncture of Dalton and Skelmersdale and named after the beacon, an iron basket on a pole at the highest point of the hill, erected in the time of Queen Elizabeth as part of a chain of such beacons across the country to give warning of the arrival of the great Spanish Armada. Ellen was grumbling at not knowing where to put the stuff though being glad of the extra commodities while the children stood around looking lost and Marie was making her heartfelt thanks to the kindly husbandman.

The next few days were not easy as they all tried to settle into unfamiliar surroundings. The children were constantly under Ellen's feet for there was only one room that was both living room and kitchen and it was too cold to play in the patch of land outside the back door while Marie often felt the sharp edge of her mother's tongue. "If you hadn't been so willing to open your legs at sixteen to the first man who asked you then you wouldn't be in this predicament now," she said. Marie gave her a pleading glance that Richard was listening but Ellen continued, "I knew from the first that Edward Webster was no good."

"He wasn't no good, he was good to us and he loved us," Richard interrupted passionately, "and he's gone to get some money for us and then we are all going to go and live with him in a beautiful place like Heaven where we can all be Catholics."

Ellen laughed scornfully, "Yes and pigs might fly. Why couldn't you have married a decent man who could keep home and hearth together like your sister Margaret."

"Margaret's husband stinks," Marie said, (Thomas Blundell was a tanner). "Edward has been a good husband to me, a good father to the children, he worked hard and he isn't the only one leaving the country at this difficult time. I encouraged him to go, I didn't want him to be put in prison and I told him we could manage until he came back."

Ellen snorted and turned her attention to Richard. "You have too much to say for yourself. When the weather improves you can go and work with Tom, you can pick weeds and stones, help pay for your keep."

Later as Marie tucked them up on the pallet in Tom's chamber James said, "I don't like Grandma Swift."

Marie sighed. She knew her mother had had a hard life. Coming from a poor family herself she had married James Swift who was only a labourer on the land. She had lost several children beside the four who had survived and when her husband died, at the time Marie married Edward, Tom was less than ten years old. Though he had been put to work on Ashcroft's farm she also had had to take any work she could find in order to survive, on the land when there was work, taking in washing, taking in itinerant workers as lodgers to share Tom's chamber, a practice which was against the law. She had never asked for charity, had managed to pay her rent, had continued in the Catholic religion in which she had been reared and which she had passed on to her children. At fifty-five years old she looked older than she was, her skin wind-burnt, her hands rough, her hair beneath her coif grey, any trace of the good looks she once possessed marred by a carpace of bitterness.

Aloud Marie said, "She doesn't always mean what she says. It is good of her to give us a place to live and you do get enough food and a warm fire now that it's so cold."

"It's cold up here," James muttered.

"Well you can keep your jacket on. And curl up to Richard." Turning to her eldest she said, "I know what Grandma said about you working in the fields and I do think we should try and contribute to our keep here, I'm going to find work for myself, but I also want you to continue with your reading. I shall help you as much as I can but I'm not very good myself and I have been thinking. Nicholas Turner can read and write and I think you should go over and ask him to help you a couple of times a week."

"It's a long way now," Richard moaned.

"It's no more than an hour walking and you will run part of the way. You are nearly eight now."

"Some of the boys round here go to a school in Upholland. I could go there," Richard said hopefully, thinking it might keep him out of the way of his grandmother and wouldn't be quite so far as Parbold.

"The school in Upholland is held in the church. You would have to attend church and your lessons would include Protestant beliefs. As a Catholic you couldn't do that," she said firmly.

"How did father learn to read and write?" he asked.

"When your father and I were growing up the civil war had just ended and there wasn't the persecution of Catholics as there is now. Master Nelson kept a priest at Fairhurst Hall who was also a tutor to his children and he encouraged all the local Catholic children to share in the education. Of course poorer children couldn't go all the time, they had to work as did your father, but they could attend some of the time when it was convenient and your father learnt enough to be able to read and write. It is a great advantage. Your father occasionally wrote letters for workers who couldn't write and sometimes had to sign things for them." *It did put ideas into his head,* she thought to herself. *Perhaps if he hadn't been so clever, believed himself superior to many of his companions, he might not have wanted something more from his life.* But to her son she said, "So you must persevere with this. You might have to work in the fields for a while but as soon as you are old enough Grandma Webster is going to have you apprenticed to one of the weavers in her family and you are going to be a craftsman not a labourer. It is important for a weaver to be able to read and write for he has to write out bills and sign receipts and read orders for commissions."

So Richard set off willingly one fine day for the house of Nicholas Turner in Parbold. When he returned a few hours later it was in a state of excitement. "I've got a letter from father," he cried, running into the house and finding his mother preparing a stew with his grandmother nowhere to be seen. Marie flung down her knife and wiping her hands on her apron rushed to take the folded piece of paper from him. She sat down on a stool and with trembling hands broke the seal, at the same time asking, "How has this arrived here?"

"Nicholas says that it arrived at his house in a packet with a letter for the Turners from John and another letter to be delivered to the Guests in Langtree. He had received the packet by a messenger from Liverpool where it had been brought in one of Sir William Blundell's ships," Richard repeated what he had been told.

"It will take me a long time to read it," Marie apologised but Richard just shrugged and sat down on another stool to wait patiently.

My dearest Marie. I have arrived safely in the island of Barbados where I am staying with my brother John. It was a long unpleasant voyage of nearly 8 weeks with many storms that we feared we might not survive. Many people were sick and it was unutterably tedious with nothing to see but turbulent water for days on end. John Turner and I were glad of each other's company to keep ourselves hopeful. However the Barbados is the most beautiful place you could ever imagine. There are sandy shores with gentle waves, wide green spaces and strange tall trees, it is warm all the time with gentle breezes. In the town are large paved squares and splendid mansions.

My brother John has a modest house but with 5 acres of land and a black slave. There are many black people here, men, women and children. Some of the planters have more than a hundred acres with many servants and slaves. John thinks he will be able to have more in time. He and Susanna have just had a child who they have called Anne. I have also met some of the Guest family from Langtree who are Quakers and have left England because of persecution. I witnessed a will for John Guest, as I am one of the few who can read and write. I wish you could see this beautiful place. You would think you were in Heaven. I wish I could stay here with John but I am contracted to a planter called Mark Cordea in Maryland who paid for my passage so I must move on and John Turner and I are awaiting a ship to a place called Boston in the New World. I hope that you and the children are well. Give them my love. I do love you Marie and only wait until we can all be together again.

I pray for you all daily. God keep you in His care. Your loving husband Ned.

It took Marie a long time to read, some of the words she had to guess at and some she couldn't read at all, perhaps Nicholas Turner might read it for her if she could get to Parbold. She held the letter in her hand, overcome by the knowledge that Edward had held it in his hand, his smudges were on the paper, it was a tangible link with him. Emotion washed over her in a wave of contradictory feelings – love, relief, anger. She was glad he was safe but angry that he dared ask if they were well without bothering to know anything of their circumstances. While he was basking in the warm sunshine of an idyllic island they had been freezing cold and almost starving. She thought back to those terrible days in November and December, her walk to ask for charity from the Justices, the dependence on the goodwill of neighbours, those neighbours who were now suffering in the renewal of the penal laws persecuting Catholics. How could he be so thoughtless.

She called James and Mary to join Richard and read parts of the letter again to them. They were excited and happy and asked her lots of questions. She replied to them as best she could–"Yes he would come back," "Yes he would take them all to this wonderful place," "Yes it was very exciting to have a father who had travelled so far."

Inside she couldn't suppress her resentment. She had to live on the charity of others and must seek work to keep the family together while he was enjoying the hospitality of his brother John and friends, basking in the warm sunshine, receiving the gratitude of others for signing a document. Yet she still loved him – reckless, thoughtless, irrepressible Edward Webster, she still loved him and missed him. She wondered if she would ever see him again. She doubted it for she now had proof that he was so far away but knew she must not let the hope flee entirely from her heart.

The baby Edward had been sickly almost from the time he was born and throughout the winter with all its privations she had feared she might lose him. She had kept him as warm as she could, even to depriving herself, and given him the greatest share of the milk but he couldn't shake off a persistent cough and intermittent fevers and often kept her awake all night either with his crying or his gasping for breath. She had almost reconciled herself to his loss, knowing that most people suffered the loss of a proportion of their children, it was a fact of life and none of her friends and family had witnessed the survival of all their offspring. However death is no respecter of persons and sometimes the weak survive while the strong are taken. The child she lost in that terrible winter was not Edward but James. James aged five who had always been strong, mischievous, irrepressible, most like his father. Taken by a strange fever in a few days while a shocked Marie and his frightened siblings looked on. Tom Swift ran to Upholland for a physician who came promptly, even though aware he would probably not get paid, but there was little he could do except ease the child. All the family were in total shock as they viewed the little corpse that only a few days previously had been fighting with his brother, tormenting the cat and trying to distract Ellen's attention so he could sneak a piece of oatbread she was cutting up. Richard and Mary were heart-broken and unbelieving that their brother was no more. Mary couldn't stop crying but though Richard felt as if the world he knew was crumbling around him he tried to hold back the tears threatening to choke him, he was the man of their family. Ellen was roughly sympathetic but it was a tragedy she had faced more than once and she couldn't help the treacherous thought that it was one less mouth to feed.

"Harry Woodcock will make us a coffin cheap," Tom said. He was a Catholic carpenter. The simple, quickly prepared box of cheap wood looked very small when Tom went to collect it. "I'll borrow a handcart to take it to Upholland," he told his sister.

"You don't think the rector will make any objections?" Marie asked anxiously.

Sometimes the Anglican ministers could be difficult about burying Catholics.

"The rector at Upholland is sympathetic, he has buried a lot of us from Dalton and he certainly won't refuse the burial of a child," her brother assured her. But it had been known for rectors to refuse to bury Catholics and sometimes they had to resort to burials on private land or even by the roadside. It was when a body had resurfaced on the roadside during heavy rain that William Blundell had arranged for a Catholic burial ground in the woods on his estate at Little Crosby but it was small and a long way away.

"I want to come with you," Richard said.

"It's a long way for you to walk and all uphill coming back," his mother tried to dissuade him not thinking it a good idea for him to share the grief of the burial.

"He was my brother. I want to stay with him to the end and say goodbye to him. I am in father's place now," Richard said firmly. "I want to help carry the coffin."

"Perhaps the last few yards down the steps," his mother granted him.

The little group made their way down Mill Lane on an April afternoon when the pale sunshine and the burgeoning trees and grass bright with daffodils seem to make a mockery of their sadness, the new life of spring contrasting with the premature end of the life of little James Webster. It was all downhill to the pleasant village of Holland dominated by the sturdy tower of the ancient stone church, once the chapel of the 13th century Benedictine priory destroyed at the Reformation. When they reached the steps leading down to the graveyard Tom Swift parked the handcart and let his nephew take hold of the end of the small coffin as he lifted it up. The service was brief and quick and as the box was lowered into the ground Richard felt tears scalding his cheeks. His brother James was gone into the earth, James with whom he had fought and played for nearly all his life, they had shared a bed, shared their pastimes and competed for supremacy. He felt very much alone, felt the burden of being the man of the family.

As they walked back to Dalton, subdued and weary, they were ignorant of the fact that on that day Edward Webster had boarded the ship "Nathaniel" from Barbados on his way to Boston and the new world.

Chapter 5

Spring–Summer 1680

The Websters had now been in Dalton for more than a year. It was uncomfortable and terribly cramped with three adults and three children in the one living room which was also the kitchen and more so in the sleeping chamber where Marie with Mary and Eddy had to share with Ellen, and Richard and James slept with Tom in his half, separated by a rough wooden partition. Marie hated having to live under the dominance of her mother who ruled the household and not being able to please herself after living independently for seven years. Now that she was no longer resident in Parbold she could not claim assistance from the Overseers of the poor there for Dalton was in a different parish. Although close with boundaries that often overlapped, the villages were in separate parishes–Parbold and Wrightington in Eccleston parish, Skelmersdale, Lathom and Newburgh in Ormskirk parish, and Dalton and Upholland in Wigan parish, all of which made organisation difficult. She could make a fresh application but dreaded having to go through the whole process again with the stigma of being classed a pauper, officially paupers had to wear a 'P' on their sleeve though it was not always done. She was determined to try and manage. She could just about scrape together the amount she had been given on parish relief by taking on any employment she could find – a few hours each day scrubbing pots and pans after dinner in one of the big houses plus helping on the land at busy times, all made possible by the fact that Ellen could look after the younger children, helped by Richard when he wasn't needed in the fields. Tom paid the rent for the cottage from his own labouring and it was subsidised by the farmer for whom he worked while Marie contributed to their share of the food. There was no money to spare for extras, food was simple and not overly plentiful but at least they weren't starving and Tom managed to bring wood enough for the fire. Marie didn't mind working hard because she was desperate to have her own house again and needed to be able to pay a rent though she was sorry to see so little of the children and knew they didn't enjoy their grandmother's supervision. Ellen was naturally sharp-tongued and impatient and although she was never cruel she was unable to show any warmth. Marie tried to make it up to them in her spare time and on Sundays when there was no work. And wherever there was a mass celebrated she went and took them with her, even though it meant a long walk.

The terrors of the past year had now abated. After months of fear for Catholics and constant apprehension about what was going to happen, the so-called Popish Plot had finally been discredited as a malignant invention. The perpetrators, chiefly Titus Oates, had lied in their account of murder and mayhem being organised by Catholics, especially priests. But the Whigs in the government and those strongly opposed to Papists had leapt at the chance to destroy the hated religion and chosen to believe the worst. It had taken a year of trials and hearings before the allegations of a plot to kill the King had eventually been proved false, a product of one man's bigoted, torturous imagination. The cost had been great. In just three months of the summer seven Jesuits and four priests had been executed together with three Catholic laymen. Over the year other priests had joined them, convicted on insufficient evidence, some very old like seventy-eight year old William Atkins and eighty year old Nicholas Postgate, while two of them, John Wall and William Barrow, had been born in Lancashire. Many more had died in prison, often just ministering priests. No-one knew how many ordinary Catholics had been imprisoned, some dying there or losing everything they had. Some Catholics had fled the country in desperation, including Lancashire gentry like members of the Blundell family. It had shaken Catholics to the core and taken a long time for them to regain their equilibrium. There were still rumblings of unease but the heat had passed and Marie and her family recommenced their attendance at mass though the masses were held with even more circumspection. Because Fairhurst Hall was now further for them they sometimes went to either Mossborough Hall at Rainford where the Lathoms lived, a walk which took about an hour and a half, to Burscough Hall which was a little more distant or to Wrightington Hall owned by the Dicconsons which was slightly nearer, whichever was fortunate enough to be visited by a priest when news was passed around by the grapevine.

Richard had now got used to living in Dalton and he liked it. It was a bigger place than Parbold but scattered over a large area, without a discernible centre but with houses and taverns grouped along the several roads and lanes, many farms and both flour mills and water mills near the river Douglas. There was a large population of which about a third were Catholics. People had large families and there were a lot of children to play with, many boys of his own age who welcomed him into their fellowship once they had come to know him. When they weren't having to pick weeds and stones in the fields, scare birds from the crops or ensure that animals didn't wander, tasks they performed in groups, they were free to make their own enjoyment. Dalton was a boy's paradise, especially in summer. It was a mixture of pasture and woodland, winding lanes with banks and hedgerows, small irregular-shaped fields, many natural ponds and countless streams and rivulets falling through wooded cloughs into the River Douglas. Although the river was farther away than when they had played in Parbold there was nonetheless no shortage of water in which to amuse themselves. It was a place of endless exploration with a network of winding tracks and pathways that enabled them to reach the surrounding villages faster once they had familiarised themselves with the secret ways. They plotted together how they could help priests escape the authorities if ever the hard times came back.

One Sunday afternoon an unexpected visitor arrived at the Swift's house, a weaver by the name of George Taylor who lived on the main road to Parbold. There was a large group of weavers in Dalton besides trades like tanners, cordwainers and shoemakers, wheelwrights and carpenters, a tailor, a cooper, a whitesmith, a baker as well as farmers, husbandmen and farm labourers. Nearly everyone knew everyone else. The weavers were clustered together, often sharing workshops, and most of them were related by marriage, even if only slightly and going back a couple of generations, and nearly all of them were Catholics. George Taylor was a man of about fifty years and related to the Aspinwalls, a prolific weaving family scattered over Wrightington, Parbold and Dalton and of which Mary Webster was a member. He spoke of her now and explained how she was responsible for his visit to the Swift household. Addressing Marie he said, "Your husband's mother, Mary Webster, has made contact with me expressing a wish that I take her grandson, your eldest Richard, as an apprentice in the weaving trade. She is concerned that he should not be merely a farm labourer but that he should learn a skill, especially as his father is absent, and knows that I am at present beginning to teach my own grandson. I would be very willing to take on Richard also if it is in accordance with your wishes."

Marie felt a surge of hope, it seemed now that there might be a turn for the better and she said eagerly, "That would be very good of you. I also want to see him more than a labourer."

Ellen nodded her approval adding, "He's nearly ten years old now, tall and strong and ready for work."

"I would take great care of him, teach him the trade and never abuse him," George said. "He would get a fair share of free time and I would nurture him in the faith."

Marie nodded her assent but then George turned to Richard who was listening intently and said, "But how do you feel about it, lad? Is it according to your wishes?"

The news had surprised Richard and for the moment he was speechless and Ellen interrupted irritably, "The decision has nothing to do with him, he's too young to know what he wants, he must do as he's told."

But George Taylor said, "You're wrong there, Goodwife, the boy must decide for himself. An unwilling learner is neither good to himself nor to me. I want workers who like what they do, pleasure in the work shows in the finished product."

Richard looked at the bluff middle-aged man with his grey curling hair and discerning eyes in his jowly pock-marked face and decided that he liked him, there was something trustworthy about him. "I would like that, sir," he said.

"You will live with us and I will provide you with bed and board and give you a penny a week for yourself. When you have free time you may come home and do as you wish. Is that agreeable to you all?" he asked.

Marie voiced her agreement and after details had been settled, general news exchanged and refreshment offered, the weaver took his leave saying to Richard, "I will expect you at my house tomorrow then at the hour of eight."

When he had gone everyone began to talk at once, Ellen re-iterating how fortunate he was, Marie saying she was sure he would do well with Goodman Taylor and Mary wailing that she didn't want her brother to go away. Richard's feelings were confused, it had all happened too suddenly. He didn't want to leave his mother, he had never been away from her before. But he would be glad to leave his grandmother's house. Though he didn't know what the Taylors' house would be like. Yet Goodman Taylor seemed kind and he had contradicted

Grandma Swift which had earned Richard's admiration. But Mama would be left alone with Eddy and Mary without his help. Yet Mary was nearly seven now and could look after Eddy who was three and no longer a baby. His mother would miss his occasional earnings but when he had learnt to weave he would be able to earn much more and that would help her. He would miss playing with his new friends. But he would have free time when they could be together again as he would still be living in Dalton. He might make new friends too as there would be other boys learning to weave. By the time he went to bed he was feeling excited about his changed circumstances.

Next morning when he was due to leave his mother held him close. "I am so proud of you," she said. "Your father will be proud of you when he knows. You must work hard and pay attention so that you will be as good a weaver as he was. And I shall see you on Sundays."

He hugged her thin shoulders though she wasn't quite so thin as she had been. But her skirt was patched and worn and he wanted to work so that he could get some money for her. Then he hugged Eddy and kissed Mary saying, "I'm not going far, I shall be backwards and forwards all the time, especially if you need me for anything. Anyway there will be more for you to eat with me gone," he laughed.

He bade his grandmother a polite farewell then ran off towards the road where the Taylors lived, a linen bag with his few belongings swinging on his shoulder.

The Taylors' house stood on the road leading to Wrightington at one end of a row of three stone houses, two-storeyed and solidly built with a roof of small tiles. Some weavers lived in family groups and shared a loom workshop which was often adjacent to their property but George Taylor worked independently. Next door was a shoemaker Peter Blundell and at the other end of the row was the shoemaker's brother Alexander, a cordwainer who ran a complementary business making bags, belts and horse harness. The houses were much bigger than the Swifts' cottage because all had the front room as their business premises and because light was important the Taylors' house had a window at the side as well as at the front, though the windows were not big and were composed of many small panes. Richard could hear the clacking of the looms before he knocked on the door then hesitantly walked inside where he saw two large looms being worked and a smaller one standing by. George Taylor was working at one of the large looms and waved him a greeting but saying he couldn't leave his work at the moment he called loudly above the noise of the loom to someone through another open door. The inner door into a room beyond opened and a woman came out. She was middle-aged like George, her skirt and bodice of brown wool hugging her buxom figure and beneath her neat linen coif could be seen a fringe of grey curls. Her cheeks were a patchy red with some skin discolouration but there were lines of good humour around her blue eyes and she had a cheery smile as she introduced herself as Jane Taylor.

"You'll be Richard," she said, eyeing him approvingly. "Welcome to our house, I hope you'll be happy here. My grandson Will is about on an errand but he'll be back shortly and you can make his acquaintance, you'll be working together and I reckon you'll get on like a house on fire. Come now and I'll show you where you are to sleep, you'll be sharing a bedchamber with Will."

She led him through a room which was obviously where they lived as a family for it was furnished comfortably with two chairs with arms set beside a large open hearth, a long oak settle alongside one of the plastered walls and a scrubbed pine table with two more chairs and several stools in the middle of the room. Even with a spinning wheel by the fireplace and a large coffer against another wall the room wasn't cramped. Richard could see a separate kitchen beyond with a bake oven, a great luxury to his eyes having only lived in a house where the kitchen was part of the living room and lacked an oven, and there was an open door into a larder. A sturdy wooden staircase at the side of the kitchen climbed to the upper floor and Jane Taylor led the way to a small landing with two doors facing each other. Opening one she ushered him into a small chamber where the bare stone walls were whitewashed but not plastered. The tiles of the roof were visible between the ceiling beams and through the casement window could be seen waving trees. There were two pallet beds covered by woollen blankets, divided by a pine chest on which stood a candle in a wooden candlestick. Richard looked around fascinated, he had never lived in such luxury. Their attic bedroom in Parbold which they all had to share had no window, blankets were thin and sparse and they only had rushlights not candles.

Jane did not notice the amazement on his face and said, "The chest is for you and Will to store your belongings. The candle is for emergencies, you must never leave it lit at night. Now unpack what you have and go and join George in the workroom."

He took his things from his bag, they seemed too few to put in a chest and his spare shirt was patched so he left them on one of the pallets with his book of Aesop's Fables on top and went downstairs.

When he entered the workroom George had now been able to leave off his weaving and greeted him warmly. "This is Pete who works with me," he said introducing him to the man working on the other loom, a tall thin stooping man in his forties with yellow skin and matching straw-coloured hair. "This is Richard who is going to be a weaver."

Richard felt comfortable with these older men and said seriously, "I want to work hard and learn to be a good weaver so that I can make a lot of money."

"Eh lad, tha'll not make a lot o' money but tha'll ave a respectable trade and enough to see ye through," laughed Pete, showing toothless gums as he grinned.

"Well let's start straightway," George said, and began by explaining to Richard the different parts of the loom and how they worked.

A short time later George's grandson Will arrived, bursting through the door noisily and earning a frown from his grandfather. He was ten years old with an impish grin that seemed permanently settled on his round freckled face beneath a thatch of unruly sandy hair. He stopped in his tracks looking at Richard.

"This is Richard Webster who will be working with you and sharing our home," George said. "This is my grandson William Taylor, Richard. I hope you will be good mates and both work and play together because it will be miserable here if you aren't."

The two boys stood weighing each other up. Although Will was a year older Richard was taller, Richard was serious and reserved while Will was brimming with mischief and self-confidence, Will Taylor was family and

Richard Webster an intruder. They stood making judgements, assessing if they could trust each other and could be companionable. It was Will who grinned first and grasped Richard's hand. Richard took it and smiled back at him. In that moment they knew they were going to be friends.

That night in their bedchamber they talked easily together. Will was surprised at how few belongings Richard had but impressed by the book as he realised his new companion could make an attempt at reading. But they were boys of the same age with the same interests. Will was an orphan who had come to live with his grandparents a year ago and he was fascinated by the information that Richard's father had gone to the new world across the ocean, a point Richard felt he had scored against the older boy. Soon he was able to talk with him as he had done with Jamie whom he still missed and Will helped to fill the gap his brother had left.

Learning to weave linen on a loom was now to be Richard's life. It was a long boring day for a young boy. Sometimes when he was trying to master the intricacies of the loom he would listen enviously to the shouts and cries of children outside on the road. When the sun was shining and he would be struggling with threads that always seemed to break he would think longingly of exploring the woodland tracks and playing in the streams. But he had Will as a companion and he had the incentive to learn a trade so that when he grew up he would never again be a pauper and he could help his mother so that she wouldn't be poor. George Taylor was a kind master, rarely impatient and he treated Richard equally with his grandson Will, who in fact was less skilled mainly because he lacked Richard's seriousness and determination. George would enliven the work by talking when it was possible and he explained to them why the weavers worked in linen in this part of the country.

"The weaving of wool has always been England's main industry, our main export, for many hundreds of years and because of your name, Richard, your ancestors must have been weavers in the earliest days of our history when surnames first began to be used so it is your heritage, you are following in the footsteps of all your family who have gone before you. But though England's weavers have usually worked with wool, here around Ormskirk it is linen that is important. This is because we do not have very many sheep here like in the upland areas. The ground is marsh and fens up to the sea near Scarisbrick, as you know, but this is ideal for the growing of flax and also a damp climate is necessary. Much linen is needed for shirts and shifts and collars for everyone but also the big houses use linen for sheets, napkins and table covers and the merchants of Liverpool, like the Blundells, export it to the new world and the West Indies where it is in great demand because of the hot weather."

Richard determined to ask him more about these exports one day because he might be able to find out more about his father who had gone away on one of William Blundell's ships. George Taylor was clever and knew a lot. He had two books, a herbal by Thomas Culpepper which Richard loved to browse through looking at the drawings of plants and herbs, and a book by the Catholic poet Richard Crawshaw – 'Steps to the Temple' – which was too difficult for him. He did try to read his Aesop's Fables, which he liked because it reminded him of his father and the woodcuts helped him to understand better. Will was filled with admiration and often said, "Read the stories to me," but Richard struggled and when George saw them together he made a decision.

"I am going to send you both for some education," he announced. "It is important to know how to read so that you can check documents and receipts and know you are not being cheated. And you must learn to write so that you can sign your names on agreements and not rely solely on making a cross while someone else signs for you. You must also learn to do simple accounts so that you know if you are making money or losing it, this is good business practice." However being Catholics he knew they could not go to school. He put his mind to the problem and it was a few weeks later before he announced to the boys, "I have made arrangements for you to have a little learning, sufficient for your work as weavers. I have an acquaintance through work and through our religion with a mercer called Edward Lathom. He is distant kin both to the Lathoms of Mossborough Hall and to the family who used to live at Parbold Hall. Before the civil war the Lathoms of Parbold were a wealthy and important family hereabouts and Parbold Hall was the most important mass centre, Christopher Lathom entered the priesthood. But they were fined so heavily after the war because they were Catholics and Richard Lathom was an active Royalist fighting for the King, that they lost everything they had. They were forced to sell the Hall and became very poor, Peter Lathom even had to resort to begging from his former tenants. Edward Lathom is related to this family and a mercer as I said. I have arranged for him to have some linen at a low price and in return he is willing to have you once a week to help your reading, show you how to write your names and teach you some accounting, skills he needs himself as a mercer. But because he cannot spare time from his work during the day you will have to go to his house in the evening."

Will groaned at this loss of their free time and his grandfather fixed him with a warning frown as he continued, "However to compensate I will give you an afternoon free from weaving in lieu." Will's impish features creased into a delighted smile, only to be quickly repressed as George went on, "This will be spent working on the living room table at what you have learnt with Master Lathom."

Life in the Taylor household was more comfortable than anything Richard had so far known. Jane Taylor supervised her charges strictly, they had to be polite and obedient, go to bed early and rise early and she would brook no laziness nor impertinence. But they were fed substantial, though simple, meals and Richard, as part of the rules of an apprenticeship, had been issued with a warm blue coat and breeches, a linen shirt and wool stockings while the cobbler next door had made him a stout pair of boots.

"You must be comfortable on your feet if you're standing a long while," George had said on noticing his broken shoes that were obviously cramping his toes and rubbing his stockingless feet.

George and Jane ensured they made their devotions regularly with evening prayers and meditations, especially on saints' days, and George never thought they were too young to understand the political problems of their religion and explained it to them. Catholics were living in hope of having a Catholic king when the present king, Charles II, died. Charles had no legitimate children so the next heir was his brother, James Duke of York who had converted to Catholocism several years previously. However James was not much younger than his brother and might never inherit the throne while his only heirs were two girls by his wife Anne Hyde and they were Protestants. However on her death he had taken as his second wife the Italian Catholic princess Mary Beatrice of Modena. So far she had not borne him a son but she was very young and there seemed to be no reason why she should not in the near future produce a son and heir. Consequently the government were growing increasingly worried about the prospect of having a Catholic king and were trying to pass an act of Parliament excluding James from the succession, an unconstitutional procedure which nonetheless had the support of a great majority.

"Who would be the next king then?" Richard asked.

"Some people are talking about supporting the Duke of Monmouth who is the King's illegitimate son. Not the son of the King's wife Queen Catherine," George explained seeing the boys' incomprehension. "Others are suggesting the Dutchman William of Orange who is married to James's eldest daughter the Princess Mary. However neither of these pretenders are the rightful heirs to the Crown which is passed on only through the will of God, the divine right of kings. We believe that the Duke of York is the rightful heir and so we must pray for him and pray most ardently that the Parliament will not succeed in their attempt to exclude him from the succession."

"Will there be enough Catholics in the Parliament to stop this ex......," Richard couldn't manage the word.

"There are NO Catholics in Parliament because they are not allowed, no Catholics are allowed to hold public offices," George said bitterly. "However several of the nobles are secret Catholics and many more are sympathetic. But most importantly King Charles is determined that his brother should succeed to the throne as the rightful heir so the opponents will have hard work on their hands. King Charles will definitely not support his illegitimate son and he would not want a Dutchman on the throne of England. Anyway it is unlikely that anything will happen just yet because the King is only fifty years old and in good health but we must not slacken in our prayers for the Duke and we must always try to keep aware of actions against Catholics so that we are prepared. Fortunately the gentry in the big houses receive regular letters and communications from London which they can pass on to us at our masses."

As Richard grew up he was beginning to be aware of how many problems there were with being a Catholic. The non-Catholics of Dalton and Parbold showed little animosity and were often willing to help in times of hardship but there was always a consciousness of being different–they didn't go to the parish church, they didn't go to school, they had to get used to being secretive about many things like hiding missals and crucifixes from view and sneaking in at the back doors of the gentry houses to hold religious services. His mother used to say, *"We are different, we are special, chosen by God to do His will and hold the true faith in a land that has spurned it. As you grow up you will be responsible for holding that faith and passing it on to your own children so that it will never die."*

On Sundays when there was no work he went to visit his mother and the family in Beacon Lane. On his first visit they were filled with admiration at his new clothes.

"I like your new jacket, Richard," said Mary, touching the thick wool enviously. "Can I be a prentice too?"

"No, only boys can be apprentices," Richard replied smugly. "Girls have to do housework." His sister's face puckered with disappointment and she pouted. "Eddy might be able to when he is old enough," he continued, making Mary even more disgruntled. He was full of his new life, telling them about his bedchamber and his warm bed and the regular meals he was fed. Richard was usually sensitive but he was too excited to curb his chatter at first. Then he noticed the worn clothing of his siblings, Mary's skirt not reaching her bare ankles and her thin arms sticking out of her bodice, his mother's darned and patched clothes while Eddy was muffled in a gown much too big for him. It was one that had once belonged to Mary as he had not yet proceeded to wearing boys' clothes.

"This jacket is only my uniform for an apprentice, I won't get another for a long time," he hastened to add, and because he had belatedly noticed the expression on his mother's face when he talked about Jane Taylor's motherly care of him he launched into an account of how he had to work hard for long hours and how it was often tedious. He went to his mother and put his arms around her neck saying, "I do miss you Mama and wish I could be with you. When I am a weaver and make some money I will come back and look after you all, I will buy you all new clothes and we shall have a lot of food."

Marie smiled at his earnestness but tears pricked her eyes as she held him close.

"I am so proud of you," she said. "I know you are the man of the family now but I do not expect you to support us, that is not why I sent you away to be an apprentice. I want you to make a good life for yourself, to do well and not be poor."

"I shall still look after you Mama until father comes back," he insisted.

Although he liked living with the Taylors and the inducement of learning a skill offset the long hours of tedium, he always looked forward to Sundays with his family.

They would leave the Swifts' cottage and walk together through the pastures and sit by the woodland streams, enjoying the different colours of the seasons, apple and elder blossom giving way to fruit, wild flowers with their hues of yellow, blue, pink and violet, leaves on the trees turning from green to gold then brown, the small irregular fields making a patchwork of brown ploughed earth, green shoots of peas and beans, the gold of wheat. Even in winter they would leave the drab cheerlessness of the house unless the weather was too bad. Sometimes they would climb the hill and see the extensive views from the beacon, even as far as the sea across which somewhere a husband and father had sailed to an unknown land. Marie would stand for a long time thinking about Edward, wondering where he was and what he was doing, wishing he were there sharing their walks. She didn't think she would need anything else. Anything would be bearable if only he were there to share it with her instead of having to return to her lonely existence. She longed for his chatter about so many things and she longed for his arms around her in bed, she was still only twenty-five years old. Only her faith sustained her. If there was news passed around of a mass at any of the Halls they would go. They all looked forward to Sundays, their enjoyment increased by the fact that Jane Taylor usually packed up a food treat in a linen cloth for Richard to take home with him – some oatcakes, griddle scones or honey bread.

One day he brought with him something even more exciting. One of George Taylor's weaver associates who had some business with weavers in Parbold had been handed a letter by Nicholas Turner who explained that a packet of communications to various people had been brought to Liverpool on the 'Mary and Anne' returning from Boston and amongst them were letters from John Turner and Edward Webster.

"Take this to your mother," he said to Richard.

Marie was excited but apprehensive as she broke the seal and looked at the closely-written scrawl while Richard stood beside her. She knew it would take her a long time to read it and with great difficulty and as Richard longed to be able to help her it made him even more determined to read well. Tom Swift arrived back from where he and his friends had been up to the beacon, the usual Sunday afternoon meeting place for girls and lads, and his sister showed him the letter.

"Why don't you take it to Wrightington Hall tonight when we go up for the mass, I'm sure either William or Roger Dicconson would only be too happy to read it for you," he suggested. Tom was unable to read at all. Marie was impatient and loath to wait so long but after struggling with the script she decided to take his advice.

Edward had been helping her to read but since he left she had not had the desire nor the time to continue and lack of practice had made her forget much of what she had learnt.

Wrightington Hall had now taken the place of Fairhurst Hall for their regular services as it was slightly nearer being on the north side of Parbold village on the hill towards Wrightington and Standish. They used the bridleways to Appley Bridge where they crossed the river Douglas by the bridge which had been repaired in recent years following many petitions as to its safety and after acts had been passed in Parliament for the repair and maintenance of many bridges essential for passage across rivers, and from there it was a short uphill walk to the Hall, a timber-framed Elizabethan manor house with a moat, ponds and a park. In earlier times the Dicconson family had adhered to the Anglican church until the brothers William and Roger had converted to Catholocism in recent years. Theoretically conversion to the Papist religion carried the death penalty and from this time on the Dicconsons became some of the most fervent Catholics in the area, several of them entering the priesthood.

Roger Dicconson was pleased to be able to help Marie by reading Edward's letter to her, especially as he was interested in what was happening in the Catholic colony of Maryland in the so-called new world.

My ever-dear Marie. I have now arrived at St. Mary's city in Maryland. John Turner and I left Barbados in April in a small ship called the Nathaniel, only nine passengers, some planters, some fleeing religious persecution–three Quakers and a Scots Covenanter. It was a pleasant calm voyage, unlike the voyage from England, the winds and currents from Barbados being most advantageous. The ship docked at a very large busy port called Boston and from there people divided to go to different colonies. John and I joined a small boat to Maryland, water being the usual method of travel because it is too dangerous to go overland because of the native red men and wild beasts. We sailed for miles along the coast and by small inlets, the sky and the gentle waters blue, the grass greener than I have ever seen though beyond the coast were dark unexplored forests. Finally we sailed down St. Mary's river into St. Mary's city, the centre of the colony but no city. The settlement is hundreds of acres with scattered houses and cabins including some Indian huts. The wooden houses are well-built with large plots of land and many trees. The centre of St. Mary's has four streets with a shop, an inn, a court house and a lawyer's office. The most amazing building is the Catholic church, very large, built of brick with a beautiful altar and people worship openly here and I pray for you often. But not everyone is a Catholic because anyone here can follow their own religion without hindrance, and there are people of other faiths fleeing persecution. Most people live outside on the tobacco plantations. I was met by my employer, a Frenchman about forty years old called Mark Cordea. He is the most important planter here. I work on his tobacco plantation St. Elizabeth's at a place called Smiths Creek, some way from St. Mary's so I only go there occasionally. John Turner is on another plantation so I don't see him. The workers live in communal houses but they help each other to build houses so that they can move out. It is hard work farming tobacco, much harder than working in the fields at home and it is unbearably hot. They say in winter it gets unbearably cold. But at the moment I am surviving and I have done a little part of my four years. I will write again when I can but it has taken me weeks to write this. I love you all and miss you all, it is lonely here. I hope the time passes quickly so we can be together again. Love to Dickie, Jamie, Mary and Eddy and to you dear Marie. Your loving husband Ned.

As Roger Dicconson read the letter he was interested in the import, especially about the splendid church in this free colony so far away. He knew about Maryland because Richard Gerard of the Catholic gentry family in neighbouring Bryn had been one of the founder members of the colony, but it was instructive to have news from such a direct source though he felt pity for the young woman who was eagerly listening to every word, seeing the hardship she was suffering with her young children. He folded it carefully and gave it back to her. He wondered if she would be offended if he offered her a shilling but decided to take the risk and pressed a coin into her hand saying, "A token of my solidarity with a fellow-Catholic," and hoped she would understand his attempt at saying he sympathised with her predicament.

On the way home Marie was deep in thought. Now that the letter had been read to her she would be able to struggle through it herself, which she would do many times until she knew it by heart. She was envious that he could follow his religion freely without harassment, worshipping in a beautiful church with all Catholic symbols openly displayed and sharing the rituals with others of his faith. Shivering as the chill night air pierced her shawl as they walked the pitch-dark trackways she wished she could have some of the heat and burning sun he talked about and remembered bitterly that he had not asked how they were faring, he didn't know of the death of Jamie. But she guessed he was as lonely as she was and that he was finding the work harder than he had envisaged. For a moment a treacherous fear engulfed her that he might forget her and find someone else to salve his loneliness. She hoped and prayed that they could all survive and be together again.

Chapter 6

1685–87

The King was dead. No-one could believe the news as it spread from London by messengers, news sheets and letters. He was only fifty-five and had been in robust health with no signs of weakness until a stroke had overtaken him on the second day of February. He had died on the sixth after suffering four days of agonising pain and even more torment from the medical treatment of his physicians. The King is dead, long live the King! The new king was James II and he was a Catholic. The news was on everyone's lips in towns, villages and the countryside, wherever people gathered together in workplaces, fields, markets, churches, their own homes from the greatest manors to the humblest cottages. No-one could talk or think of anything else. The news was greeted with differing reactions- the Protestants were aghast and fearful, the Catholics jubilant and hopeful.

George and Jane Taylor were amongst those in Dalton who rejoiced as they passed on the news to their apprentices. Richard was fourteen now and Will fifteen, old enough to understand the implications of this momentous change.

"There will be no more persecution, no more secret worship, no more fines and hiding of missals and crucifixes," George said, almost beside himself with happiness.

"Under this new king Catholics will no doubt be able to hold official positions as constables, magistrates, lawyers, teachers, Justices, enter Parliament, the universities and the army. We have waited for this for years and now God has heard our cries of lamentation and delivered us from the oppressor."

"Will all this really happen"? Richard asked, not able to comprehend the different course their lives would now take.

"I can't see why not," George continued, his red face alight with excitement. "Go take a holiday today. Go home to your family Richard and share the rejoicing with them."

Marie and Mary and Eddy were still living in the cottage with Ellen and Tom Swift but in slightly improved circumstances. After five years of apprenticeship Richard and Will were now familiar with the skill of weaving and able to make a useful contribution to George Taylor's business. Although the days were long and the work often tedious it was mitigated by their mutual companionship and life with George and Jane Taylor was comfortable enough. The boys welcomed Sundays and festivals but their experience had now brought more variety into their work as they were sent to collect stocks and deliver commissions to people. Also their personal tips had increased to three pence a week and Richard gave two pence to his mother, happy to help with the family finances. One day he had been sent to deliver a roll of linen to Ashurst Hall, the large manor of Sir John Ashurst which stood in its own grounds behind an impressive gatehouse on Mill Lane. Whilst there he had picked up some information from one of the servant girls who had relieved him of his parcel and taking a fancy to the good-looking young lad had stood chatting with him. The next time he saw his mother he told her about his visit and said, "While I was at the Hall I heard that they need another house-servant, mainly to help in the kitchen and do light work like cleaning silver, trimming candles and repairing linen. Why don't you go up there and see if there is anything you can do."

"They're Protestants and were Roundheads in the civil war," Marie said shortly.

"Ma, the civil war has been over for thirty years," Richard said, half in amusement and half in exasperation. "And you have worked for other Protestants like the families at Swifthouses. It would be easy, clean work, a lot better than scrubbing floors and abrading heavy cooking pans and working in the fields as well. I don't like to see you doing such hard, dirty work. And I expect they would pay you more. I know it's a little further to walk but I'm sure it would be worth it. Please go and see, for my sake." He was pleading in earnest and at last she gave in to him and promised to go and find out.

So one morning she had put on the best clothes she had, the only skirt without a patch, with a newly-washed linen collar and coif, and walked up the hill to the Hall. Standing in front of the gatehouse and viewing the stone mansion with its gables and leaded windows, the huge tithebarn and the dovecote to one side, she was filled with apprehension but reminded herself that she had been inside the Halls of Fairhurst, Wrightington and

Mossborough and it couldn't be much different. She avoided the main oak door with its iron studs and huge bell on a chain and went instead to the back of the house used by servants and tradesmen. It was open showing a flagged passage and as she stood tentatively in the doorway an elderly woman with an enveloping blue canvas apron and a linen turban covering her hair came out. When Marie told her business she invited her inside, saying she would call the housekeeper. Marie followed her into the anteroom to the kitchen, a large limewashed room with a scrubbed pine table covered with fresh vegetables being chopped by a young girl, cupboards and dressers with pots and pans, thick oak beams hung with bunches of herbs and game, brooms, besoms and wooden buckets stocked along one wall. A woman whom she presumed to be the housekeeper–middle-aged, dressed in a matching bodice and skirt of good quality grey wool with a pointed linen collar and a coif with long lappets–arrived promptly, her brisk steps sounding businesslike on the flagged floor. Introducing herself as Goodwife Prescott she looked Marie up and down then led her along a narrow passage to a small parlour. Marie was intimidated at first by her questions but although her square face was stern her eyes betrayed a reassuring gentleness and she herself liked what she saw in the young woman, thin and pale but with no disabilities and hands that showed evidence of hard work. Her plain skirt and bodice of brown wool was neat, her collar and coif clean, her manner modest and her speech soft and without vulgarity. She was offered work and asked to begin as soon as she could.

So Marie had found work at Ashurst Hall in an environment much pleasanter than anything she had been used to since Edward left. It was a long day with the walking there and back and although she wasn't paid a lot she still had no need to supplement her wage by taking on less agreeable jobs and the work was light and varied. She saw little of Sir John and Lady Ashurst for her work was supervised by Goodwife Prescott who soon appreciated her dilligence, and the other servants, all local men and girls who were aware of her Catholic religion, were neither hostile nor companionable. Together with her brother Tom's wage and the odd pennies from Richard they had enough to eat and she was able to buy second-hand clothes for the children. While she was working her mother looked after Mary and Eddy, a task Ellen undertook with relief after spending so long in back-breaking toil herself and she enjoyed never having to leave her house apart from shopping, while supervising her grandchildren was less arduous than anything she had known in the last few years.

Marie's life had been unrelentingly hard until she had found work at Ashurst Hall and her unhappiness intensified by the fact that since the second letter from Edward she had heard nothing further. She had now begun to fear the worst for his four year contract of work with the planter Mark Cordea must have long-since ended. If all had gone as he had planned then he would have either returned home with money or have sent for them to join him. Hope had begun to seep from her heart. Either he had found someone else or he had died, both possibilities too dreadful to contemplate.

By the time King Charles died, Edward had been away for six years. If he was coming back then he should have returned by now. But then she salved her worries by reminding herself that he had to make some money first and it was a long voyage and perhaps he couldn't find a ship immediately. He might have written and the letter gone astray, ships sank and messengers entrusted with letters were unreliable. She tried to keep hope alive in her heart because it was the only way she could exist.

When Richard arrived at the cottage on Beacon Lane he found his family in no less a state of euphoria at the momentous news than the Taylors had been.

"Too late to help me," grunted Ellen though there was an uncharacteristic softness in her eyes.

His mother however was ecstatic, saying again and again how wonderful it was going to be now with a Catholic king and that all restrictions against Catholics would be overturned. "We won't have to go in secret any more to the Halls," she cried, her blue eyes sparkling, her thin face full of more joy than Richard remembered having seen it for a long time and taking years from her so that she seemed like the young girl he had known in his childhood, especially when she uncoiled her hair.

"We shall still have to go to the Halls for mass because there aren't any Catholic churches," he said.

"Yes but it won't be in secret. People will be able to get married and baptised openly like they do in the parish churches. And who knows, they might start to build Catholic churches, like the one your father told us about in Maryland." If only Edward were here how he would appreciate this freedom she thought. If only she knew what was happening in Maryland. Was he making money and had decided to stay there with someone he had met, making a new life for himself with another family or was he dead. Either possibility drove a knife into her heart and cast a shadow on the most wonderful news they had heard for a long time.

"Will father come back now that we can all be Catholics?" Eddy asked, seeming to read her thoughts. He was seven now and though thin and small for his age he was continuing to thrive although his cough still bothered him, especially in winter, and he was not yet out of the dangerous stage of childhood. His mother didn't answer because she didn't know what to say but although Mary and Eddy often asked about their father it was more a matter of habit than real concern. Eddy couldn't remember him at all while Mary's memories were growing vague and she had difficulty remembering what he looked like. They had got used to being without him and their Uncle Tom was the man in the family since Richard had gone to live with the Taylors. Richard had been older and he carried a clear picture in his mind of his father on the day he left – his handsome face, his habitual smile, his quick movements and the way he walked with a spring in his step. He remembered how he always had a story to tell, whether it was true or not, and how he made people laugh. He tried to keep this picture fresh in his mind and tried not to lose faith in his father's promise to return but now he was older he had begun to share some of his mother's doubts. And George Taylor had taken the place of a father for him after living in his household for five years. He advised him and disciplined him, taught him his craft and shared his experiences of his long life, all the responsibilities his father should have had. He still came back to the Swifts' house every Sunday and festival days and loved his family dearly. He gave his mother two pennies out of his three and brought back scraps of linen that were waste or had gone wrong, for her to use. At the last harvesting when there was feasting and games afterwards he had won a running race and proudly presented his mother with his prize, some duck eggs. He played with Eddy, teaching him the games he and Jamie had made up and tried to include Mary in some of them though she was eleven now and more interested when he brought her strips of linen tape for her long straight hair. And now on Sunday afternoons instead of walking out with the family as he used to do, he and Will Taylor would go up to the beacon to look for girls, groups of them parading with their friends and trying to attract young lads. Will managed to get stolen kisses but Richard was too shy, he was a year younger than his friend.

The happiness felt by Catholics at the new reign was not shared by everyone, nor did all Catholics behave with restraint. After having been derided and subjugated for so long some of them took pleasure in flaunting their new freedom, wearing crucifixes and singing ditties about Good King James and the new world to come, especially in groups in the streets and alehouses.

"Not a wise thing to do," George Taylor said. A moderate and tolerant man himself he was getting worried about the animosity building up between Protestants and Catholics, more than there had ever been before when they had lived and worked amicably together, not letting their differing faiths divide them. The new reign was not turning out to be as smooth as they had expected. And the King himself was not helping matters. There had been a Protestant rebellion to his accession led by King Charles II's illegitimate son James Duke of Monmouth. Although he had the support of many people, the actual rebellion was composed mainly of poor craftsmen and agricultural labourers from the south-west. They had been beaten at the Battle of

Sedgemoor by the Royalist forces and the King was ruthless in his reprisals. Despite the Duke of Monmouth being his nephew and pleading forgiveness, he was publicly and brutally executed, the executioner taking five strokes of the axe to sever his head. The King's chief Justice, Judge Jeffreys, supervised what later became known as the Bloody Assizes where over three thousand of Monmouth's supporters were sentenced to death and another five hundred transported and sold into slavery in Barbados.

"This doesn't bode well for building up an alliance with our opponents in this new reign," George Taylor said sadly. "Many of those executed or transported were poor weavers like us. The south-west of the country is known for its woollen cloth, most of the workers down there are wool-weavers," he explained to his apprentices.

The boys talked about it together in their bedchamber. Richard remembered his father's stay in Barbados and that his uncle John had a black slave working for him.

Now these poor weavers had to be slaves like the black men, separated from their families not because they were in search of a better life but because they had given their all for their principles, not working to support their dependants but toiling for nought to enrich wealthy planters. His heart went out to the families they had left behind, remembering how hard his mother's life had been as she had tried to take care of them alone.

"Do you think religion really matters if we love God and try to live good lives," Will asked his friend.

"I don't know," Richard said. He was only fourteen and confused. "We have always been Catholics so I don't know any other religion and I don't understand why people wanted to change it for something new."

Will repeated his question to his grandfather one evening when they were all talking together in the parlour as they usually did after supper while Jane busied herself with her habitual tasks of patching linen and darning stockings.

"Yes it does matter," he said emphatically. "People have different ideas about what makes a good life and what loving God means. Protestants have persecuted us Catholics in God's name and Catholics, God forgive us, have also persecuted non-Catholics during the reign of Queen Mary and the Spanish Inquisition, all believing they were doing God's will. We must have one faith that binds us together in love and unity. This is the old faith, established by Jesus Christ and venerated all over the Christian world except here in England where it was ruptured by King Henry for pride and greed, him wanting to be head of the church instead of the Pope who is Saint Peter's heir named by Christ Jesus, and coveting for himself and his supporters the wealth of the religious foundations. We have kept the old faith and must continue to do so as a sacred trust, trying by our example to convert others to the truth. We have now been blessed with a King who will help us to do so but we must pray for him that he will rule with wisdom. He has always believed in tolerance and I think this present harshness is a result of bad advice. He is hoping to convert England back to the true faith by reason and good example and we must do our best to share his dream. So remember, lads, don't gloat and don't get drawn into quarrels. This could be the beginning of a new age."

Richard was always inspired by George's fervour. He recognised how fortunate he was to have him as a mentor. Not only was he a kindly master who talked to his apprentices like equals but he was a skilled weaver. He was pleased with Richard's progress, more so than with his grandson's. Richard had learnt quickly, remembered what he was taught and was quick, not hasty and careless but deft. He had decided from the beginning that he wanted to be a success at a skilled trade that would enable him to earn a respectable wage. It was in general a tedious existence because the Taylors restricted their activities, in accordance with the rules governing apprentices.

They were not allowed to frequent ale-houses or horse races, forbidden to gamble or fight or play football. When he and Will had free time they would sometimes look longingly at groups of boys having mock fights or kicking a pig's bladder around, but on Sundays they fished in the streams, swam in the Douglas and George would let them play cards in the house, though without gambling on them. Festival days were looked forward to – Easter, Whitsun, May Day, Harvest, and Christmas when they had several days holiday. And Sunday was going home.

Now with a Catholic king on the throne they could walk openly to the big Catholic halls. King James had made a Declaration of Liberty of Conscience which allowed both Catholics and Non-conformists, who had also been persecuted in the previous reign, to have their own worship centres. Because they no longer had to visit the Halls secretly under cover of darkness, masses were held in the mornings. Marie and her children were at Wrightington Hall when William Dicconson made a momentous announcement. Bishop John Leybourne was making a tour of the whole of England to visit as many places as possible and to confirm children between the ages of seven and fifteen. There had not been a Catholic Apostolic bishop in England for fifty years and therefore there had been no confirmations. Wrightington Hall was one of the centres chosen for his visit but because there were so many places on his itinerary he was only going to arrive there in the summer of the following year. There was great excitement over all the area for no-one had ever seen a bishop. Until recently even working priests had to stay hidden and now there was an apostolic bishop coming openly and in great state. Even though they had to wait a year the occasion was something to look forward to and Marie was filled with happiness. "I am sorry you are going to be too old Richard," she said regretfully, it was the only cloud on her horizon.

"It doesn't matter, Ma, I am old enough to be confirmed in my faith without the Bishop laying his hands on my head. After all you and father never had the blessing of confirmation and it hasn't made any difference to you. I shall come to the service to watch Mary and Eddy."

It was going to be a great festive occasion as well as a spiritual one, because besides those who were to be confirmed people were planning to come from miles around to share in the occasion and catch sight of the bishop. The anticipation of the promised visit kept the Catholics jubilant as they waited. It wasn't often that anything unusual broke the routine of living in Dalton where only Sunday recreation, seasonal festivals, and occasional visits of itinerant musicians, pedlars and mountebanks, provided any relief from continual labour. Tedium was a fact of life and working people had to get used to it, accepting monotony as their lot. Consequently any opportunity for diversion was eagerly seized upon. Weddings were attended by all and sundry, irrespective of any close relationship to the couple. If there weren't enough cakes and ale for bystanders there would be music, good humour and the opportunity to gossip about the participants and comment on their "fine" clothes. Weddings were a social occasion and a communal activity and a 'private' wedding was frowned upon. Similarly funerals were public events and there were more of them. These were sorrowful occasions if the corpse was a child or a young woman dead in childbirth who left other young children, but there could also be celebration on the death of a long-liver or even satisfaction with a less than popular inhabitant. And beneath the compulsion to attend a funeral lay a morbid fascination with the inevitability of death and the random nature of its stroke. There was also the added incentive of the refreshments usually served afterwards, unless the deceased was very poor, for it was proof of good reputation to draw a large number of mourners and to reward them generously afterwards. Because funerals entailed attendance at the parish churches several miles away many of the older people needed transport. Most of the farmers and husbandmen owned horses and others could often find room on a cart but Will Taylor had discovered a way of making himself a little extra money as well as enjoying time off work. He would borrow a horse and offer to take a passenger pillion for three pence each way. He was trying to persuade Richard to do the same but although at fifteen years old he was now getting bold enough to go girl-chasing with Will he didn't consider himself competent enough to be in charge of a borrowed horse.

What he did enjoy as a break from spending all day in one room with the loom was to be entrusted with deliveries to the big houses. As well as the walk in the fresh air he could usually find someone to talk to, servant girls only too eager to spend time in conversation with a handsome lad and dally for a while. He enjoyed even more the occasional times when he and Will were sent to Ormskirk market to sell cloth and buy supplies. George would hire a pony and cart for them and they would amble through the country lanes and on the way pick up passengers who usually had news to impart. When they arrived at the weekly Thursday market all was bustle and noise as people came from miles around to buy and sell. The four streets around the market cross were packed with stalls and booths selling all sorts of food and goods, some not usually available on a daily basis. As well as bargaining purchasers, gossiping housewives, scavenging dogs, beggars and thieves, there were travelling preachers and strolling musicians, while the constable made his rounds, checking everyone had paid their dues and no-one was cheating with weights and measures and the standard of their goods. Richard got the opportunity to use his reading and writing when he filled in receipts, a task Will was only too glad to leave to him, they had finished their tuition with Edward Lathom years ago. One day before they left for home Will drew Richard's attention to a preacher declaiming loudly from the steps of the market cross, a black-suited Puritan holding a Bible aloft, and with a large crowd attending to his words. They were too far away to hear him completely but caught the words, "Whore of Babylon......the

Papist king who wants to make us all Papists........all positions of power going now to Papists......making us slaves to Spain and France..........the anti-Christ Pope now sending his bishop openly into our midst."

Will made to go and heckle him but Richard put a restraining hand on his arm. "Let it be. You'll only cause trouble. It's what most people are thinking."

Will was still uncertain but then he shrugged angrily and turned away but they both felt disturbed as they made their way back to Dalton.

The Bishop's visit came at last and on a warm Friday in July they made ready to go to Wrightington Hall. Marie had ensured that Mary and Eddy had new clothes, spending what money she could on them and Richard was now earning a few extra pennies to help. They had been well-schooled by the priest at Wrightington and Marie had taken great delight in preparing them for the momentous occasion. They couldn't believe the number of people gathered at the Hall, both inside and in the grounds. It was said there was to be a thousand communicants as well as spectators. People had come from far and wide. When the Bishop arrived everyone pushed and craned to get a good view. A man of early middle age, he was seated in a sedan chair carried by priests and attended by a retinue of Jesuits. When he descended from the chair his full splendour could be seen–garbed in a white cassock richly embroidered and edged with green and gold with a long cloak of identical costly material. Round his neck was a large gold cross on a black ribbon, he carried his shepherd's crook and on his head he wore the distinctive mitre. People gasped in awe at their first sight of a Catholic bishop.

THE YEW AND THE ROSE

The ceremony was long but everyone revelled in the unique occasion, the prayers, the ritual, the confirmations, all performed openly and without fear. Marie thought her heart would burst with love and pride as Mary and Edward went forward to where the Bishop placed his hands on their heads with a blessing then anointed their foreheads with the holy chrysm of oil in the sign of the cross, lastly giving a light punch on the cheek in a reminder that they must be willing to endure persecution should it come to pass. Afterwards there was much celebration with friends and family. It was a family occasion for Ellen and Tom were there, Marie's other brother James and sister Margaret with their families, Edward's mother Mary Webster was dead and the wonderful occasion came too late for her but her son Thomas and his wife and children could share in it as well as uncles, aunts, cousins and family friends. It was a momentous occasion that was to remain in the memories of all those present, a unique gathering of blood and faith such as had not been experienced for half a century. Everyone believed it to be the beginning of a new age and had no presentiment that it would soon all come to an end.

Two days later was a Sunday mass at the Hall and Marie and her family made their way there with a new joyfulness. When the service had ended Roger Dicconson approached them and said to Marie, "The priest here today has come from Maryland, from St. Mary's city." Several years before Edward had left for the colony a priest had arrived in west Lancashire from Maryland and it was not unusual for priests to make long journeys both from Europe and from the New World. "He would like a word with you, Marie," Roger continued. His voice was gentle and there was something in his face that alerted her and made her heart lurch. He introduced the young priest as Father Anthony who took hold of her hand. Her heart was pounding but whatever news it was, either good or bad, she needed to hear it.

"I'm afraid I have some bad news for you," he said gently, all too accustomed to having to deal with these situations. "I have been in St. Mary's city, as Master Dicconson said, and when it was known that I was returning to this part of Lancashire I was asked to see if I could find anyone who knew Edward Webster and to inform them that he had died." Marie gave a little gasp and her hand flew to her mouth. "It would appear that Edward died quite a long time ago but no-one knew how to contact any of his family, the planter he worked for, Mark Cordea, also having died. I am afraid that many English settlers in the colony die and it is not possible to keep track of all of them," Father Anthony said. Marie's shoulders began to heave as she tried to stifle her sobs and the priest understood she was unable to ask the questions she obviously wanted to know so after a pause he continued, "It would seem he died of what they call there 'the sickness.' This is a general term used for the many ailments caused by an unfamiliar climate. Settlers from England cannot tolerate the extreme heat of the summer and the severity of the winter and our bodies do not have the resistance to native diseases. Half of the settlers who come to Maryland die."

Marie looked up with tear-filled eyes and said softly, "I don't think he expected that."

She wiped her eyes with the back of her hand then asked, "Do you know how he died? Was it a painful death?"

"I'm sorry I know nothing else. As I said, it happened some time ago. I was just asked to convey a message when it was known I was coming to this area. It will perhaps be of some comfort to you to know that he is buried in the churchyard of the Catholic church in St. Mary's city. During the time he was in Maryland he was able to follow his religion freely and worship in a beautiful church and he is now at rest there fortified by the rites of our faith."

Marie thanked him and turned to go. "I am sorry and I shall pray that God's love and the comforts of our faith will sustain you at this time," said the young priest, laying his hands on her head in blessing. Roger Dicconson joined them and offered his own condolences.

Marie saw the children standing apart and went to join them. They looked at her questioningly and she said, "Your father is dead. He died in Maryland." She could say no more because tears were choking her and she did not want to break down in front of them. They looked stunned and unbelieving. Then Mary began to cry followed by Eddy. Richard was determined not to cry. He was sixteen and now head of the family in reality not only in name but he felt as if his heart had frozen into a solid block of ice.

On the long walk home all Marie could think about was him dying there alone, all his dreams of making money and returning home shattered. She gave no thought to herself, how she could manage without him permanently. Despite her faith wavering at times she had never really believed that he wouldn't come back, that she would never see him again. He had lost everything in a foreign land so far away. He was thirty-five years old. His image surfaced as clearly as if he were beside her so that she felt as if his spirit had joined her to take a last farewell. How she had loved him, how happy they had been before he went away. How she still loved him and the knowledge that she would never again see his face, never feel the closeness of his body, never hear his laugh, tore through her whole being in an agony of grief that she did not think she could survive. She felt her own life had ended. Eddy put his hand into hers and she could hear him snuffling. She had to survive for them, for the children Edward had given her. They would be a constant reminder of him. Mary was still crying and Richard put his arm around her.

When they arrived home Marie gathered them around her and related to them the details she had been given by the priest. They all sat in silence for a while, overwhelmed by what they heard. Eddy had never known his father, had no remembrance of him but had always believed that he would make his acquaintance one day, accustomed to saying to his friends, "When my father comes home." Mary remembered little of him but her daydreams had always been coloured by the possibility that when her father returned they would be rich and she could have fine clothes and a comfortable house. Richard remembered him well and that night lying on his bed in George Taylor's house he relived his childhood. The Taylors had shown their sympathy and when he retired to bed Will had left him to his thoughts realising he didn't want to talk. Unable to sleep he relived all his memories of his father, their outings, the things he had made them, the stories he had told. His spirit had been adventurous and he had risked all on a gamble to have a better life. He had survived a perilous voyage and several years' hard work on a tobacco plantation, only to die alone, miles away from his family, before his dreams could be realised. Richard had refused to let tears overwhelm him, he was head of the family now and had to act like a man. But now tears rolled down his cheeks and he was powerless to stop them. Of one thing he was certain. He would not let his father down. He would look after the family and do as well as he could for himself.

Chapter 7

1688–89

The visit of the Bishop had brought great contentment to the Catholics of west Lancashire but not everyone was in accord with King James and his Declarations of Indulgence. However Protestants were aware that the King was in his late fifties with no son and heir so it seemed his reign would be mercifully short and they only had to put up with it temporarily. The next heir would be his daughter Mary who was married to William of Orange Stadtholder of the Protestant Netherlands.

Then in June of 1688 came a bombshell that completely changed the picture. After thirteen years of marriage the King's young Queen, Mary of Modena, gave birth to a healthy son – a Catholic succession was secure. The Protestants, especially those in positions of power, the government and the aristocracy, were panic-stricken. Some went so far as to broadcast a tale that the child was no royal babe but had been smuggled into the Queen's bed in a warming pan, even though there were fifty spectators in the birthing chamber to witness the event, including Charles II's widow Catherine of Braganza. No time was to be lost. A number of politicians signed a document inviting William of Orange to come over and save England from the spectre of permanent Catholocism.

The news reached Dalton in two instalments. Firstly there was great joy at the birth of James Edward Stuart, a Catholic heir, announced at a mass at Wrightington Hall. Then six weeks later rumours were spread abroad about an invitation to William of Orange to come to England, no-one being quite sure of what he was to do. The Catholics in Dalton began to be aware of changing attitudes from their neighbours, a certain lack of friendliness and sometimes downright hostility, especially by young lads cat-calling and making threatening gestures as they walked to mass. When they met together they talked about what this might mean. Richard always relied on George Taylor's practical wisdom and asked him, "William of Orange's visit to England, is this a danger to King James?"

George frowned and bit his lip as he said seriously, "We don't know what the import is. Some people are saying he is coming to discuss with the King about measures to unify Catholics and Protestants even if it means the King having to relinquish some of his concessions to us. Others are considering a more sinister interpretation."

"Does this mean there could be another civil war?" Richard asked.

He knew little of the war but his father had occasionally told him stories that *his* father had told him and the events had been corroborated by George Taylor who had been about the same age as Will and Richard when the war began in 1642. Edward Webster had been born in the closing stages of the war after King Charles I had been executed but his father, another Richard Webster who had been a young man when the war was at its height, had told him tales that he had passed on to his own son. He told about Lord Derby recruiting troops for the King's army from among his tenants and labourers and marching them off to fight in other parts of the country. A lot of the local gentry had followed Lord Derby including Richard Lathom of Parbold Hall who had fought at the battle of Preston and his participation had cost him everything he had. Farmers and family men had not been expected to leave the area though most of the men under forty years of age had been summoned from time to time for local skirmishes and all had been involved in some way in the siege of Lathom House. When the army of Parliament attacked Lord Derby's great fortress the Roundheads had made all the local men dig trenches and heave boulders for defensive fortifications as well as requisitioning their animals and food supplies to feed the besiegers and laying waste the land. Everyone in the area had suffered, some having their houses destroyed by misplaced cannon shot, their thatch burnt by accidental musket fire, their provisions and bedding taken away for the soldiers or else compelled to take officers as non-paying lodgers. The fields had not only been stripped of their produce but turned into a wasteland of hastily-constructed ramparts, mud and grooves by the march of the army and heavy artillery. His grandfather had seen Prince Rupert come with his cavalry to lift the siege, a splendid figure, tall and handsome in a scarlet cloak and the Roundheads had fled, leaving devastation in their wake. Then three years later the Roundheads had returned when the King's cause had been lost and slighted Lathom House, leaving it uninhabitable and a shell of its former glory. Local people couldn't believe that the great edifice which had dominated their landscape for centuries, a symbol of Lord Derby's power over them but also the main centre of employment for the people who lived on his lands, was no more than a decaying ruin. It stood as a permanent reminder of a war that had lasted nearly ten years and brought universal hardship. It had taken another ten years for the country to recover.

Richard did not like the thought of a war beginning all over again but Will was saying impulsively, "If there is a war then I'm going to fight. We have always been told that we might have to fight for our faith."

"Let's pray that we don't have to," his grandfather said. "A war between Catholics and Protestants is unthinkable. We live amicably with most of our neighbours except for the fact that we worship in different ways. During the civil war neighbours fought against each other, fathers against sons, kin against kin. We don't want to see that again."

Throughout the summer there was tension as people were unsure what was happening and news took time to get from London to west Lancashire even with newsletters, which all the gentry subscribed to, and travellers. It was a repeat of the summer of the Popish plot ten years before. Work continued in workshops and fields in the hot weather, children paddled in the streams and housewives sat outside their houses gossiping with their spindles and knitting needles, men stayed long in the alehouses in the light evenings discussing and arguing about the possible outcome. Everyone tried to keep as merry as they usually were in the summer but it was as if a thundercloud hung overhead threatening the pleasant season. There was a perceptible tension in the air like the heavy pressure of an approaching storm. Harvest came and went with all its attendant hustle and bustle, the haste to get the crops in before rain arrived followed by the festivities of decorating the last hay wain and the harvest supper. Michaelmas brought rain and winter approached, lowering the spirits with the spectre of cold weather, little food and unnavigable roads.

On the 5th of November William of Orange landed in Devon with what was undoubtedly an invasion force. The date had been specially chosen as a reminder of the Gunpowder plot in the reign of James I in order to stir people's memories as to the perfidy of Catholics. It was all over very quickly. James II would not fight, refusing to inflict another civil war on his subjects. The Queen and the baby prince were sent to France for safety. A short time later the King followed them accepting the hospitality of his cousin King Louis X1V.

It was a sad Yuletide for Catholics. Richard had gone home, glad to leave the Taylor household where he was worried both by George's uncharacteristic silence and Will's angry talk of retaliation. They tried to keep merry. Tom brought a small Yule log from the farm and they collected evergreens to decorate the house though there was a shortage of berries this year. Marie and Ellen mulled the ale with the poker, adding some garden herbs as they couldn't afford expensive spices, boiled a ham shank and made some mince pies which they took to the Plumb's cookshop to be baked but there was no money for new year gifts. Yuletide was a time for making and receiving visits before the weather worsened after Epiphany and they walked to Wrightington to see Uncle Thomas Webster and his ever-increasing family, and to Parbold to visit their old friends there, everyone devastated by what had happened.

At Nicholas Turner's house, where his wife Anne had just given birth to their fifth child, Nicholas told them that his brother John had finished his apprenticeship in Maryland and was starting out on his own, claiming land that was now due to him.

"I'm sorry our parents died before they knew that he has done well for himself," he said. He expressed to Marie his sorrow about Edward which brought about a new wave of grief at his loss, exacerbated by the knowledge that John Turner had survived and was now ready to claim his reward. This together with the realisation that the long-awaited age of freedom for Catholics seemed to be coming to an abrupt end with the deposition of King James seemed a burden almost too much for her to bear. Everywhere they went people were saying, "I can't believe what has happened. How can the Parliament depose a lawful monarch, a King divinely appointed by God, and replace him with a foreigner whose right to the crown is unfounded and any claim of inheritance comes through his wife."

This was a declaration made more forcibly by William Dicconson when they went to midnight mass at Wrightington Hall on Christmas Eve.

"We must not yet be downhearted," he commanded the congregation when the service was ended and they were about to leave. "At the moment William of Orange is not King. King James has left the country because he was not willing to be the cause of another civil war, a sentiment which shows his care for all his subjects. There cannot be two kings so for the present there is an Interregnum. We must pray that King James will be returned, perhaps even with the help of France, and Parliament's original avowed intention of seeking only William's help to advise on issues will be upheld."

As the communicants walked home on the moonlit frosty night they were more confused than comforted. They were Catholics but they were English. Despite officialdom's suspicions to the contrary, most of them put their patriotism before their religion when it came to the crunch. They had continued to serve Queen Elizabeth when the Pope had excommunicated her and had not supported the Armada in the planned invasion by Spain. In the civil war they had unanimously followed the King. The thought that King James might only be restored by the aid of France, England's long-term enemy, sat uneasily in their minds. They wanted an English king but not one planted by either Holland or France. The new year seemed set to begin on an unsettling note.

The first of January did not make a change of date which only occurred on Lady Day the 25th of March. However momentous changes began from the outset. In January a special Parliament was summoned which declared that King James had abdicated after trying to subvert the constitution, two allegations that were denied by many people, including Protestants. But in view of this it was agreed that Mary, James's daughter and wife of William of Orange, was to be crowned Queen. Her husband however disputed this. If he wasn't made King then he was returning to his own country, he was not willing to accept only a matrimonial entitlement. He was determined to be king in his own right. The next month the Parliament backed down and offered the crown jointly to William and Mary who were to be equal sovereigns. The coronation ceremony took place in the spring.

William Dicconson warned the Wrightington Hall congregation. "I do not expect we shall have many more of these open services when we can hold masses with impunity," he said. "We must expect a return to the penal system and without delay. From everything we have heard this new king will be far less tolerant than King Charles was." A shiver of apprehension rippled through the congregation coupled with a great sadness. "However that does not mean we need accept the situation meekly without attempting to change it," he said ambiguously, leaving the more mentally alert to ponder on the significance of his words.

"I think he might be plotting something," Will opined to Richard when they were alone and later he repeated his thoughts to his grandfather.

"Well it won't be the first time our gentry have involved themselves in such," George Taylor admitted. "There were a few plots around in Queen Elizabeth's time. Two of the Stanleys tried to rescue Mary Stuart and secure her in the Isle of Man, Sir William Stanley organised Catholic conspiracies from Flanders and it was a local plot involving the Heskeths of Rufford and Aughton that caused the death of Ferdinando Lord Derby. It would be out of character if they didn't do something. But remember you two, no getting involved in anything. You've finished your training now so keep your noses clean and don't throw it all away by ending up in gaol or worse."

Richard had turned eighteen and the two boys had finished their apprenticeship. Will Taylor as family would continue to live in his grandparents' home and because Pete was too ill to do much weaving his grandfather had taken his grandson on as a partner. George was apologetic to Richard that he did not have enough work and not enough looms to be able to employ him now that he would be entitled to a proper wage, especially as he considered the boy the better of the two. However he sought around for weavers needing workers and discovered that Robert Shaw who lived in Dalton was expanding his business with another couple of looms and was willing to take Richard on trial, especially as George had emphasized his skill and dexterity. Richard was sorry to leave the Taylors after having lived and worked with them for eight years but George and Jane offered a warm welcome whenever he wished to visit, George assuring him that he was always available for help when needed, while Will made him promise that they would continue their friendship.

"Robert Shaw will probably be a stern employer," George warned him, "but he is known to be a fair man and will always give you your due. Work hard and you will do well and don't forget you are learning all the time, constantly improving your skills."

Now that he was no longer an apprentice meant moving back to live in the Swift household, not something he was looking forward to. He had always enjoyed his Sunday visits but to live there permanently was different. The house was unbearably cramped, he had to share a bedchamber with his Uncle Tom and Eddy and he desperately missed George's interesting conversation and the companionship of Will. Tom had little to talk about except his work on the farms, Eddy at twelve years old was too young and his grandmother was constantly complaining, her increasing ailments making her more irritable.

"There's not room for another adult in this house," she snapped. "Why don't you look for another husband,

Marie. Take you all off our hands. You're only.... thirty-five is it?......though by all the saints you look a lot older. Come to think of it, I don't know who would take you on."

Richard saw the expression on his mother's face and said, "You are beautiful, Ma. As soon as I know Robert Shaw is going to employ me permanently we will look for a house of our own to rent. With both our wages we will have enough to pay the rent and buy some furniture."

Consequently he was determined to gain the weaver's approval. The first two weeks were hard. He had to put up with his master's harsh criticisms, didn't complain about not being allowed regular breaks and suffered the suspicions of his fellow-employees who mistrusted the arrival of a new broom who appeared to be more efficient than they. Robert Shaw had a large workshop, a weaving shed separate from his house in which were five looms–three for linen weaving, one for fustian (a mixture of linen and wool) and a linen tape loom. All the looms were capable of weaving broad widths where more than one weaver was needed and he already employed three weavers as well as working himself. He was not a Catholic. Richard missed the talk he had known with George and Will to help pass the time. But after the first week he had come to appreciate his master's skill and business acumen and realised that his apparent hardness was a way of testing him. For his part Robert Shaw had seen that George Taylor's commendations had been true and in the young Richard Webster he would find a valuable employee especially as his experience increased. After two weeks he offered him a permanent job and a small regular wage commensurate with his youth and inexperience but it was more money than Richard had ever had and he felt the satisfaction of having earned it himself with his own efforts. Now the first stage of his ambition could be realised – a home for his mother.

Between them they set out to look for a suitable house in Dalton near to his work. The new landlord of the 'Millstone' tavern was moving out of his cottage to live in his recently-acquired premises and when he was assured they had a regular income to pay the rent he was willing to have them as tenants. The small half-timbered cottage was an old building constructed of a frame of oak beams, the spaces between filled in with wattle and daub, and thatched with a roof of reeds. It stood on its own, the front door opening from the lane but with a vegetable plot outside the back door. There was only one large room downstairs but Joseph Rimmer had had a brick oven added to the hearth. The cooking area was a stone sink with a stone slab and shelves in an angle of the room. A wooden ladder led up to two separate chambers. Marie was overwhelmed with joy because it was the first place of her own that she had had since Edward left ten years ago and she immediately set about removing their few belongings from Ellen's house. The cottage had been left sparsely furnished with a table and stools, and Tom Swift helped them carry their pallet beds and their old chest from his mother's. They would buy more things as needed and when they could afford but there were always people selling second-hand goods either if they were improving their living or someone had died. Richard was happy because his mother was happy and her face shed years as she busied herself cleaning and preparing their new home. Richard would have to share a bedchamber with

Eddy but Marie was ecstatic at the thought of having her own room after so long without privacy as Mary was to continue living with her grandmother. Ellen's health had deteriorated badly, her rheumatism rendering her practically immobile and in constant pain and she was unable to manage on her own with Tom out working all day. When Richard suggested that his sister go out to work as she was now fourteen and his mother take the easier option of looking after Ellen, Marie gave one of her rare laughs saying, "Dear Richard, I would much rather spend my days at Ashurst Hall, enough said!" Mary never seemed to mind her grandmother's sharp tongue and increasing bad temper due to the unrelievable pain. She was a quiet uncomplaining girl and had always been caring, looking after the baby Eddy when she was only a child herself. Ellen was fond of her in her undemonstrative way and Mary contributed to her keep by doing some spinning at home for the weavers. Eddy was about to start an apprenticeship now that he was eleven and arrangements had been made for him to work with a weaver called William Crosse, a relative of their Crosse friends in Parbold and a Catholic. Eddy was older than Richard had been but he had never been strong and Marie had kept him at home as long as possible. For this reason she did not want him to live in the Crosse household so he was to return home each evening. Richard would have liked his own room in their own house but he knew his mother still worried about Eddy and wanted to keep him close and he intended to make her as happy as he could.

They were finally getting on their feet ten years after Edward Webster's ill-fated journey to Maryland. They had been hard ten years and there was still a lot of hard work to come if they were to escape permanently from the trap of poverty. Richard was aware that much of the burden fell upon him. It would be a long time before Eddy was earning a wage even if he could survive his apprenticeship and his mother might not always be able to work. He was now a trained weaver but working for someone else, a state of affairs that would continue for some time. One day he was determined to be an independent weaver, his own man.

The dark cloud covering their lives was the deposition of King James II and the possible end of what had seemed like the fulfilment of their dreams – the reign of a Catholic monarch and the abolition of all penalties against Catholics. The euphoria had lasted such a short time and now there was confusion and uncertainty again. William of Orange, now King of England, had invaded the country with the sole intention of destroying Catholocism so it would not be long before he began to take steps.

It was as they feared. In William's first Parliament freedom of worship was granted to all except Catholics. Non-conformists who had shared their persecution previously were now at liberty to abstain from attendance at the parish churches and were permitted to make their devotions in their own way, even build places of worship for themselves. They included Baptists, Quakers, Presbyterians and Independents. All previous penalties against Catholics were to be revived even more harshly. This was a blow that struck them severely, especially after the brief idyll of freedom. It was more bitter because the Non-conformists of Tunley, a part of Wrightington, had been given permission to build a chapel for themselves there and the Dissenters of Rainford were arranging for a meeting house.

"We will not give up the fight," William Dicconson said.

Masses now had to be said clandestinely once more. Of course many people in Parbold, Wrightington and Dalton were aware of those amongst their neighbours who were Catholics and it was not possible to completely ignore the numbers entering the Halls of Fairhurst, Wrightington, Burscough and Mossborough at specific times. But the authorities had to find proof of illegal activities and suspicion was not proof. Catholics were discreet and of necessity cunning. They continued to use the back ways and go in the dark and had ways of clearing up evidence swiftly. Unless officers of the law could disturb a mass actually in progress, or see a priest on, or near, the premises, or find an individual with a missal or crucifix on his person, then they couldn't apply punishment. Church wardens were supposed to make note of anyone not attending the parish church for the stated number of times per year but even those who were scrupulous, and not everyone was, found it genuinely difficult to keep track especially as there were several parishes in the vicinity and even Protestant locals tended to use whichever was most convenient at the time – a lift on a cart to Ormskirk for a baptism was preferable to a walk to Upholland.

"I was at Ormskirk on that date," or "Eccleston" or "Upholland" or "Douglas Chapel" (when it was in use), "Lathom chapel" or even "Croston" were common untruths that were difficult to pursue. It was easy to confuse the church wardens. Some Catholics were what were called "Church Papists" who followed their own religion in private but continued to attend Anglican church services to avoid being fined while others kept their faith so secret that none of their neighbours knew.

However most Catholics in the area, including the Websters and their family and friends, refused to pretend otherwise and although times were not always dangerous they lived with a threat hanging over them and the possibility of pursuivants infiltrating their circles, often posing as Catholics, and informing on them. Consequently William Dicconson was always careful with his pronouncements but in the urgency of the present situation he was more than usually forthright.

"In the Bill of Rights passed by the Parliament is a clause stating that no Catholic may ever become Sovereign of England. But King James is already our lawful Sovereign. He never abdicated and it is not in Parliament's power to depose a Divinely appointed king. I have it on good authority that he does not intend to stay inactive in France nor has he given up his right to the throne. He will return and when he does then we must prepare to come to his aid. The Lancashire coast is one of the best places for an invasion, at the time of the Spanish Armada the fleet was expected to land here, and so we must get ready for such an event. For the moment several of our trusted neighbours are in communication with the King at the Palace of St. Germain near Paris where he is living as a guest of the French king."

Richard and Will had kept up their close friendship even though they no longer worked together. After work they often walked over to each other's houses and on Sundays and festivals they continued to pursue their usual activities, activities which now often involved seeking out girls to share their diversions. Now that they were no longer apprentices their activities had widened into visits to the alehouses, playing dice and cards and occasionally gambling a penny on something that seemed to offer favourable odds. They usually attended the meetings and masses together.

"So it seems as if there could be a war," Will said to Richard as they walked home from Wrightington Hall together. "If there is going to be an invasion on the Lancashire coast then it seems definite we shall be involved though I don't suppose it will be immediate. I'm ready for a bit of excitement, aren't you?" Before Richard could reply Will nudged his arm saying, "Walk on and let me have a word with Anne Berry there." He disengaged himself and Richard watched him retrace his steps to where a young woman was following them with her friends, the group whispering and giggling together. A few minutes later he caught his friend up and Richard laughing said, "No luck?"

"On the contrary, very promising. Listen can you compose me a letter to her, I think that would do the trick."

"Write it yourself."

"You're better than I am."

"Not really," Richard demurred. "I can't do much more than write my name, I read better than I write. Hey is this so I'll get the blame if she doesn't like it?"

"We'll write it together then," Will compromised. "She seems very encouraging."

"Are you fond of her?"

"Not really. She's rather fat but she looks buona roba."

"Where did you get that expression from?"

"I heard somebody use it. He'd been to London," Will smiled knowingly, his face full of mischief. "Mary Haughton has her eye on you. God's bones why do all these Catholic girls have to be called either Mary or

Anne? I'm bound to get into trouble one way or the other by mixing them up. Shall I put a word in for you?"

"No thanks. I don't like her."

"You don't have to like them, Richard. Just get yourself a bit of experience. God knows there's little to do around here except try to find willing girls and hope for Catholic plots. Let's go and spend an hour in the 'Black Bull' before we go home. I can only afford one drink but there will likely be some music. Another boring week of weaving starts tomorrow."

Richard didn't like to admit that he liked his work, he liked to set challenges for himself on how fast he could be and he was learning a new pattern from Robert Shaw. Though Richard missed George Taylor's company he found the change of scene welcome and was beginning to get to know his new workmates. They made fun of him both for his proficiency and his religion but it wasn't malevolent and there was always a spirit of solidarity amongst those in the same occupation. He wasn't sure what he might be asked to do if there was an armed response to what had been called "The glorious revolution" but at the moment he was content because his mother was, and the family were united in their own house again. He wanted to keep it so.

Chapter 8

1694–96

They had decided on a stroll by the River Douglas to talk, they could be overheard in any of the alehouses even when the noise was deafening.

"It's going to be a big rebellion, they are all in on it – the Dicconsons of course, Standish, Molyneux, Blundell, the Gerards, many of the lesser gentry. They've been sent commissions of array by King James and made Colonels."

"How do you know this?" Richard asked his friend.

"I sometimes take messages, I've told you that. William and Roger trust me and I have to know some things. Other information I pick up," Will Taylor replied.

"They've failed before, two years ago."

Will said nothing. Since the beginning of the reign of William of Orange, Catholics had been plotting to bring back James as king. Several attempts had been made to smuggle arms from France onto the Lancashire coast but they had been betrayed by either informers or negligence and the participants arrested. But while King William had been involved in a war with France in Flanders there had been moves in Lancashire for an uprising while he was out of the country with his army.

It had been considered an opportune time but had come to nought when William had beaten the French so decisively that they were in no position to aid a Jacobite rebellion. Then plans had been made for King James to land on the Lancashire coast from Ireland but the defeat of the Jacobites by William at the Battle of the Boyne had made this impossible. However they had not given up and King James continued to place his trust in the Lancashire nobility and gentry. He sent his chief agent Francis Parker to help them in their efforts and they were in constant touch with his court at St. Germain to which they sent regular envoys.

"This time could be different," Will said at last. "There are people other than Catholics who are willing to join us."

Since Queen Mary's death that year her husband had become more unpopular for she had always been the one to win the approval of their subjects. William had never been liked for his dour and arrogant demeanour while his open preference for his Dutch entourage and the way he rewarded them with lands and benefits at the expense of the English had alienated many of the upper echelons. Consequently a hybrid alliance had been formed between Jacobites and Whigs. The politics were not known to the two Dalton weavers but the situation had been assessed and seized upon by the local gentry – the Dicconsons, Nelsons and Lathoms – who occasionally would give a simplified explanation to the congregations who gathered at their Halls. They would be the natural leaders in any enterprise as in the previous civil war but they needed the co-operation of the lower classes for the rank and file of an army.

"Would you be involved, Richard?" Will asked his friend.

"If an army is raised, yes. We shall all have to fight. My grandfather had to fight sometimes in the other civil war. But I'm not willing to get involved in clandestine activities when the outcome is uncertain. It's different for you. Working with your grandfather means you can take time off with no questions asked. But I work for an employer who is not a Catholic. Also you are single with no responsibilities, living in your grandfather's house. I on the other hand am the supporter of my family and cannot leave them bereft again."

His grandmother Ellen Swift had died and been buried in Ormskirk churchyard. Richard was ignorant of the fact that in the parish registers her burial had been inscribed as 'unknown wife of James Swift.' It was uncertain whether that was because the clerk could not hear her son Thomas say her name clearly or because she was a Catholic and not a regular member of the church and therefore not worthy of note but Richard would have been angry had he seen the entry. Thomas Swift could not read or write and would not have noticed the omission. His mother's death now left him the only occupant of the cottage as Mary returned to her family so he had set out to find a wife. It had not taken him long but then he had to wait for a visiting priest before it was possible to marry Jane Topping, a widow with two young children. There was a brief ceremony at Mossborough Hall followed by a quiet family celebration though Marie could not completely hide her exasperation that her brother with only a labourer's wage had chosen to burden himself at the start with a ready-made family. Jane Topping had been fortunate to find another husband so soon after her husband's decease and Marie thought of how she had had to struggle alone. But for a long time she had not known whether Edward was dead or alive and when the truth was made certain she had realistically acknowledged that few men would wish to take on an impoverished woman with three remaining children. Now she was more or less independent and not yet forty years old and she was aware that some local widowers tried to engage her attention. But she was now content enough living with her children in their own house and did not relish having to accommodate herself to a man and taking on the responsibilities of another family. It would have been different years ago when she needed help. And a part of her heart still belonged to Edward. Despite his desertion, and she still believed he would have come back for them if he could, she did not think she could replace him with someone else.

With the death of her grandmother, Mary at sixteen had been left free to look for work. Their landlord, Joseph Rimmer of the 'Millstone', offered her work in the tavern but Richard refused. She would be cleaning the premises and washing jugs and tankards but would also be serving drink to the customers and Richard considered it wouldn't be an appropriate environment for his gentle sister who had spent most of her time within the family circle and lacked the boldness to hold her own against groups of raucous men. Eventually she had been offered a place with Goody Marclew who sold second-hand clothes from the front room of her house and needed help with washing and repairing them. Mary was quite happy with the buxom gregarious widow who chattered nonstop about the doings of her neighbours whose private lives she was amazingly well-acquainted with, a consequence of the nature of her business. Mary was also able to pick up bargains for herself and her family when they needed anything, clothes in particularly good condition that were newly-arrived in the shop and which Goody Marclew let her buy at a reduced price.

The planned insurrection, called "The Lancashire Plot" in official circles, was discovered. There were always informers and the plotters in their enthusiasm were not always discreet. People had heard the Dicconsons talk openly in their supposedly secret meetings and Will said that letters had passed freely among their supporters, he had delivered some of them himself. The local gentry were rounded up by the militia – Lord Molyneux of Croxteth, Sir William Gerard, Sir Rowland Stanley, Sir Thomas Clifton, William Blundell, William Dicconson and William Standish of Standish Hall as well as many lesser men. They were conducted to Manchester where they were to await trial on a charge of High Treason. Everyone knew that the penalty for treason was death without exception, the cruellest death of hanging, drawing and quartering unless the nobility were granted the merciful privilege of death by the axe. The news spread like wildfire through the villages of west Lancashire and people were talking of nothing else. In the past important individuals had been imprisoned for recusancy like Sir William Blundell and Sir Thomas Hesketh of Rufford Hall but never in such large numbers. Not only Catholics were horrified but also the Protestants, these men might be Catholics but they were *their* gentry, *their* landowners who gave them employment, and local support tended to veer in their favour against the anonymous administration of the Court and the Parliament. There were less tolerant men who preached vehemently that the prisoners were planning an invasion by King James and had been stockpiling arms to instigate another civil war and install not only a Catholic monarch but a permanent succession of Catholic rulers. But many people saw only the genial faces of the Dicconsons, Standishes, Blundells as they rode around, doffing their hats and donating food and drink at their festivals. The Catholics who frequented the services at Wrightington and other Halls were horrified and met in friends' houses to pray, saying the rosary without the benefit of their beads. Some of the labourers and artisans, including Will, were worried that their own small part in the abortive uprising might be discovered but the authorities were more interested in the big names.

Then to the amazement of everyone, at the trial in Manchester all the defendants were acquitted, all of them. No-one could believe it. The judge and jury declared there to be insufficient evidence and the informers were indicted for perjury. The Catholics were jubilant but whispers rustled around the community. Someone had pulled strings. Was it Lord Derby? In the time of Queen Elizabeth the 4th Earl of Derby, William Stanley, had been accused by the Queen of turning a blind eye to the activities of his Catholic tenants; Ferdinando the 5th Earl was blamed by the same Queen for being sympathetic towards them; and the officials in London had expressed their disapproval to William the 9th Earl for not ensuring the penal laws were more strictly enforced at the time of the Popish plot. This Earl had refused to call out the County militia in support of William of Orange's landing and was a close friend of Roger Kenyon, the Tory member of Parliament leading the investigation into Jacobite conspiracies. Although not Catholics themselves the Earls of Derby had always shown a modicum of sympathy. Had it happened again? Nothing was known for sure but thoughts travelled towards Knowsley Hall. The 9th Earl, the forty year old William Stanley, was the grandson of James Stanley who had been Lord Derby at the time of the civil war and for whom most of the inhabitants of west Lancashire had fought. His execution at Bolton by the Parliament in 1651 was within living memory and still aroused strong feelings. It was conceivable that his grandson had come to their aid.

For a time all meetings at the Catholic Halls were suspended and no secret visits made by priests. The Catholic gentry lay low. William Dicconson left the country and afterwards it was learnt that he had gone to join the Jacobite court at St. Germain where he had been made one of the tutors to the young prince James Edward Stuart. But apart from this rupture in their religious lives, ordinary life in Dalton and the surrounding villages returned to its usual routine, the monotony only broken by the seasons. Marriages and deaths continued with unceasing regularity. A death that caused much sorrow to Richard and Will was that of George Taylor. They mourned him for the way he had taught them, taught them more than weaving, and dispensed his care and his wisdom to them. His death made a hole in the weaving community of Dalton for he had been respected by all for his skill and his fair dealing and a crowd of mourners attended his funeral at Upholland. Afterwards they all made their way to the Abbey tavern to drink to his memory.

"He never recovered from the failure of the plot to reinstate King James, not that he was ever in favour of violent action but for the near-escape the conspirators had," Will said. "He was worried about me too because he never liked me putting myself in danger."

"At least Jane has you to care for her," Richard said, noting his widow who was trying to keep a good countenance as she accepted the condolences of their acquaintances.

"I shall be in sole charge of his weaving business now and I don't relish all the responsibility," Will said. "How about coming in with me and we could run it between us."

"I thought it was more or less arranged that Pete could bring his son," Richard said.

Will grimaced. "Pete's not well enough to do much and I don't want to have to train someone. And I'm not really that good at business dealings, you know my grandfather always thought you better than me."

"So you want me to come and do most of the work then," Richard said wryly.

"No, I don't," Will protested. "We'll share everything. We'll share the profits and you will make more than working for Robert Shaw."

We shall have to make sure we don't share the losses, Richard thought to himself. They were both young, he was twenty-four and Will a year older, with no experience of running an independent business.

"The trouble with you is that you are not really interested," he said aloud.

Will shrugged. "It's a job. Better than some. A way to make enough money to live adequately without the fear of starvation."

Richard thought about it carefully. He wanted to make himself independent one day. But that would mean having a loom made, buying stock and renting premises. He needed to be able to save money and he couldn't do this working for Robert Shaw, he was paid a wage which was all used up on living expenses. If he joined with Will he could work extra hours and put away money for future use.

"Yes I'd like to work with you," he said at last, "but with one proviso. What we make together we share. But if I want to work extra hours on my own then I must take that money for myself."

"You're already a hard businessman," Will laughed. "Yes I agree to that. But why you want to be always working beats me. There are other enjoyments in life you know. I've got a promise of one for tonight."

Richard eyed his friend, half in amusement, half in exasperation but said, "I'll tell Robert Shaw that I wish to leave his employ and as soon as gives me permission, I shall have to wait until he finds a replacement so it may be some time, then I'll join you. It will be strange working in George's place."

Richard put his decision in action immediately and though the weaver was sorry to lose him he did not refuse his request while demanding that he work another month to show a replacement what was required of him. When he was finally ready to join Will his friend had some news for him. "I'm getting married," he said.

Richard was taken aback and his surprise showed on his face. "This is very sudden. You never mentioned the possibility before. Has the fact that you're now an independent weaver gone to your head?"

Will scowled. "I didn't mention the possibility before because I hadn't thought of it until I received some news. Betty Plumb is pregnant. Go on, say it."

"I told you so," Richard said obediently. "I'm surprised it hasn't happened before." His friend continued scowling and he took pity on him. "It can't be so bad, you're of an age to get married and you have a house of your own and a business, it's time you settled down instead of philandering. I take it you have an affection for her?"

"God's bones, Richard, you are so high-minded. It will happen to you one day. Or perhaps it won't, you live like a priest."

"I don't and you know it. But I believe there should be love between you before you go so far and I have never found anyone I could love. Do you love her?"

Will sighed. "I do have an affection for her, she's good natured and hard-working. She can cook, she works in her parents' cook shop and," he smiled suddenly, "she's very willing and good in that respect which makes up for the fact that she isn't exactly blessed with brains. She will be useful in looking after Grandma Jane."

Richard shook his head in resignation, not knowing whether he should laugh or commiserate.

The wedding however was celebrated in grand style with no sign of the fact that it had been precipitated by unwelcome events. To avoid any suspicion that they were entering into matrimony by duress they decided against a clandestine Catholic ceremony and were married before scores of spectators in Ormskirk parish church after making sure the event was well-publicised.

Richard signed the register as chief witness. He had to poke Will once to remind him of the correct response but Betty was all smiles, the skirt of her leaf-green gown flowing full from her waist to hide her swelling stomach and her dark hair falling in loose waves over her shoulders as befitted a virgin. She borrowed Will's knife to cut the love-knots loosely sewn on the skirt to hand out to the girl spectators as wedding tokens, smiling triumphantly. Will's natural exuberance was complemented by his new clothes, a thigh-length jacket with pewter buttons and matching knee-length breeches in a yellowish tan called 'Lion's colour' appropriate to his mop of sandy hair on which sat a high-crowned hat of brown felt. White stockings and a newly-made pair of brown leather latchet shoes completed his outfit which drew many admiring glances. (Richard knew that George Taylor had left him a small amount of money, some of it earmarked for his wedding expenses.) Betty basked in the awareness that many of the local girls envied her for Will Taylor had always been popular while her parents, the Plumbs of the cookshop, showed their evident satisfaction that their unremarkable third daughter had gained a young man who had his own business as a weaver with a house of his own. Richard caught his eye and Will cocked his eyebrow but even though Richard smiled he found himself wishing he would find a girl he could love and one day he would have such a wedding. After the ceremony everyone crowded into the 'Bell' for liquid refreshment then later when the general public had made their way home, riding on horses or in carts, ambling through the country lanes or staggering unsteadily, Jane Taylor had provided a supper for the wedding guests proper, supplemented by the Plumbs' baking. The Taylor's living room was packed to capacity with people spilling over into the back garden as it was a fine evening and many of them had brought instruments – rebecs, tabors and pipes, flageolets and small bagpipes while Rafe Forshaw, a joiner, had a hurdy-gurdy that he had built himself. Everyone knew everyone else and Richard's family were there to enjoy the day, Marie, Mary and Eddy together with Tom Swift and his wife and children.

After the wedding Richard moved his employment and went to work with Will. With his new responsibilities as head of a business, husband, and finally father, some of his friend's exuberance had left him, for the activities that had provided his enjoyment for the last ten years were of necessity curtailed. But when the child was born, a boy whom they named George, Will was prouder than Richard had ever seen him while Jane was in her natural element with a grandson named after her husband.

Richard enjoyed working with Will and when the new husband retired to his family in the evenings he continued working. He was also learning much about the administration of a business for Will left the accounts and the receipts to him. Some of their work was 'outwork' when agents brought them yarn and then collected the linen after it had been woven into pieces paying a set price based on weight. Some of it was individual commissions and if there was any time left then they would buy yarn themselves from the spinners or the markets and weave lengths which they could sell independently. This was something that Richard put his mind to because he was determined to save up some money for the future.

THE YEW AND THE ROSE

For the Catholic community of west Lancashire the failure of the plot to reinstate King James had resulted in their having to be more circumspect in their religion but they had not given up hope of toppling William of Orange and the gentry were in constant touch with the King at St. Germain, boosted in their hopes now by the young prince James Edward Stuart as heir. In the year 1696 came an attempt to assassinate William. The King rode in Richmond Park on Sundays and the plan was to await his arrival in a country lane leading there. However the plot was revealed by informers and the assassination thwarted. The plot was led by King James's illegitimate son the Duke of Berwick and did not directly involve the previous Lancashire plotters but naturally they came under suspicion and a search was made of Standish Hall. This time the protagonists, including a priest Ambrose Rookwood, were executed– hanged, drawn and quartered as the punishment decreed for the crime of High Treason, and the previous local plotters realised what a lucky escape they had had. Ordinary Catholics suffered the repercussions as legislation was tightened against them. Two manservants, a groom and a gardener, were dismissed from Ashurst Hall but no complaint was made about Marie and she was glad for she liked working there. It wasn't arduous work and the money was essential. Richard paid most of the household expenses but she expected him to marry soon though Eddy had nearly finished his apprenticeship and would soon be bringing a wage. Mary contributed a little though circumstances were soon going to change for her. While working in Goody Marclew's second-hand clothes shop she had met a young man called Benet Bimson who worked for a cooper. He had come in looking for a canvas work shirt and when Mary had found him something satisfactory he returned a short time later for a pair of boots. After that he seemed to be always in need of an item or other, though he didn't always buy but busied himself looking through the stock. Even Goody Marclew noticed his regular appearances and commented to Mary that he seemed to be looking for more than clothes. Mary blushed. But she had noticed that he stayed talking longer to her than his visits warranted. The courtship took a long time because Mary was quiet and reserved, lacking the talent for flirtation while he was nervous about declaring himself with a slight stammer in his speech. Eventually it was Goody Marclew who suggested they took a walk together and this progressed into regular Sunday outings in the fields and to the Beacon. Gradually it became accepted that they were courting until at last Benet plucked up courage to ask Mary if he could approach her mother about a marriage between them.

"You had better ask my brother Richard too, he is the head of our family and has always looked after us," Mary said.

So she made sure Richard was at home with their mother when Benet came to call on them one Sunday afternoon. Marie was happy that quiet little Mary whose life had known much hardship had found someone to care for her so early in life. Richard questioned them both about their feelings for each other and Benet about his work and his ability to support a wife and family. But he liked what he saw of the humble young man and there was no doubting his obvious affection for his sister. Mary was twenty-two years old and he was sure she could find no-one more suited to her temperament. It would be a life without luxury but she had never asked for much. He believed it would be a life where she would be given affection and to which she would bring her own talent of caring for others.

The wedding was a quiet affair very different from the jauntiness of Will Taylor's nuptials. Marie was determined they should be married by a priest with the Catholic sacrament so they had to wait until a travelling priest arrived secretly at Mossborough Hall. Consequently it was a rushed event without much time for preparation although they had wedding clothes ready. Mary had seen a gown she liked in Goody Marclew's shop but Marie was determined she should have a new one and got the tailor Thomas Prescot to let her pay in instalments for a skirt and bodice in popingay linen, a bluish-green shade. It was the only new clothes Mary had ever had apart from the one she had worn at the Bishop's confirmation ten years earlier and for the first time in her life felt beautiful with blue ribbons in her straight fair hair. Afterwards Joseph Rimmer made a simple supper in the 'Millstone' for family and a few close friends for which Richard used some of his savings. Then they bade farewell to the newlyweds and Mary left her home for the last time, with some tears, to live with Benet and his widowed mother not too far away in their house in the little hamlet of Skelmersdale.

"Isn't it time for you to get married, Richard," Marie said when they and Eddy were alone in their own cottage. "You are twenty-six."

"I haven't met anyone I could love," he replied.

"Don't bother about love. Find yourself a good Catholic girl who will keep house for you and bear you sons to carry on the faith and help you in your work."

"I couldn't marry anyone I didn't love," he reiterated. "Someone I couldn't live without."

"That's not always a good thing. I want to see you settled and comfortable. Love is a deceiver. It brings as much grief as joy."

He was surprised at the bitterness in his mother's voice.

Chapter 9

1698–99

At twenty-eight years old Richard was feeling in a rut. His sister Mary was happily married, having found someone to reciprocate her devotion and in her usual manner willingly accepting Benet's widowed mother into her care. Soon she had someone else to care for when a little girl was born whom they named Ellen. Marie was happy in her new role as grandmother and went to visit as often as she could, Skelmersdale being only a short walk away. Eddy was on the verge of completing his apprenticeship and would soon be earning a wage. Will was settling into being a husband and father, he and Betty had another child besides George whom they named Edward. Kindly Jane Taylor had died to the especial regret of her grandson and Richard who owed her much, but Will and Betty now had the house to themselves with plenty of room for their growing family. Will's spare time was no longer in the alehouses or competing in horse races but walking out with his family and frequenting the markets and consequently his leisure time with Richard was curtailed.

For a time Richard had entertained a vague idea about going to Maryland. Once he was sure his family were settled satisfactorily he had thought of trying to make a new life for himself in the Catholic colony where his father had gone. Nicholas Turner occasionally brought news of his brother John who now owned a hundred acres of land which he had named 'Turner's Adventure.' Richard could see little hope of ever bettering himself beyond becoming an independent weaver one day and the prospect of being a land-owner was tempting. His father had died in the attempt but Richard was sure that if John Turner could do it then so could he. Four young people had recently gone to the new world from Wrightington–Thomas Roper, Ellen Fisher, Margaret Lavinsley and Mary Howard, and the tailor Thomas Prescot's son John had gone from Dalton together with young Margaret Lamb and Richard Berry which had provided a talking point for some time because everyone knew everyone else. There was news that others had gone from Upholland, Ormskirk and Lathom. All had bound themselves in service for a set period in a colony called Virginia because the colony of Maryland was no more, another victim of the deposition of King James. Buoyed up by the 'glorious revolution' in England a group of Protestant colonists there had led an uprising against the Catholic Calvert owners of the province and succeeded in removing them from the control of the colony, an act legitimised by King William. Maryland as an independent Catholic colony had ceased to exist. King William had put his own royal governor in charge there and by an Act of Government the Anglican church had been made the established church of Maryland and practising Catholics forbidden. St. Mary's city was destroyed and Catholic settlers had moved away to find refuge in other colonies like

Virginia, the newly-developing Kentucky or in a new colony called Pennsylvania. This had recently been established by an English Quaker called William Penn and though the motivation had been to create a refuge for Quakers, Penn's liberal principles on religious freedom granted welcome to all settlers irrespective of their faith. Richard wondered what his father would have done had he still been alive, he had made acquaintance with Quakers in Barbados.

But now that Maryland no longer seemed an option and he was still bound to supporting his family Richard decided that the time had come for him to set up as an independent weaver. He had been saving money for several years and reckoned he had enough for a loom and yarn and the rent of some premises. Will was sorry to have him leave their partnership but it was no surprise as he had known for a long time that his friend had been planning this.

"You won't have any problem finding someone in my place and it will make no difference to our relationship, we shall always be friends," Richard told him.

Once he had accepted this, Will considered it might actually be an advantage to be an employer who could state his own conditions to a newcomer. He had matured with his new responsibilities as husband and father and learnt a lot from Richard. Provided he could find someone who didn't need supervision it would mean he could work fewer hours instead of trying to keep up with Richard's schedule. But he felt it necessary to warn his friend of the risks he was taking. "Are you sure you will be able to manage financially, it will be hard at first trying to find work for yourself and you will have to work long hours."

"I'm used to that," Richard said.

"There's a danger you could lose money as well as make some but if things don't work out you can always come back," Will assured him after wishing him luck in the venture.

Richard's next task was to find somewhere to live and work. There were always cottages to rent in and around Dalton as people moved around – losing their employment as labourers, not being able to pay the rent, moving elsewhere for work, marriages and deaths, but he needed something larger. It took time but then a weaver called John Finch died and his widow decided to go and live with her married daughter in Lathom. Jenet Finch would be willing to rent the house, which was owned by her husband's family, but wished to sell the two looms and his assistant Samuel Jolly was hoping that the new inhabitant would continue to employ him.

"I only have use for one loom and I'm afraid I can't employ anyone else at this time," Richard explained. "However I know a fellow-weaver William Taylor who would be glad of an experienced assistant and I will mention Samuel's name to him. If you could possibly let me buy one loom, Goodwife Finch, I'm sure you would find no difficulty in selling the other."

Jenet Finch was not eager to do so, looms were cumbersome and not easy to dismantle and convey elsewhere. She tried to persuade him to take the two on the grounds that he might require a partner one day but though Richard was tempted he knew he could not afford. The rent for the house was much more than they were paying for the cottage. Eventually they reached a compromise that if he could find a buyer for the other loom then he might take over the premises. Richard went immediately to his former employer Robert Shaw knowing that he was always seeking to expand his business and the offer of a large loom at such a price well below its value would be too tempting to refuse.

Richard was well pleased with the arrangement. The house stood on its own at the crossroads where the roads to Newburgh and Parbold diverged and was built of irregular stone of all shapes and sizes with a roof of hand-made tiles. The door was set at one side of the frontage with a window of small-paned glass beside it and another casement above it with panes of yellow horn. The door opened directly from the road and led immediately into the workshop, spacious with only one loom now and plenty of room for yarn, rope, rolls of cloth etc., and though the window had small panes it was big enough to provide good light, essential for working. The living room behind the workshop had white-washed stone walls, a stone-slabbed floor and a brick hearth. A casement window of four glass panes overlooked a patch of ground planted with vegetables where two apple trees stood sentinel and a fenced pen awaited domestic animals. The door into the back garden was through a small kitchen which opened out of the living room and was lit by another window. There was a brick bake-oven and stone sink and an alcoved larder with wide stone shelves. Beside the back door a staircase led up to two inter-connecting rooms of a good size. The chamber at the back had a window of small-paned glass which overlooked the garden with open fields beyond while the adjoining chamber overlooked the road at the front with a casement of translucent horn so Richard decided he would take the back room for his own.

Now that he was satisfied with his accommodation he informed his mother that he was leaving their cottage to take up his own abode. "I'll continue to help with the rent until Eddy is getting a full wage," he assured her.

"Are you planning to get married, Richard?" she asked eagerly after assimilating his news.

"I'm not planning anything, Ma, except setting up on my own," he replied.

Marie was disappointed but not entirely convinced. Why else should her son be moving into his own house if he wasn't planning on taking a wife to share it and the possibility excited her enough to compensate for his loss.

"Will you be able to take Eddy to work with you eventually?" she asked hopefully.

"I don't know," he replied guardedly. "It depends how well I do. He must get some experience first and then we'll see how things work out."

Marie considered he was thinking of how he could support a family and the idea gave new impetus to her conviction that he was planning to marry, so much so that she couldn't avoid saying, "Now you have a house of your own you must find a good Catholic girl to keep it for you and fill it with children."

Richard moved into his house as soon as it became vacant though he was woefully aware of how poorly supplied he was. Will came over and they shared a bottle of ale between them to celebrate the occasion, bringing his own tankard as Richard only had one. They sat on stools as there were no chairs and only a rough pine table.

"Mother of God, Will, I never realised I would need so much stuff," he groaned. "You had the house ready furnished from George and Jane but I have nothing of my own. Ma gave me a few pots but I've had to buy bed linen and blankets. I'll gradually furnish it as and when I can, make it more comfortable, but at the moment it will do for me."

"So you are not keeping us all in the dark by planning marriage, as Betty insists you are?"

"Will, you know me better than that. How many times must I tell you I haven't met anyone I could spend my life with."

"Betty says you should find a good Catholic girl to keep house and bear you children and that would make your life so much more comfortable."

"Sweet Jesus, she sounds just like my mother."

"All women think about is marriage. They don't realise it's not quite the same for men. If we could get our pleasures without it, it wouldn't be worth considering." The rueful tone of Will's voice didn't escape Richard. He now had three children, Betty lately having given birth to a girl they had named Jane. "But what are you going to eat? Can you cook?"

Richard shrugged. "I suppose I shall frequent Betty's parents' cookshop. Or go around to my mother's. More likely I shall live on bread and cheese or ham and eggs."

"Sounds good," Will said wistfully and they laughed together. "Listen, I've heard there's a horse race at Newburgh on Sunday. How about us going?" he suggested as he prepared to depart. "I fancy a day away from the family. I only wish I could borrow a horse and race as I used to." Their minds travelled back to the times they had occasionally disobeyed George Taylor and gone to the races that were periodically held in various places on Sunday afternoons. Whenever he could borrow a horse, a colt, even a pony, Will would take part and persuade Richard to put a bet on him. Once he even managed to win and Richard collected his winnings for the first time. "I've half a mind to find a mount but realistically I think I'm a bit too old at nearly thirty, the competitors will all be young lads. But we can make bets and have a tankard of ale. It's a time since we had a day out together."

Richard agreed, being in the mood for some diversion himself especially as the weather seemed set to be fine for early April.

The following Sunday they set off from Dalton to Newburgh, soon joining the crowds flocking to watch the horse racing. Anyone who had a horse or could borrow one could participate so there was a lot of local competition, most of the spectators putting money on their neighbours rather than on who were considered favourites. There were several races over the afternoon and the alehouses were taking bets as well as dispensing large quantities of ale though the company was good-natured and well-behaved if boisterous. Anyone who could get to Newburgh did so for the races were a festival in themselves and any diversion was eagerly snatched at by the inhabitants of the cluster of villages. Costermongers sold pies and gingerbread, pedlars were taking the opportunity to sell ribbons and ballad sheets to the girls and there was a musician with a hurdy-gurdy. Richard and Will made small bets on what they considered the best horses, some were little more than nags and some small animals more resembled donkeys than ponies but some were good well-formed colts. The riders also were of differing standards – farmers' sons and husbandmen used to riding contrasting with young lads who had never ridden before and on finding a mount were willing to risk accidents for the sheer excitement of novelty. Many a tumble resulted and caused as much enjoyment to the spectators as a successful winner. Sometimes fate was capricious and a young lad clinging helplessly to his pony's mane overtook a more experienced rider to win the race much to the spectators' amusement.

Richard was enjoying one such escapade when his attention was caught by a girl standing a little way to the side of him but in his line of vision. She was laughing at a young lad who was trying desperately to keep his seat as his lively colt bucked and tossed but refused to go anywhere and she seemed so carefree that his attention was caught by her rather than by the unfortunate rider. She was young, he reckoned she could not have been twenty years old, and he continued to look at her, admiring her pleasantly rounded figure neatly proportioned to her more than average height. She was dressed in a tight-fitting bodice of buttercup yellow over a full kirtle of bright grass-green and in her natural spontaneity she seemed to him to represent the very spirit of springtime. She turned to pick up a child of about four years old standing beside her and the curtain of shining chestnut hair reaching almost to her waist fell over her face as she lifted him up. Richard didn't think she was old enough for the child to be hers and if she had been married she wouldn't have been wearing her hair flowing loose. She put the child down on the grass again as he was obviously too heavy for her then after saying a few words to him she turned her head and saw Richard looking at her. As if she could feel the intensity of his gaze she kept her eyes fixed on him and Richard was able to see her face, wide expressive eyes under arched brows, sun-kissed skin with a healthy rose tint in her cheeks, curving sensuous mouth. For a moment their eyes locked and as if sensing his appreciation she smiled at him, a warm natural smile devoid of self-consciousness or flirtation. He didn't return her smile but doffed his hat in salutation and she dropped her eyes in embarrassment. Then she turned away again to talk to the three children gathered around a plump woman in her forties whom he thought must be her mother and siblings.

"Who's that girl there?" he asked Will who had returned after collecting their winnings from the 'Wheatsheaf'.

Will squinted in his direction then replied, "Dick Crane's eldest. I don't know her name, there are a lot of Cranes. Too many some would say. They think they own the place."

"They nearly do," Richard said wryly. The road between Lathom and Ormskirk was called Cranes Lane, showing how much land they owned in the area.

Will lost interest and they moved on. But the image of the girl stayed in Richard's mind and he didn't quite know why. Her natural loveliness and her joy of being had made an impact on him. Somehow he thought of his sister Mary at that age – poor, thin because she never had too much to eat, never able to beautify herself with new clothes, always working with little leisure time. The Cranes were farmers with an abundance of good food to hand, yeoman farmers who had money enough to afford fine clothes, people to work for them so that they could enjoy leisure time. Still he could not free his mind from the fleeting glimpse of the girl in the yellow and green gown.

He wondered if it was coincidence or fate that he saw her again a few weeks later. He had gone to Ormskirk market with a parcel of linen for a mercer there and as usual had been given a lift for part of the way by a husbandman taking in some fresh vegetables. But if he had to walk all the way home it was another two hours so he decided to stop at the 'The Plough' and drink a tankard of ale to help him on the way. It was a fine day and seeing some acquaintances he joined them at one of the tables set outside. They made general talk for a while – the rising price of wheat, how long the fine weather would last, the growing unpopularity of King William and the burning down of the royal palace of Whitehall by a maid who had left clothes to dry too close to a fire, a fact eliciting some ribald comments. Then they set to go their separate ways and Richard was rising to return his blackjack tankard to the tap room when the girl came into view walking beside a man. She wore the bright green kirtle again but with a short untabbed bodice of a darker forest-green wool fastened with wooden toggles, the full sleeves of her white chemise turned back over the cuffs. A small linen cap with an edging of lace was set far back on her flowing brown hair and tied under her chin with ribbons. The man was dressed in homespun with a felt hat and carried a large wicker basket filled with goods she had obviously purchased at the market. They made to go into the inn and Richard surmised they would be picking up a horse they had left in the stable while they shopped. She glanced at him with a little frown wrinkling her brow as she wondered where she had seen him before but when he raised his hat to her she appeared to remember him for she smiled in acknowledgement before they went their separate ways. A little way out of the town she passed him, riding pillion behind the man whom Richard decided was one of the farm servants given the enviable task of taking her to the market although she was not holding onto his waist but cradling the basket as she rode confidently sidesaddle. They had soon disappeared from sight but when the road curved around she saw him striding vigorously as he left the stony path to cut across the fields. As he walked home the brief encounter lifted his spirits as much as the money he had earned and he wondered if they would ever meet again in such an unexpected way, pondering on why it mattered to him.

It was about two weeks later and Richard was working on the loom in the front room of his house when a knock on the door signalled a visitor and he called to come in. "I can't leave what I'm doing at the moment, just give me a minute," he shouted above the noise of the loom and it was only when he had finished the line that he was able to lift his head and see who had come through the door. To his amazement it was the Crane girl except that today over the green kirtle she was wearing a sleeveless bodice of scarlet wool with a white smock showing beneath, the swell of her breasts revealed above the low neckline. Her hair was tied back from her face with a red ribbon but hung loose over her shoulders.

"Give you good day, Mistress Crane, how can I help you?" He was flustered by her presence in his workroom and conscious of his working clothes, a sleeveless black leather jerkin over an open-necked linen shirt.

"I heard you were the best weaver in Dalton," she said. It was the first time he had heard her speak and he liked the voice that was clear and firm with flat vowels like his own.

"I am," he said and she laughed, opening her mouth and revealing even white teeth. He smiled ruefully at his own conceit and in explanation said, "I've been doing it for nearly twenty years."

Her wide eyes, which he could now see were hazel with gold flecks in their depths and fringed by thick lashes, showed her surprise. "You must have been very young," she said and there was a trace of sympathy in her tone.

"Just a young boy, not much more than a child really." He felt an urge to tell her why he had had to start work so early but he said nothing more.

"Can you weave a piece of linen for me?" she asked.

"Certainly. How big? Enough for a kerchief, or a smock?"

She blushed and he thought *I shouldn't have said that*. It sounded impertinent but she didn't seem to mind.

"Only for a collar, a large collar that will cover my shoulders, almost like a little cape. I have a length of beautiful lace that I want to use, it was a present from my grandmother but it isn't long enough to trim a petticoat or a smock. But I want a piece of beautiful fine linen to do it justice and I haven't been able to find anything fine enough with a special weave. Could you do it for me? I'm sorry it won't be a very big piece for you to do and I'll understand if it isn't worth taking on."

"I can't actually weave wide pieces, that takes two people because you have to have someone else to throw the shuttle back at the end of the line, you can't reach it yourself. It's usually a job for an apprentice. So don't worry about only wanting a small piece. I can do anything to fit your requirements."

"I have the money to pay," she assured him earnestly.

"I'm sure you have, Mistress Crane," he hoped he didn't sound sarcastic.

"My name's Debra," she said but he made no comment and she continued, "How long will it take?"

"Not long, but I have a lot of work." He didn't want to appear too eager to do something for her.

"I'll come for it in a week then?"

"I'll deliver it for you. I usually do," he said.

"No, I'll come for it," she said, "Newburgh is quite a walk when you are busy."

"And also for you. Did you walk here today?" Richard asked.

She shook her head. "My father had some business close by and I rode pillion with him. I'll come back in a week."

"Very well if that is what you wish, Mistress Crane."

"My name's Debra," she said again but he merely nodded and bade her a courteous farewell.

When she had gone he didn't feel that he could continue his work immediately, it was as if the light had been extinguished. He went into the living room. His most recent acquisition had been a chair with arms, his only chair, and he sat with his elbows resting on the table. What was happening to him? He had never experienced such turbulent emotions before – confusion, loneliness, an indefinable longing – all for the sake of a girl he had seen a couple of times and talked with once, about business. He was twenty-eight years old and had seen and known dozens of girls, some of whom he had liked, but none had ever affected him in the way that Debra Crane did. Yet he knew nothing about her except her father was the farmer Richard Crane. He didn't even know how old she was or if she was betrothed to someone, a likely prospect. His heart was pierced with an unidentifiable pain and yet at the same time the image of her sent his heart soaring as if on wings. He would weave the most beautiful piece of linen he had ever made and in the weave would be something more that would make it special.

The days passed slowly, waiting for her return which was almost a week to the day. When she walked through the door it was as if the room flooded with sunshine. She was wearing the red sleeveless bodice again but with a linen kirtle of a shade somewhere between bluebells and wild violets and her face was alight with anticipation. Richard thought he had never seen such a lovely face, serene in repose but vivacious when she spoke, a smile ready on her lips. She was thrilled with the piece he had made, fingering the delicate stuff and exclaiming, "This is so beautiful, almost like silk, just what I wanted. When I have made the collar I will let you see it."

She paid him the money he had asked, taking the coins from a little bag hanging at her waist and although he almost said she could have it for nothing he knew this would not do. She seemed in no great hurry to depart and asked, "Do you live here?"

"Yes I do," he replied. Whilst realising it was not according to the rules of propriety he found himself saying, "Would you like to see my living accommodation?"

When she accepted with unselfconscious eagerness he led her through the workshop into the living room and she looked around curiously. Although he had been gradually adding to his stock of necessities the room was still barely-furnished with its pine table and stools, the one chair and a few shelves, one of which held three books, and a wrought-iron candlestick.

"Do you live alone?" she asked, then added hastily, "I'm sorry I shouldn't be so impertinent but I thought you must be alone because it lacks comforts."

He was taken aback because to him it was eminently comfortable, especially the armed oak chair which he had never had before. "It's much more cheerful when I light a fire in the hearth," he insisted.

"Curtains on the window would make it warmer and you could weave a mat for in front of the hearth. And what about colouring the walls instead of the whitewash, we paint some of ours with oxblood."

Richard couldn't help laughing as he said, "Yes I know it's basic but the problem, Mistress Crane, is also money."

It was her turn to look abashed and she apologised hastily saying, "I am so sorry, my mother is constantly reprimanding me for being too forthright. I was out of order, I have no right to pry into your private life." Then contradicting herself she couldn't forbear asking, "You aren't married then?" She was curious as to why a handsome man of twenty-eight and an independent craftsman should not have a wife.

"No I am not married. I live alone," he answered, half of him happy at her questions but the other half feeling embarrassed by her disingenuous manner. Yet he liked her natural easiness, her curiosity a part of the joy of being that emanated from her.

"Aren't you lonely?" she persisted.

"I'm not lonely most of the time. I work long hours so I don't have much time in the evenings. I have several friends who come around occasionally, we play cards and some of them bring musical instruments, sometimes I go to visit them or meet them in the alehouses and during the light evenings I can read though I only have three books." When George Taylor died he had left Richard his Herbal and during the few years of Catholic freedom in the reign of King James when Catholic books and artefacts like crucifixes and rosaries were sold openly he had bought a book of saints' lives from a bookseller in Ormskirk which had joined his father's copy of Aesop's Fables on the shelf.

She looked surprised and said, "I can't read. My father thinks it isn't necessary for girls to read and write."

"That's a pity. Reading can give you great pleasure and it's always useful to know how to sign your name. Even my mother who hasn't had many advantages can sign her name and read a little."

Debra was finding the weaver even more interesting because he was different to anyone in her circle of acquaintances and she thought him the most handsome man she had seen – taller than she with a well-proportioned figure, pleasant regular features with intelligent grey eyes and a gentle smile that betokened a kindly nature, thick fair hair that was beginning to darken swept back from his forehead and falling to his shoulders in a natural curve. But even though Debra's nature was naturally frank and open she realised she had overstepped the bounds of propriety with a single man she hardly knew.

"I'm sorry, I haven't been polite asking too many questions," she apologised. "I've wasted your time when you are busy. Please forgive me. Thankyou for making my linen and for showing me where you lived."

"There is nothing to forgive," he assured her as he led her back through the workshop. "It has been a pleasure."

At the door she turned and said, "You are very kind." She left and neither of them said goodbye.

Afterwards Richard's emotions were more disturbed than ever but he took irrational comfort in the fact that neither of them had said goodbye. But the chances of seeing more of Debra Crane were slim in the extreme. She would be unlikely to visit him again and he could hardly go to Newburgh and hang about in the hope of catching a glimpse of her. Most people met either through work or church. Weavers' daughters and sons married into other weavers' families, farmers' children with sons and daughters of other farmers. Debra Crane was most probably engaged to someone. Protestants married Protestants and Catholics married Catholics and the Cranes were Protestants. *Why on earth was he thinking of marriage or even of any closer relationship just because his emotions had been touched for the first time by a girl? Debra Crane was out of his reach. He didn't know how old she was but he doubted she had reached twenty years and he was turned twenty-eight and, more seriously, of a different religion and a different class of society. He must put her out of his mind for it was impossible she could think more of him than being the best weaver in Dalton.*

Nonetheless it was perhaps some deep-seated desire to see her again that made him accept Will's suggestion to go to the Whitsun Ales at Ormskirk. He hoped it might be an opportunity to catch a glimpse of her there though he couldn't confess to Will even though he was his closest friend and almost a brother. He told himself he needed some relaxation. Spring was the time for festivals but Easter and Mayday had gone almost unnoticed by him as he had continued to work to pay the rent of two houses and furnish his own home better. Easter had seen a mass at Wrightington Hall with the welcome arrival of a priest, and he had shared a meal with his mother and Eddy on Easter Sunday but the next day when they had gone to watch the egg-rolling at the Beacon with all the attendant merriment he had stayed home to work. Similarly on Mayday when there had been maypoles in Wrightington and Lathom he had refused several invitations to join the festivities. Mayday was a time for lovers and a day when marriages often took place and this year for some reason they didn't appeal to him.

Less than two months later the Whitsun Ales was the last of the spring festivals. There was too much work on the land in the summer for workers to take time off and there would be no more relaxation until Harvest home so it was always an occasion for merrymaking. Will told him that he was going to hire a pony and cart to take his family for an outing, there was now another infant girl named Elizabeth to make his brood up to four, and suggested that Richard also borrow a horse and accompany them.

"We can choose either Upholland, Eccleston or Ormskirk," he said. The Whitsun Ales, as well as being a festival for the parish was a way for the parish church to make money for themselves by selling their own ales at a slightly inflated price justified by the entertainment provided, music, dancing, and sideshows. "Upholland would be the nearest."

"Ormskirk would be most likely to offer the best entertainment, being a bigger town," Richard commented, not willing to acknowledge his real reason for the suggestion. Dalton where they lived was in Upholland parish, Parbold and Wrightington where they had a lot of family and friends was in Eccleston parish, but Newburgh was in Ormskirk parish and this was where the Crane family would likely be.

Will accepted the reasoning and Richard decided that he would also hire a cart with a horse so that he could take his mother and Eddy to enjoy the festivities as well.

"Why aren't we going to Upholland, it's nearer?" Marie asked as she and Eddy climbed into the small cart which was equipped with two facing plank seats. Richard thought how happy she looked in her best kirtle of brown wool with a plain orange-tawny bodice, a linen cap with the edge folded back and gathered in the nape of her neck. She wasn't quite so thin and her light brown hair showed only the odd thread of silver.

"I thought you would enjoy a pleasant longer drive through the fields while the weather is so warm and it's such an unaccustomed treat for you," he replied as he climbed onto the board at the front of the cart and took up the horse's reins. "Also as I am not an experienced horseman I didn't fancy the long hill with the cart, it's flatter to Ormskirk and you're not as likely to get overturned."

The road to Ormskirk was crowded with horses, carts and walkers and they picked up a grateful labourer and his wife. The crowd increased as they reached the town which was already full with people of all classes and ages. The activity was centred around the church and the churchyard where the ales were being sold but sideshows, stalls and entertainments were set around the streets and in the grassy spaces. Betty took the children to watch a puppet show and was grateful when Marie accompanied them to hold the baby. Eddy joined Richard and Will to sample the ales then they wandered over to where a group of musicians, the town waits, were playing, joined later by a team of the traditional whitsun morrismen. Richard stayed watching them when Will and Eddy went off in search of more ale, Will also determined to try his skill at the archery butt which had been set up in the churchyard. The morrismen finished their turn and the musicians turned to playing dance tunes which soon drew groups of people, not all of them young for middle-aged dames took the opportunity to reawaken nostalgic memories of their youth in their more reluctant spouses. Richard felt a light touch on his arm and turning he thought he was in the middle of a dream as he found himself face to face with Debra Crane. She was dressed in her blue kirtle with the yellow bodice she had been wearing the first time he had seen her but she had untied the sleeves from the bodice to show her smock, filling in the eyelets with blue ribbons. Her hair was flowing loose and her face had a healthy glow. Although he had been hoping against hope that he might see her, the shock took him by surprise.

"Give you good day," she greeted him. "Were you thinking of joining the dancing?"

"I'm afraid I can't dance," he said lamely after returning her greeting.

"Everyone dances at a festival," she said smiling mischievously and with a challenge in her eyes. "It's a communal activity and a perfect way to socialise for anyone who lives on their own."

"Well then why aren't you dancing, Mistress Crane?"

"I'm looking for a partner," she replied. She was looking at him expectantly but there was no trace of flirtation in her manner. "Anyone can dance a brawl. You just hold hands in a circle and go round to the left and then to the right. That's all. I'll show you if you wouldn't mind obliging me."

She waited for his response and because he didn't wish to appear churlish he held out his hand to her and they went to join the circle of dancers. Many of the dancers had already drunk too much ale and there was a lot of shambling and going in the wrong direction with howls of laughter so that Richard's ineptitude went unnoticed and all he was conscious of was Debra's hand in his and her obvious enjoyment as they capered about. When the dance had finished to the accompaniment of much laughing and clapping Richard asked, "You are not alone here are you?"

Debra shook her head saying, "Oh no, all the family are here, well except father who isn't at home with this sort of thing and besides he's always busy. But mother has taken my brothers and my sister Esther to watch the puppet play and I wanted to dance. I suppose the show will be over by now so I had better go and find them. Are you alone?"

"No, I also am with friends and family," he replied, feeling foolishly glad that she did not seem to have a young man in tow.

"Do enjoy the rest of the day," she said gaily, feeling involuntarily happy that he did not seem to be with a girl. "By the way my mother would like some linen for sheets and I told her about you. When she is sure about how much she needs I would like to come and give you an order if you are willing."

"I would be very happy to do so," he replied and they bade farewell.

Will and Eddy were walking towards him and they saw her depart. Will raised his eyebrows interrogatively. "Her mother wants some linen for sheets," Richard said in answer but added nothing to it. Will narrowed his eyes and a slight frown crinkled his brow but he said no more and they made the rounds of the stalls and entertainments together, stopping often to sample the ales.

Back home in his own house Richard was torn between hope and despair. He knew now without doubt that for the first time in his life he had fallen in love. Debra Crane had captured his heart as no-one had ever done before though he had to admit he knew hardly anything about her. But why should a lovely young girl from a good family feel the same way towards a weaver who once had been poor enough to be classed as a pauper, a weaver with a life skill who worked hard but had few possessions and whose family and social circle were in a different class to affluent farmers? Yet she seemed to like him. She was without guile and had demonstrated a natural warmth towards him. She was the one who had twice sought him out. He had no idea where to go from here. He couldn't go wandering around Newburgh in the hope of seeing her or stand outside her home like a lovesick swain. The chances of meeting her by accident were minimal and there was no reason for him to contact her, she might be offended if he did. He could only wait and see if she kept her word about coming with another order for him and even that was only business. It was no use telling himself to forget her when he had been looking for her for so many years and though it seemed impossible that anything could come from his desire he did not want her to slip from his life. He drew consolation from the fact she had mentioned coming to see him about an order for some sheets for her mother and although he knew he was being foolish his heart leapt every time the door into his work room opened.

He had almost given up hope although it was only a week after Whitsun when she walked into his workshop wearing her red sleeveless bodice and green skirt with her lace-trimmed cap perched at the back of her head.

"Good day, Mistress Crane," he greeted her formally though his heart was racing.

"My name's Debra," she said with a trace of annoyance in her voice.

He inclined his head and asked, "What can I do for you?"

"At the Ales I told you my mother wanted some good linen for sheets. I now have the measurements if you could do them for her, Sarah Crane." She watched him as he wrote down the figures and the name on the top of a sheaf of papers he took from a shelf. "How long will it take?"

"I can weave about ten yards a day but I have some other commissions I must finish first. I will deliver it to you when it is ready. It will be too heavy for you to carry yourself."

"I could ride over with one of father's men, it would save you a long walk," she offered.

"I walk nearly everywhere, I'm used to it," he said.

The business was over and he expected her to depart but she lingered.

"Are you busy?" she asked.

"I'm always busy," he replied.

She was hesitant but still made no move to leave and he asked, "Did you walk here?"

She shook her head, "No, I rode the pony."

He didn't know what to say next but found himself asking, "Could I offer you some refreshment? There's ale but I suppose you might prefer elderflower cordial, my mother brought me a jug, she still thinks I'm in need of looking after."

Debra gave a slight smile. Richard knew she must be thinking, as indeed he was, that it was hardly proper for him to entertain her when they were alone. But then she said, "That would be very welcome, thankyou. You are very kind."

He led her through into the back room and she took a stool at the table while he went into the larder. He returned with a pewter tankard of ale and an earthenware beaker of cordial and took the stool at the opposite side of the table.

She looked around and he knew she noticed that against one wall was a cupboard with open shelves on which were set a few drinking vessels, some wooden bowls and an earthenware jug, and by the hearth a set of fire-irons.

"Yes I have collected a few more things. I shall get it all together in time," he said in response to her interest.

He didn't know what to say next then Debra asked hesitantly, "Is it true you are a Papist? Is that why I have never seen you at church?"

He didn't answer and she was full of remorse, her cheeks turning pink as she stammered, "I'm sorry, I shouldn't have said that."

"Yes I am a Catholic. We were all brought up in the faith," he answered her then.

"I've never known any Catholics," Debra said in some awe. "The Cranes are all Protestants, strong Protestants, some of them go to the new non-conformist meeting houses though we don't."

Richard knew some things about the Cranes for the extended family had been prominent in the area for many years, John Crane had been constable. He almost told her how her uncle Robert Crane had chased his own uncles, John Webster and Thomas Swift, out of Lathom, but decided against it.

"I know something about your life," she admitted. "I know how you have looked after your family since your father went away."

He looked at her sternly, his eyes narrowed and a frown on his face, "How do you know all this?" his tone was brusque.

"People talk," she stammered, ashamed that she had trespassed on his personal circumstances and a little nervous of his reaction. "I'm sorry if I have offended you, it was not meant." He remained silent as he wondered what she had heard and from whom.

"You have known troubles which you have overcome and made a good life for yourself which a lot of people couldn't have done and I think that is admirable. And being a Catholic must take a lot of courage. You are different to the people I normally meet and it has been a privilege to make your acquaintance. I have led a sheltered life and you probably think me a silly girl so I'll go now and I won't disturb you again."

She rose from the table and he rose with her. "You have neither offended nor disturbed me," he said, "but I think you have too exalted an opinion of me. Perhaps some day I might be able to give you my version of my life, it is neither romantic nor worthy, just based on necessity. I certainly do not think you a silly girl, indeed if I may say so, Mistress Crane, I think you are intelligent, honest, and compassionate."

Her wide expressive eyes rested on his face then the flicker of a smile touched her lips as she said, "Can you not call me Debra? Mistress Crane is my mother."

He capitulated at last. "Then Debra it shall be. And I am Richard." He escorted her to the door and promised to have her commission ready by the beginning of the following week.

When she had gone he relived their time together. No intimacies had been exchanged, everything had been said within the bounds of polite conversation. But it seemed as if something had passed between them, some implied regard, some mutual feeling. Was it only a single moment of contiguity? A brief spark as from a tinder box that once extinguished would not be relit. He would have to wait until he saw her again. She had said she would send one of her father's men to collect the linen so it might be unlikely that she would accompany him.

However on the appointed day to his great delight Debra walked into the workshop making the room seem brighter with her warm smile and her vitality.

"Give you good day Richard, I've come for mother's linen," she said, completely unselfconscious about using his name.

"Good day to you Debra," he replied. "You have got someone to accompany you and carry the parcel I trust."

"I thought you could do it," she said. "No, I'm jesting, I know you are too busy to leave your work for a couple of hours. I rode pillion behind one of our men,

Nat. I thought I should come in person and not leave it to him in case there were any problems."

He showed her the linen to ensure her satisfaction then he began parcelling it up.

"I haven't brought the money to pay because I didn't know how much it would be," she apologised. (She kept to herself the fact that her mother had offered her a sum of money anyway.) "If you will send her an account I will bring the money another time, if you don't mind waiting a day or two."

"Most of my customers don't pay immediately and sometimes I have to wait for instalments," he said ruefully, "but I am sure Mistress Crane will reimburse me speedily."

Debra was unable to tarry as 'Nat' was waiting and obviously had other tasks to perform at the farm so their farewells were brief but Debra promised to return at the earliest opportunity and Richard understood and welcomed her little stratagem to ensure another visit though still somewhat puzzled as to her eagerness to do so.

A couple of days later he heard her pony on the cobbles outside. "My mother was determined I came with the money immediately," she explained as she swept into his workshop bringing with her some of the fresh air and sunshine outside. "She is really pleased with the linen and says she will order from you again the next time she has need. The only problem is that I shall now be given the task of sewing it into sheets."

She was in no hurry to go so he brought a stool from the living room so that she could talk to him while he worked. She watched him with interest as he moved the shuttle in a complicated pattern of several differently-coloured threads.

"Who spins the yarn for you?" she asked.

"There are many spinners," he said, "my sister Mary used to do some spinning from home and when I work for agents they have spinners of their own of course."

"I have a spinning wheel, it was my grandmother's but I am not very proficient, I've never been really interested. But I could try and improve and I could do some spinning for you."

He laughed. "Without in any way insulting your abilities, Debra, I doubt you would be fast enough for me."

"I like to see you laugh," she said.

"And somehow I don't think your father would approve." She pulled a face and he continued, unwillingly but feeling he ought to say it, "There could be a problem with you coming here often, it won't be seen as proper, you know that. I am a bachelor living alone and you are a single girl."

Debra thought for a moment then taking a deep breath but looking him in the eyes she said, "I know you will probably think me forward but I like to be with you, you are different from my usual set of acquaintances."

He was at a loss what to say. How could he explain that he wanted her company more than anything in the world, that the sight of her filled him with joy and longing, but he felt it was not right to encourage a girl younger than he with no experience of love, or life, and from a class and a religion so different to his own. Yet he couldn't bear to let her go and the compulsion was so great that he found himself saying, "Would you like to walk by the river on Sunday? We could exchange stories about our lives, I would be interested in learning something of yours, and it wouldn't be so compromising as your coming here alone."

"I would like that very much," she replied.

"Would your family object? You ought to tell them," he warned.

"Do you think I should bring a chaperone? I could get my sister Esther to accompany me." Her expression was serious but then she burst into laughter. "I think you are a very respectable person and I am nineteen years old but don't worry I will make it right with them," she promised, unobtrusively crossing her fingers. She had no intention of making her family privy to the meeting, especially her father, and would invent an excuse.

"I could meet you by the bridge at two of the clock," he suggested.

Her eyes were sparkling and he wondered if his eyes were revealing the emotion he felt. She departed with a promise and he was left wondering what he had done. He knew it was not a wise thing to do but caution had flown out of the window. Despite choosing a walk by the river instead of one of the more popular locations for a Sunday afternoon, he was aware that they would most probably be seen together and wondered what mischief the gossips would make. He was more worried for Debra than for himself but she had promised to gain her family's permission and there was always the chance that she would not come. This possibility helped to salve the guilt which lay like a bedrock of stone beneath the bubbling stream of his happiness.

Sunday was a torment until the appointed time with not even a meeting at one of the Halls to occupy his mind. When he arrived at the bridge across the Douglas she was already there. He noted she had deliberately chosen not to wear anything that might be construed as courting dress–a kirtle of dark forest-green that showed signs of wear with a black velvet sleeveless bodice that laced at the back emphasizing her trim waist and rounded hips–and her hair was braided in a long thick plait. Richard appreciated her good sense though he was unaware of the little prevarication she had made. He had left his better clothes at home and was bareheaded, a sure sign of the lower classes, because he also did not want to give any impression of courtship. From a distance he looked to be chaperoning a young woman taking a walk, as one of her father's workers might have done.

They strolled along the riverbank and though at first they walked with long silences Debra was soon encouraged to talk about her life. "Because I told you I have led rather a sheltered existence you must not think me idle," she said. "I have jobs to do on the farm like feeding the hens and collecting eggs and my father makes me look after my own pony. I help in the dairy and the garden. My mother teaches me about herbs and I help her with making recipes and simples and I do a lot of needlework. I also help with my brothers and sisters as I am the eldest. My next sister Elizabeth died when she was a child, Esther is fourteen but she is somewhat slow and not capable of doing much, John is ten and James is five. My brothers William and Peter both died as infants which upset my father very much."

She stopped for a time and Richard said, "I had a brother James who died when he was six. We called him Jamie and he was always into mischief. He was my best friend when we were children and I missed him so much. He was strong and had never been ill. I helped to carry his coffin to the churchyard. I realised for the first time how uncertain life can be, how death can catch us at any time and how we should make the most of the life we have, every minute of it."

"I think so too," she said. "I think when we want something we should strive to get it, not wait until the time is right because the time might never come."

There was silence again, both pondering on what had been said and whether the other person had meant to imply what lay beneath the words. Richard wanted to ask if she had a suitor but desisted because it would reveal too much of his hidden feelings.

Then Debra said, "Tell me more about your life."

Richard didn't know how much she knew about him, she had said she had heard about his life so he didn't say any more about his childhood, much of it was too painful to recount, but began to tell her about his life as an apprentice with George Taylor. "I owe him so much. He was kind and wise. He made me learn to read and write and was a skilled weaver who taught me my craft. But more than teaching me the technique he taught me to take pride in my work. George loved his work and found enjoyment in creating something that was useful and the best he could make it. And he passed that on to me so that the pleasure of creation, even with something simple as a piece of cloth, takes away the tedium, the monotony, the repetition. Every piece of cloth I make I try to make better than the last one." He smiled ruefully, thinking how old and pompous he sounded but Debra was feeling even more drawn to him. "Working with George I also met his grandson who was to remain my best friend and take the place of my brother Jamie. His name is Will Taylor and we were apprentices together."

"Is he the person dearest to you?" she asked.

"No not really. I think that must be my mother and I have a real brother and a sister though they are younger than me. But Will and I understand each other, we can be honest with each other, we have shared so much together, the good times and the bad."

"I'm glad you have a really close friend," she said but there was a trace of envy in her voice.

They didn't get as far as Appley Bridge, they had strolled leisurely and stopped often and were aware that they had to walk back. She expected him to say something about meeting again but he didn't and she was disappointed. "I thank you for the walk, I enjoyed my Sunday afternoon."

"So did I, I thank you for your company," he replied.

The intimacy had gone and there was a formality between them as they realised the afternoon was over and they must make their farewells, both a little confused about the situation.

"I can't walk with you next Sunday, I have an appointment I must keep," he said.

There had been news that a priest would be at Wrightington Hall and he had promised to go to his mother's cottage and go with her and Eddy and stay for a meal after.

Her face showed her disappointment and he knew he had to see her again.

"I could meet you at the river bridge again the following Sunday if you would like," he suggested, grasping at the chance that this was perhaps the only way he could see her again. The eagerness with which she accepted gave him hope to believe she found as much pleasure in their mutual company as he did.

As he walked home Richard suffered a feeling of anti-climax. He was more in love than ever with Debra

Crane but he hadn't resolved the problem and didn't know what would happen next. He thought she was attracted to him but he feared it was the novelty of knowing someone older and different to her usual circle of acquaintances who would be farmers and farmers' sons, while his history of misfortune elicited her sympathetic interest and his forbidden religion added an aura of mystery. Her lovely face was imprinted on his heart in the days that followed and he put all his energy into his work so that the the two weeks would pass quickly until he could see her again.

When he met her again at the bridge she was wearing over her black bodice a wide cape-like collar with an edging of fine lace and she pointed it out to him with pride saying, "This is the collar I made from the linen you wove for me, I told you I would show it you when I had finished it. I decided not to put any embroidery on it because it would detract from the fineness of the weave and the lace." He showed his appreciation and complimented her needlework and she said with satisfaction, "This is something we have made together."

Their walk was a repeat of their previous excursion and they were both surprised at how the time flew as they talked, he venturing into reminiscences of the adventures he had shared with Will Taylor when they were apprentices and Debra telling him more about her daily life and the many aunts, uncles and cousins she had in Newburgh, Lathom and Dalton, all from farming families.

"Do you have family apart from your mother, brother and sister?" she asked.

"Dozens of Websters, Swifts and Aspinwalls and all weavers and all related to all the other weavers around here," he replied.

"Are they all Catholics?" she asked.

He hesitated then said, "Yes they are. We have kept the old faith despite being penalised for doing so."

"Have you been to a mass today?" she asked in some awe.

"Not today. We have to wait until a priest can come and that isn't very often, usually on festival days. I went last week but I will not tell you where, for your safety, it would not be good for you to be considered an accessory, there are penalties."

"But also you think I might accidentally give away some information."

He didn't reply and she was hurt that he might suspect her of this. "I only want to safeguard you, Debra," he insisted but he was aware again of how much divided them. They were both a little subdued when they parted but he put his hand on hers as he said, "God keep you safe until I see you again."

She kept hold of his hand as she said, "You too."

Loving Debra, for his love for her was growing, shed a radiance on all his daily tasks and although he longed to be with her constantly, the image he kept in his mind and the memory of the brief times they spent together were repeated over and over again in his memory. Although worried, he walked on air.

One evening he went over to see Will Taylor as he often did and was met by an altercation between them over how much money Betty had spent at the haberdashers accompanied by the wailing of four small children.

"God's bones, squalling brats," Will groaned, "Come on, let's go to the Millstone." They left the house with Betty shouting after them, "And how much money are you going to spend on ale?" but before they reached the

Millstone Will's habitual good humour had re-asserted itself. Because it was a fine evening they eschewed the smoky interior and sat at a bench outside with their tankards of ale, catching up on their doings and general news. They had been there some time when Will said, "You have been seen with Debra Crane."

"What do you mean 'seen with'?"

"Walking out with her." Richard said nothing. Will waited for a response then continued, "Tell me it isn't true. That there's nothing in it."

"I've done some work for her," Richard said.

"Which doesn't include walking out with her on Sundays, an activity which most people would call courting. Sweet Jesus, Richard, are you mad? She's under age, a Protestant and the Cranes are a class above us."

Richard remained silent and Will's forehead creased in a frown. "You're not denying it, are you? Is there something in it? Because if there is then I advise you to put an end to it. It just won't do and you're making trouble for yourself. If you are intent on courting Debra Crane then you are going to upset everybody – the Catholics, most of all your family, because she's a Protestant, the Protestants because you're a Catholic, our friends and fellow-workers because you're out of your class, not to mention what the Cranes will do and Dick Crane isn't known for the sweetness of his temper, plus general condemnation because she's under age. Is that enough?"

"She's nineteen."

"Is that all you can say? Mother of God I'm seriously worried about you Richard. You're heading straight for trouble, can't you see that?" Richard still didn't speak and the fact that he didn't attempt to deny or justify worried Will even more. He felt like shouting at him in frustration but decided to be reasonable saying, "I speak as a friend, you know that, and if my words sound harsh they are only meant for your own good. I admit that for years I've been telling you to get a girl but no-one could be less suitable on all accounts than Debra Crane. And what's so special about her? She isn't strikingly beautiful, merely prettily-dressed and brimming with good health that comes from all the advantages of a farm upbringing. Forget her and find a Catholic girl who can cook and is good in bed and try her out first."

"You're a good friend Will and I appreciate your advice but because you are my friend I have to be honest with you and say that as long as Debra Crane is willing, and that is the only factor that counts with me, I have no intention of giving her up no matter what it costs me." He couldn't say any more, was unable to articulate his feelings, to confess even to Will how deep and all—consuming his love for her had become, the fact that to him Debra was the most beautiful girl in the world. The emotion was too raw and until he was absolutely sure that Debra felt the same it seemed a violation to discuss her. He believed she was at the very least attracted to him and their relationship was warm and comfortable. But because of all the dividing factors Will had mentioned he could not assume her feelings were strong enough to be called love.

Will was unhappy as he said, "Well let's hope that she has enough common sense to realise the potential disaster and backs off before it's too late. She's too young anyway to know her own mind while you should know better than to encourage her for what is probably only a flash in the pan."

Richard couldn't argue with him because this possibility was his own deep-seated fear. He had hinted at it to Debra because he still suspected she had a mistakenly romantic image of him that was a product of her youth and inexperience but he knew that if she broke off the relationship he would be inconsolable. When he and Will parted it was with less than their usual affability though they clasped hands at the door.

Despite his friend's misgivings what was left of the summer was a time of great happiness. Twice Debra found an excuse to visit him asking for some linen to make shirts for her brothers, then a table cloth for her mother. On two more Sundays they walked together, the second time Richard went to Newburgh and they walked to the ruins of Lord Derby's great fortress at Lathom, destroyed during the civil war. Richard related to Debra some of the tales of this happening, tales his father had heard from his grandfather. The eerie skeleton of this once-great stronghold straggled over the raised mound as a permanent reminder of the mutability of life urging the necessity to seize the moment, carpe diem. They talked freely but about local affairs and the routine of their daily lives and they laughed a lot as Richard told about the idiosyncracies of his customers and Debra recounted with some mischief tales of her numerous relatives. He had never been so happy. The only physical contact ever between them was on the occasional visits she made to his workshop when their hands would brush together as he handed her a drink or a parcel.

He was aware of talk and one day when he visited home his brother Eddy made mention of it. Eddy was twenty-one now and working as a trained weaver with the Crosse family, another branch of the extended Catholic family with whom he had served his apprenticeship. He was stronger than he had been but thin and with bent shoulders, with the fair hair of both his siblings, though not as thick as Richard's, and with his mother's narrow features and blue eyes. He was a little resentful that his brother had not invited him to join him but Richard was intent on being independent and had not enough work to warrant the two of them. Now Eddy had heard rumours that clarified his brother's desire to live alone and he was no more pleased than Will Taylor. He waited until their mother was away from the house until he broached the subject.

"Ma and I are very disturbed by the talk about you and Debra Crane. In fact we find it hard to believe. The Cranes are some of the strongest Protestants around and have done their share in making life hard for us. Have you forgotten that it was Robert Crane who had father's brother John humiliatingly removed from Lathom by a court order? And he also sent mother's brother, our Uncle Tom Swift who was only ten at the time, out of Lathom where he had been working with John and back to his hated employer. Officious bastard and Debra Crane's uncle."

"That's a long time ago Eddy and you can hardly blame Debra for that."'

"No she wouldn't have been born then. How old is she, seventeen?"

"She's nineteen."

"But we are not in the same class as the Cranes and they look down on us, owning a lot of land and employing half the population of Dalton and Lathom. Ma is really angry that you are not tying yourself up with a Catholic girl of our class and I must say I think you are mad to have anything to do with Debra Crane. She isn't even very beautiful, not as beautiful as Isobel Blundell who has a fancy for you, she's really beautiful and her family are Catholics and working men like us. Why are you intent on getting us into more trouble?"

"Why what trouble have we ever been in?" Richard asked angrily.

"When father left us and we had no home and had to claim parish relief."

"Well that was hardly our fault."

"And being Catholics. You can't say that isn't our choice," Eddy said obstinately.

"I'm not so sure about that, Eddy. What chance did we ever have of being anything else? As babies we were listening to Catholic rituals, in our childhood we were immersed in Catholic practices, all our family were Catholics so we never had the choice of meeting anyone else, we didn't go to school or join with the neighbourhood children in their activities. We were destined to be Catholics from the moment we were born."

"Richard, that's heresy. I can't believe what you are saying. Are you thinking of giving up the faith? Is this the Crane girl's influence on you?" Eddy was aghast.

"I am not thinking of giving up the faith and I never shall. My faith is me, body and soul, it is what makes me and what sustains me, it is the air I breathe and the roof that shelters me. I only said we did not choose in the beginning to be Catholics. But now it is my choice and I believe it to be the true faith which I shall uphold. You may tell Ma that. As for the other matter, then that is only a matter for me, no-one else."

But on the way back to his own house he was perturbed by the fact that his family and friends were condemnatory in their warnings.

THE YEW AND THE ROSE

As summer's end approached preparations were made for harvesting. This year's crops would be plentiful as it had been a good summer and all those who had time, wanted to earn extra money, or just enjoy the attendant festivities went to lend a hand at the various farms.

"I am going with my family to help at Uncle John's. You know he lives in Dalton so I thought you could come and join in the celebrations afterwards, I know you will probably not have time to help with the actual harvesting," Debra had suggested.

Richard was a little wary, John Crane was one of the wealthiest and most important members of the family but he knew there would likely be at least a hundred helpers so he considered he might not be too conspicuous. He had time to spare on Sunday so went to join most of the people in Dalton in bringing in the last sheaves. Debra was busy with her cousins for John Crane had a large family of four daughters and five sons including twin boys and all Debra's siblings were there as well as many other cousins. Richard enjoyed working in the fields for the day and thought how pleasant it might be to be a farm labourer instead of working indoors all the hours of daylight in a small noisy space, though he was honest enough to acknowledge that the fine warm weather made such an occupation enjoyable while for most of the time working outside was in rain, wind, cold and frost for a minimum wage. His father had been forced to do both because he hadn't been able to make sufficient money weaving for someone else and had to supplement this by also working on the land whereas Richard was independent and able to make a decent wage even though it meant spending all day indoors. He took advantage of the change of scene despite the back-breaking toil until finally the last sheaves had been piled on the hay wain. There was always one stalk left standing in the field and because this was believed to contain the spirit of the grain no-one wished to be the taker. Consequently a group of young men all threw their sickles together so that no individual might incur the vengeance of the deity. It was a ritual causing much merriment and afterwards, leaving the fields to the gleaners, as many as possible climbed onto the hay wain on its ceremonial procession to the barn for drink and plentiful food. When everyone was sated the meal was followed by music and dancing. Richard was acquainted with many of the young men and not short of company but whilst they were availing themselves of the pies, bread, cakes and ale, Debra came to talk with him. She was wearing an old dress of worn and faded red linen that showed her ankles with her hair tied back under a conical straw hat, her cheeks were rosy with heat and exertion and Richard thought she had never looked so lovely.

"You mustn't let any of the girls take you for a dance until you have danced with me," she commanded. Then true to her words she was beside him when the music began an haphazard jig and she pulled him into the throng of merry revellers crowding the barn floor. Neither was aware of a figure watching them intently. When Debra was called elsewhere, Richard was standing in the shadows of the barn when a man approached him and said brusquely, "I want a word with you."

He turned and saw a tall strongly-built man in his forties, his face ruddy as one who spends much time out of doors, his grey hair short-cropped. Richard surmised he might wear a wig when he dealt with the gentry or supped with the parson because he knew instinctively that this was Debra's father. There was no sign of friendliness on his chiselled features and his voice was harsh as he said, "I have been hearing reports that you have been seen walking with my daughter Debra and that she has been visiting your premises alone. I am not pleased about this."

"There has been nothing improper. Mistress Crane has only visited my workshop in the course of business and any times we have walked together have been only in a spirit of friendship," Richard said carefully but courteously.

"Nonetheless they must stop. Your family and your religion are not the sort of circles I wish my daughter to be included in. She is underage without the experience to understand the consequences of her behaviour. She is affianced to the son of a farmer in Parbold who has land which I wish to see joined with mine and I want no shadow of impropriety to cloud her name before marriage." Dick Crane's tone never softened. "I have forbidden Debra to see you again under any circumstances and I will make sure she obeys me. If you ever try to come near her again I shall take severe measures and believe me I do not make idle threats."

He strode away leaving Richard shaking and his insides turning into knots of sickness and pain. He didn't know if he should have retaliated, justified himself, declared his love. He would have done so had he been sure that Debra loved him. But was it true that she was betrothed to someone as her father had said? Were his own words true that she only looked on him as a friend? He longed to talk to her but there was no sign of her as the revellers began to disperse and he walked home thinking his life had come to an end. How could he possibly see Debra again? These past few months had been some of the happiest he had ever known but they would now have to live only in his memory. Debra would not be able to disobey her father and there was no way he could contact her. The warnings of Will and Eddy had come home to roost. It had been an impossible dream and he had no idea how he could go back to the life he had known before he met her.

Chapter 10

1700–1701

For the next few weeks Richard tried to immerse himself in his work whilst hoping against hope that one day Debra would open the door of his workshop with some excuse for linen. But she never came and he surmised she had taken her father's warnings to heart. He had been foolish to think she might have the same feelings for him as he did for her. He was unlikely to run into her accidentally because there were no festivals after harvest until Yuletide. Most young people met either through their work or at church but he didn't attend the parish church as Debra did, the Crane's parish being Ormskirk. But even had there been such opportunities he knew that Dick Crane would be keeping a close watch on his daughter. He was tormented by the possibility that she might actually be affianced to some young farmer and had reconciled herself to an arranged marriage. He tried to drown out his thoughts by working even harder, saving up a little money, but he was morose and unsociable. It didn't take Will Taylor long to notice something was wrong though on his visits to his friend he had been uncommunicative. At last however in answer to Will's well-meant enquiries he confessed that the relationship seemed to be over and admitted to Debra's father's interference.

"I'm sorry for you but you can't say I didn't warn you," Will said with a certain amount of satisfaction and Betty was of the same mind.

"It's for the best, Richard, Debra Crane was never suited to you. You will find someone else soon, many girls have a fancy for you. I would myself if I wasn't married to Will."

"But you'll have to get out and about, not sit moping in the house," Will added.

Richard couldn't bring himself to say, *"I don't want anyone else because I love her, I always have and I always will,"* because he knew that even though they were his friends they couldn't understand the strength of his feelings.

Yuletide passed in a blur. The long holiday was not welcome to him because he could not make the time pass by working hard. He made an attempt to be sociable by entering into the spirit of the usual festivities – Christmas dinner with his mother, Eddy, and his sister Mary who joined them with her family which now included a boy as well as a girl, suppers with Will and Betty, visits to relatives and friends, midnight mass. But he participated like a sleepwalker, moving as in a dream and making instinctive responses. Every event made him wonder what Debra was doing. Was she enjoying the festivities in the bosom of her large family, there would be much visiting and exchanging of gifts, hearty food from the farms and visits to the parish church. Had she put him out of her mind? Was she spending the Yuletide season with a young man she was going to marry? He couldn't write to her because she couldn't read and she was unable to write so she couldn't send him a letter. He was glad when the last celebration of Twelfth Night passed with an Epiphany mass at Wrightington Hall and a supper provided afterwards by the Dicconsons with entertainment by a troupe of travelling players. Both Isabel Blundell and Cecily Berry made much of him and were frustrated when he didn't respond to their flirtations while their mothers looked on with annoyance. But Yuletide was finally over though the following Monday, Plough Monday, was still only a half-hearted workday, easing the labourers gradually back into the daily grind. A decorated plough was dragged through the villages accompanied by music and the ploughboys knocked on doors to receive gifts of money or food.

January and February were always hard months. The weather was usually bad and many people did not possess enough warm clothes. Houses were cold and damp, hearths only heating the immediate area and bedchambers were freezing, not many could afford a brazier. Food was short as not much could be grown in fields and gardens, and many animals had been killed for the Yuletide feasts and because they all could not be fed in the winter. Churchyards were full and funerals commonplace, both of old and young. Will and Betty lost their little daughter Jane and Richard commiserated with them in their loss. There was always a shortage of work in the winter for there was little to do in the fields apart from hedging and ditching, working hours were short because of the long dark hours and because money was scarce people cut down purchases. Richard had less work and time on his hands but early twilight curtailed activities. Candles were too expensive to burn for long and rushlights gave little light so the pitch dark lanes often lacked the helpful glimmer from a window if anyone attempted an evening visit.

One gloomy afternoon in late February Richard was thinking of giving up work for the day as the light was poor and there was little to do when the door opened and Debra Crane came in. She was wrapped in a red wool cloak and her face was pale and anxious beneath the hood. He snatched off his wool cap and they stood looking at each other though Richard's heart was beating fast beneath his workaday woollen jacket.

"I can't bear it any longer, not to see you," she whispered.

Then as if drawn by forces outside themselves they instinctively moved towards each other and he took her in his arms, holding her close with her head pressed against his shoulder.

"Dear Debra," was all he could say, feeling her body against his.

She tilted her face up to him and her hood slipped from her head as she said, "Have you missed me as much as I've missed you?"

"I've longed for you so much," he said. He kissed her for the first time and she opened her lips to receive him. They were both surprised at what they had done but they made no move to draw apart and he kissed her again, slowly and gently then with more passion as she didn't resist.

"Come let's go into the back room, it's warmer there, there's a fire," he said at last, taking her hand and leading her through the door. He unfastened her cloak and seated her on the chair beside the hearth, a new acquisition, drawing up the other from the table and sitting beside her, putting his hand on hers.

She clasped his hand and said, "I am not going to obey my father any more, he doesn't own me."

"I am afraid he does, my dear Debra, until you are twenty-one."

She sighed and a look of abject misery was etched on her face. "Are you agreeing that we can't see each other? Don't you love me?" She took a deep breath then looking into his eyes said, "It might be considered immodest but I love you."

She had been the first one to say it and Richard felt ashamed. But he had never wanted to take advantage of what he thought might have been an innocent friendship on her part. He had always felt her regard but had never been sure that her feelings for him were as strong as his were for her. Now she had declared her love openly.

His emotions were crushing his heart as he said, "I love you more than ever I thought it possible to love anyone. I have loved you since the first time I saw you. I've kept silent because I never believed you could return my love."

"Why not? I have loved you since we first talked together. But you are wise and clever and I didn't think you could love a young girl like me with little to commend her."

Looking at her lovely innocent face Richard wanted to laugh but he said, "Debra you are everything I have ever longed for, everything I ever hoped for, to me you are my heart's desire in body, mind and soul."

"Kiss me again," she said, and it was a long time before they drew apart.

But Richard was compelled to say, "The fact that we love each other does not change the situation. You are bound to obey your father and he has forbidden you to see me. He told me that you were betrothed to a farmer's son, is that true?"

"No it isn't," she retorted angrily. "It's true that he wants me to marry William Barton because the Bartons have land in Parbold that adjoins ours but it is not of my choosing. There's nothing wrong with William as such but I have no feelings for him and I could never marry a man I didn't love."

"Would your father force you to do so?"

"I don't think he would *force* me. He's hard and stern and very dogmatic but he isn't cruel. But he uses persuasion, telling me how I would please him and how advantageous it would be for me, I would be well-off with a fine farmhouse."

Richard was silent for a time then he said, "You feared you had little to commend you to me but in reality the opposite is true – I have little to offer you. I'm not poor but neither am I well-off. I'm only a weaver and though I hope to expand my business in time I have few possessions and a rented house." He let his words sink in as he swept his hand around the simple room in which they sat. Then he added, "But I would love you more than anyone else could love you for all the days of my life."

"That's all I need. All I want," she whispered, tears starting to her eyes. "And I would love you in return with every part of my being, body, mind and soul."

"I haven't mentioned one more important thing," he said seriously. "The fact that I am a Catholic and you are not. I do not expect you to change your faith but neither can I ever change mine and you must accept that my religion brings with it certain penalties, certain dangers even. In some ways it sets me apart."

Debra thought carefully for a time then said, "I love you for what you are and because your faith is part of what makes you then I accept that too. I don't think I could ever change, in fact your religion frightens me a little, but because I love you I am willing to accept whatever consequences this might bring," and in her answer he recognised that Debra Crane had a maturity beyond her years.

"Would you be willing to marry me, Debra, be my wife? Despite everything? The fact that I cannot offer you as much as you will leave?"

"I want nothing more in life than to be your wife. If I do leave anything then it is nothing compared to what I shall gain by being loved by you. What use are possessions if it means sacrificing the chance to love and be loved." Her answer was firm.

"Darling Debra, if you are absolutely certain then this constitutes a betrothal between us. However it still does not solve the problem of your father. I am honour bound to go to him and tell him and ask for your hand in marriage," Richard said.

"He won't agree, he will be very angry, he might do you harm," Debra cried, her voice raised in alarm, her eyes wide with fear in their depths.

"Nonetheless I must do it," Richard insisted. "I cannot marry you without his permission."

She bit her lip in anxiety. "Go to him when he is alone in the field. I know he will be angry and it would be better if it were not in the house."

She didn't want to leave the comfort of being with him but they knew they must part and Debra must ride home before it got too dark. Their parting was a maelstrom of emotions – joy at their betrothal, sadness at having to separate, anxiety about the future, apprehension at her father's reactions.

"I won't give you up no matter what happens," she assured him.

"And neither will I give in, no matter what happens," Richard promised as they took a fervent leave of each other with kisses, and tears from Debra.

The thought of having to face Dick Crane was an unpleasant prospect but Richard decided it must be done as soon as possible and early one misty morning he set off to walk to Newburgh. He tried to free his mind from apprehension by reciting the rosary as he walked, saying the familiar words by rote to prevent thoughts entering his mind. He shunned the farmhouse and made for the fields, eventually locating the farmer with a ploughing team. As they turned at the bottom of the field Dick Crane saw him. He continued working but then at the end of the furrow he strode towards him and his aspect was not friendly. Richard greeted him politely then drawing a deep breath told him directly how he and Debra had sworn a betrothal and that he wished to marry her. Crane's face turned purple with anger and his response was immediate.

"Are you out of your mind?" he roared, "I wouldn't let my daughter marry you if you were the last man on earth – a family of paupers and damned treasonable Papists. Her husband a weaver with nothing but a loom to support him, would you make us a laughing stock? Do you know who the Cranes are, and my wife's family the Seddons? Respected in the church and in society with a long history of working and owning the land here. No Papists will ever come in our midst nor will we ever join our family with those supported on parish relief."

Although Richard had steeled himself for Crane's anger the vehemence chilled his heart but he knew he could not deny the allegation of Papistry. However he said as calmly as he could, "I am no longer poor, I am a skilled craftsman of mature age and can support a wife and family, I am not responsible for what happened in the past. Debra and I love each other and have pledged our troth."

"Debra is too young to talk about love, a romantic fallacy which is not a necessary component of marriage in any case. Position in society, a substantial inheritance and a shared religion is what matters. Debra is immature and impressionable and with your greater years you have no doubt talked your way to a seduction. This fantasy of a betrothal is nonsense, worthless without witnesses of which I presume there are none," he scoffed. Richard knew he could not gainsay him here, being well aware of the conditions of an official betrothal. A promise made between two people was legal provided it was followed immediately by sexual relations. A promise to marry in the future needed witnesses. In any case there was no stopping Debra's father for he continued in full spate, "I warned you before to stay away from my daughter. I can see she has disobeyed me but it will be the last time, I'll see to that. As for you, if I hear that you have been seen anywhere near her I swear I shall come and find you with my horse-whip and beat you to an inch of your life. Is that clear? As I said before I do not make idle threats. Now get out of my sight." He strode away back to the plough.

Richard realised it was useless to follow him to say anything further, to plead, to appeal to his better nature, to talk about love. Dick Crane was impervious to all these. It was clear he would never consent to a marriage. Richard's main thought was for Debra and the punishment she might incur. She was on his mind all the way home, he was fearful for her and though he was now sure enough of her love to believe she could not be persuaded to abandon him he had no idea how they could contact each other.

It was with a heavy heart that he approached Dalton and turned into the road where his house stood. As he got close to the house he saw to his amazement that her pony was there, the reins looped over a branch of one of the apple trees in his back garden. He opened the front door calling "Debra," and she came out of the living room, looking anxious. One glance at his face told her the worst.

"What are you doing here?" was his first question.

"My mother sent me on an errand to my aunt Jane here in Dalton, my Uncle John Crane's wife, and when I called here and found you away I guessed where you might be and decided to wait."

He told her all that had happened and as he drew her into his arms she began to cry.

"It wasn't a great surprise was it? I am just fearful about what will happen to you, that your father will punish you," he said sadly.

"That's the least of my worries," she sniffed. "He might beat me but he doesn't hit very hard, my mother won't let him. But he probably won't let me out of the house without someone accompanying me. What's to happen to us?"

Richard pulled up a chair and drew her onto his knee, her head pressed against his chest. "We wait. We wait until you are twenty-one and then you can please yourself, you won't need your father's consent to marry."

"But that is nearly a year and a half, my birthday is only in July," she cried in consternation. "I want to be with you, I cannot wait so long. And you will grow tired of waiting, you will find someone else."

"I want no-one but you, my love, and I am willing to wait. I am a patient man. I have learnt patience." He thought of the long years he had worked as an apprentice, the years he had waited for a girl to love, even weaving required patience. "I shall wait as long as it takes. My heart is yours for ever and the waiting, though hard, will be endurable if I know we can be together at the end. But what about you? You are young and the temptation to marry someone of your father's choice will be strong. You will think you are wasting your life and family pressures will be very hard to resist."

"I know that, but I am strong. You will see how strong I am. I love you more than I ever thought it possible to love anyone and if you will wait for me I promise I will learn patience and wait for you as long as it takes no matter what it costs."

Richard was overwhelmed by happiness but his mind was working. "Because we cannot be together yet it does not mean we can never see each other. Firstly there are all the festivals, and summer is coming now. It is natural to find us both in their midst and so long as we are never seen to be together there can be no gossip nor can your father suspect anything. We can greet each other, keep a sight of each other, believe me I shall miss none of them."

"My father doesn't usually go to the festivals," Debra said.

"But your family will be there and would inform him if anything untoward happened so we must still be watchful," Richard warned.

"Yes my brothers would tell him," Debra agreed. "Do you know he has told them to keep watch on me."

"What about your mother? Is she sympathetic?"

"She's afraid of father. She never goes against him in any way. But she was only about twenty years old when she married him and her family, the Seddons, are important in the church and the community."

"Well don't despair, at least we can see each other from afar, perhaps even pass the time of day. But I have another plan if you are willing. I know a lot of secret places around Dalton, well-hidden groves and copses and winding pathways that are used by no-one except those with an intimate knowledge of them, it's hilly ground and wooded as you know. I used to explore them with my friends when I was a young boy. And sometimes we have escorted priests to safety on their secret visits, yes I have done so occasionally, most of the young lads have, my father used to do it years ago because it needs someone with an intimate knowledge of the area and someone who is agile and quick-thinking. If occasionally, and I don't think we should risk our chances too often, you could find excuse to ride out with your pony then I could meet you some place where it is unlikely anyone should find us."

Debra's eyes were sparkling at the idea of a romantic tryst but Richard was thinking of how difficult it would be to arrange. "It's a pity you can't read because I could find a way to pass on messages."

"My father sends my brothers to school but said it wasn't necessary for Esther and me and my mother can't read either."

"Well my mother can," Richard said defiantly, "and my sister Mary can write her name. When we are married, love, I shall teach you to read. However if you have need of me urgently find an excuse to visit the weaver William Taylor, it will cause no comment to visit his workshop but you must only do so in an emergency, we must make sure nothing ever leaks out to your father. And you must never come here."

"I like coming here," she said wistfully.

Richard looked bemused. "Your farmhouse must be more comfortable and far bigger."

"Oh it is, we have a lot of rooms. But it is your home and that makes a difference. Do you think I shall ever be able to live here with you?"

"We must have faith that it will happen. And while we are waiting I will make improvements, more furniture, more comforts, it will give me something to do. But are you really sure that you would be happy living in this small house that must of necessity be also my workplace. Some day if I could increase my business I might be able to have a separate workshop and an assistant."

"I shall be happy anywhere with you Richard but can I see the rest of the house?" she asked.

He led the way up the wooden staircase and into the room at the back. "This is my bedchamber," he said and she looked inside at the large bed, a simple oak frame with several blankets. "I was always cold when I was a child, we never had enough blankets," he smiled ruefully. The only other furniture in the large room was an old oak chest on which stood a rushlight in an iron holder. Pegs on the wall held clothes. The window with wooden shutters looked out over the back garden and the fields beyond. He led her into the other chamber overlooking the road and it was empty. "It needs furnishing, perhaps making ready for children sometime," he smiled. "I shall try to finish the house while I am waiting for you. But go now, love, before you are seen here. I only wish I could accompany you."

Their farewells were long and passionate, bitter-sweet in the awareness that it would be a long time before they could be renewed. But a spirit of exhilaration enveloped them in the realisation that they had plighted their troth together and made a promise of marriage which was a betrothal. They had to be patient but there was every chance that the future would fulfil that promise. In another month the year would change, it would be 1700, more than a new year it would be a new century. The 17th century had seen momentous events – the death of Queen Elizabeth and the end of the Elizabethan age, a Scottish king and the union of Scotland with England, the colonisation of the new world, the long civil war, the execution of a king and the establishment of a Commonwealth, the Restoration of the monarchy then the deposition of a rightful king and the installation of a Dutch noble. The Webster and Crane families had lived through all of these. Everyone wondered what this new century would bring. Whatever changes lay in store Richard and Debra would be part of them.

The new century brought the strangest year of Richard's life. He was engaged to be married to the only girl he had ever loved but was not allowed to meet her and told no-one of the fact. Even his best friend Will Taylor thought he had given up his ill-considered obsession with Debra Crane. But the secret warmed his heart and gave impetus to the routine of his daily life. He was working for her now, saving money to provide for her. Throughout the spring and summer they saw each other occasionally, even though it was usually in a crowd of people – Easter festivities, May Day, Rogation and beating of the bounds, Whitsun Ales, racing and bowling, a visit by a troupe of travelling players, and they both visited Ormskirk market. Sometimes they would watch each other from afar but occasionally they would be in a position to exchange a formal greeting when their eyes would meet and speak volumes. They took solace from knowing they were bound together and Debra's image was kept fresh in Richard's mind though it was frustrating and at night in bed he lay longing for her and certain that she was feeling the same. Their happiest times were the two secret trysts they were able to arrange.

"Twice in six months, Richard, only half a year gone," Debra sighed as she lay in his arms in a secluded spot by a noisy little brook under a canopy of beech and ash.

"But it is half a year," he said, trying to sound positive though the strain of holding her close, feeling the rounded contours of her body beneath her light summer clothing and her warm breath on his face was stretching his control to the limits.

"Now that we are betrothed it is within our rights to make love," she said. "If I became pregnant then they would have to let us marry."

"Mother of God, Deb, don't tempt me," it was a cry of desperation. "There is nothing I would rather do, believe me, but it would not help our cause. I will not give your father any ammunition to condemn me further nor will I have people saying this was the reason for our marriage. I don't want anyone to believe you only married me because I got you with child, or that I only married you because it was the honourable thing to do. When we marry it will be because we love each other and cannot live without each other, not for necessity, and I want everyone to know this. I want to make love to you for the first time as my wife in our own bed in our own house and (*he thought of his parents and Will and Betty*) not already starting our life together with a child."

"You are an honourable man Richard Webster and I love you for it," she said quietly.

"But a very frustrated one," he laughed, "and not immune to temptation so please darling do not make a suggestion like that again."

However both were aware that the summer was ending and winter would lessen their opportunities for meeting. The next festival would be harvest and as this would be one where the Cranes would play a prominent part Richard decided he must stay away.

"Only three seasons left now, darling – autumn, winter and spring. Then it will be summer, your birthday and our wedding," he comforted her.

It was a long dismal winter again, only supportable by the fact that by working long hours he was saving up money and in his spare time trying to improve his house. He gave the inside walls a new coating of limewash over the stone, following Debra's idea of mixing ox blood with it for the living room. He was pleased with the result so got one of the dyers to mix him some yellow dye which he added to the wash for the bedchamber which gave the impression of sun shining on the stone walls. He bought another chest for this room and a long narrow table set against the wall with a pewter jug and wash bowl. He paid a visit to his former employer Robert Shaw and asked him to weave a large piece of fustian as he had looms weaving both linen and wool, which he took to the dyers to be dyed a deep blue colour for a bedcover. A neighbour was giving up his house and selling some of his furniture and he bought a settle and another chest for the living room.

Will Taylor was mystified when he came to visit. "Why this luxury, are you thinking of getting married at last?" he asked. He and Betty were constantly finding suitable girls for him and disappointed that he never furthered the acquaintance.

Similarly his mother raised the matter whenever he saw her. "When are you going to get married, Richard, you are almost thirty, I despair of you. There are many young women who look favourably on you. What is the matter with you? Even Eddy has started looking around."

Easter came late so before the festive celebrations could take place the trees were already flowering with elder, apple and cherry blossom; the fields carpeted with primroses, violets and wild daffodils; new-born lambs gambolling in the fields; the sun feeling warmer as it fingered the lacy branches of the trees. People's hearts warmed also with the promise of spring after winter's hardships. Richard and Debra had not been able to see anything of each other for three months and he was wondering desperately how he could contrive to see her when fate intervened by Will Taylor telling him of an Easter horse race at Newburgh and suggesting they go. Richard accepted eagerly knowing that Debra would contrive to be there as she would expect him to seize the opportunity.

They were both in high spirits as they made their way to Newburgh, Will because he had managed to leave his family behind, they now had another little daughter named Jane again after the child they had lost, and Richard because he was expecting to see Debra. However it took him a long time to catch a glimpse of her as the crowds were great for the occasion and he had to try and show to Will the same excitement they used to share about the races themselves while all the time his attention was focussed on the spectators. Finally he saw Debra in the company of her mother and brothers and sister as she had been the first time he had set eyes on her two years ago. They managed to gradually edge closer together at the finishing line and while everyone's attention was concentrated on the final burst and the cheering that erupted for the winner she said quickly, "My father is away next Thursday, I will come to you." She moved swiftly away before he could answer and Will hadn't even seen her. He was worried about the risk she was going to take but his heart soared at the knowledge they would soon be together again if only for a brief space of time.

Time crawled until Thursday and it was mid-morning when the door opened and Debra came quickly in, looking spring-like in her yellow bodice and forest-green kirtle, her hair in a long plait. As soon as she had closed the door they were in each other's arms and kissing hungrily after their long separation. Then he led her through into the living room where they clung together, holding each other close and drinking in the sight of each other after so long apart. "You are so beautiful, Debra, and I have longed to see you, but how have you managed to come here today?" he asked.

"My father has gone to Preston on business and won't be back until tomorrow," she replied. "I told mother I was going to visit my cousins in Dalton and she won't check up, she's too busy supervising everything in father's absence."

She expressed her delight at the colourful walls and noted more shelves and the settle in front of the hearth. He went into the larder and returned with a jug and took two pottery beakers from the cupboard.

"It's only nettle beer, I'm afraid," he said as they seated themselves at the table. She took a sip of the drink then put it aside with a grimace. He gulped his down then laid the empty mug on the pine board and took her hand. "I think it's time we made serious plans about our wedding," he said.

Debra's eyes sparkled as she said, "Although we still have four months to wait, it's now the year of our marriage isn't it."

"It is indeed," he replied happily. "We must prepare carefully because it is unlikely we shall have much opportunity to meet for any length of time before July. Even though we have waited until you come of age I expect your father will be very angry that we are disobeying his wishes."

The happiness had left Debra's face and she frowned, biting her lip. "Yes he will be angry, he hates people to thwart him. If he knew what we are planning he would do everything he could to stop us, even up to the ceremony itself. He would probably lock me up."

Richard smiled ruefully but he said, "I doubt your father would go so far, he isn't a monster."

"You don't know him," she muttered. "He is getting more insistent about me marrying William Barton.

I can't refuse him and all I can do is to keep delaying it, saying I wish to wait until I am twenty-one but he is urging me to make the announcement on my birthday."

"This is why we have to be actually married so he can do nothing about it though I hate being deceitful," Richard said. "Unfortunately I don't think it will end there. I think we are still going to have to face a lot of anger. Your parents are not going to be pleased that you have disobeyed them. Have you thought about this and what it will mean because I don't think your family will ever accept me and we shall have to face the consequences. Are you absolutely sure you can bear this?"

Debra swallowed but said firmly. "I know he will be furious and I shall have to face his anger which can be terrifying. I think he will probably disown me and say I can never go home. But if I have you beside me none of this matters. All I want is to share my life with you. The only thing that distresses me is that I am bringing trouble upon you, my father's unfairness to you hurts me deeply. I wish he could see you through my eyes."

Richard leaned over and clasped her hand. "Don't be sad about me, darling. I do wish, for your sake more than mine, that our marriage could have been easier but I can bear anything to have your love. I will make it up to you in every way I can."

She put her other hand on his feeling the strength of his grip. She knew he was strong and when she was with him she felt safe and protected.

After a time Richard said, "We shall need a special licence so that the banns need not be called for three weeks beforehand when your father would be in his rights to stop us. Also because I am a Catholic I am not a communicant of any parish church and by the same token because you are not a Catholic we cannot be married by a priest in the Catholic rite."

"Wouldn't it be against your religion to be married in an Anglican church?" she asked hesitantly.

"Although it is usual, Catholics don't *always* marry in private Catholic ceremonies, it isn't always possible. As for our own special case our marriage must be properly and officially documented so that no doubt must ever be cast upon it. A secret marriage in a Catholic ceremony might be open to dispute if anyone wanted to challenge it."

"You're doing this for me, aren't you? If you were marrying a Catholic girl you wouldn't have any problems."

."I want to marry you, Debra, no-one else and any difficulties fade into insignificance when I know that you want to marry me. But you must realise, my darling, that I will continue to worship as a Catholic with all the attendant secrecy and danger. That I cannot change. Are you sure you can accept me still."

"Nothing will make me change my mind. I love you because you are what you are and your faith must make you what you are. But where can we be married then?"

"With a special licence we can be married anywhere without having to fulfil the normal restrictions about belonging to a particular parish. We can go somewhere outside the parishes of Ormskirk, Eccleston and Upholland, somewhere where no-one knows us. So I shall see about getting a special licence."

"Won't that be expensive?"

He shrugged. "I don't know but it doesn't matter. I will make enquiries as to how to go about it in case it should take some time. There is one other thing, darling."

"Yes?" she asked nervously, wondering how many more problems they had to surmount for his tone was serious.

"You must learn to write your name. I'm not having you making a cross on our marriage record in case of unforseen circumstances, you must write your name clearly so that all may see you are in agreement. Before you leave here I am going to teach you the necessary letters then I will write your name, both Debra Crane and Debra Webster, and you must practice until you get it right. Debra Crane is easy because there is only a small number of letters, Webster will be more difficult but my mother managed it."

"I will do it," she promised.

He found some paper and a quill and seated at the table together he taught her the necessary letters and wrote her name twice. She copied it laboriously, biting her lip in concentration and when he was satisfied she folded the paper and put it in the little bag on her waist.

"I'll start to make enquiries about the licence then we can be married the day after your birthday," he said.

"Is it not possible to meet again before then?" Debra asked wistfully.

"We mustn't spoil things now we are so close," Richard warned. "I'm afraid we must content ourselves with brief encounters on May Day and the Whitsun Ales like last year." Debra looked so downhearted that he capitulated saying, "Perhaps we could get away to our secret place in a few weeks' time. What about midsummer day? Then we can make our final preparations."

"I'll find some way to be there," she promised.

The decision was made, the time would not be long now. They parted regretfully but with hope that the waiting was almost over.

Application for a special marriage licence had to be made through a bishop of the Anglican church and access to the Bishop of the Diocese of Chester was through the rector of Wigan, Sir Orlando Bridgeman. A licence dispensed with certain regulations of the church like the calling of banns and the rules of residency and could be used in any parish at any time. Richard gathered information from various sources because he wasn't the first Catholic to circumvent regulations if they wanted to marry in a parish church. However it wasn't a simple procedure and the granting of a licence was considered a privilege and not a right. Certain conditions had to be agreed and for this he needed assistance so was forced to ask the help of Will Taylor. He made sure he visited Will when Betty was out of the house and told him of his plans.

Will was stupefied at what his friend was telling him. His first reaction was fury at the realisation that Richard had kept him in the dark so long.

"You have been seeing Debra Crane for two years and you haven't said a word to me, your friend for longer than I can remember. I can't believe it." Richard understood his anger and felt even more guilty when Will's anger began to melt into disappointment, "It hurts me most that you didn't trust me, your closest friend. All the things we have shared together over the years. I must have been with you dozens of times when Debra Crane and her family have been amongst the company." His round face, usually so cheerful with a mischievous smile was set in a hard line and Richard was conscious of how much older he looked, his freckles had almost disappeared and his hair faded from its sandy colour into an indeterminate ashen shade.

"I'm sorry Will, it was to safeguard Debra, not myself," Richard said miserably. "And I knew you didn't approve."

"That's no excuse, we've always been open with each other. I feel completely let down by your lack of trust. And the way you did more than that, you actually deceived me by making me believe you had given up the idea, letting me introduce you to girls I considered suitable."

"I do apologise, Will, but honestly it was forced upon me, for Debra's sake, not mine. Her father forbade her to see me and made threats against me twice. If any rumour had got about it would have been the end."

"You thought I couldn't keep a secret, that I would have told Betty," Will was still both angry and upset.

"Perhaps," Richard had to admit honestly.

"And now you are actually going ahead with a marriage, despite everything?" Will shook his head in disbelief. It took Richard several minutes to plead for his friend's forgiveness and the need for his assistance for Will's sense of betrayal remained strong. But eventually his good nature prevailed.

"Can she cook?" he asked.

"I haven't the slightest idea. I want a companion, a soul-mate, a lover, not a housekeeper."

"Is she good in bed then?"

"I don't know."

Will's expression was comical in its astonishment. "Don't tell me you have been courting her for two years, supposedly madly in love with her and you haven't made love. What's wrong with you?"

"It hasn't been easy I admit. I love her and she loves me but we can wait for marriage." He forbore telling

Will that his main reason for abstinence was so that no-one should ever think the marriage had taken place for necessity as this touched too closely on Will's own circumstances. "But I want to get married now. And because of the difficulties I need a special licence. We don't live in the same parish and I don't attend any parish church, I am a Catholic and she isn't, yes I know Will that this troubles you, but more importantly her father is adamant that she is not to marry me. As I told you, he has threatened me more than once." He went on to confess how he had actually asked for permission to marry Debra. "We are waiting until Debra is twenty-one and then it will be over and done with before anyone knows."

"Phew, is it worth it? He could make life very difficult for you, turn people against you, you could lose trade." Will paused. "He could even make matters worse for you as a Catholic, inform on you, invent things to get you jailed, it's been done before."

"I've considered all that but I don't think he would do anything to harm Debra once we are married. He will never accept me but he must accept our marriage once it is done. Which is why I need you to help me get a special licence."

"What do I do?"

"Before I can get a licence I have to make a declaration or an allegation as they call it. I have to swear that both of us are free to marry, that we are both over age and give the reasons for wanting to marry out of our own parishes without the waiting time. I need a witness who is also a bondsman because I must proffer a money bond as security against the honesty of the statement I make. The bond would be forfeit if any part of the allegation was proved to be untrue."

"What sort of money? How much?"

Richard paused. Then he said, "From forty pounds to four hundred I believe, depending on circumstances."

"God's blood Richard, I can't guarantee you for a fortune like that."

"It will never be asked for, believe me. It is merely a formality. It would only be forfeit if the marriage did not proceed or the facts haven't been honestly declared, and neither is going to happen. So will you come with me to Wigan as soon as possible?"

Will sighed, "I think you are mad. I wouldn't like to be in your shoes. Have you also thought of the implications of a secret marriage? You are going to offend against the rules of society. Marriage is meant to be celebrated publicly with acceptance into the community. Secret marriages are frowned upon by society and both you and Debra Crane will be condemned."

"I know this too, Will. But we are prepared to take the risk. So will you help me?" Will sighed but realising nothing could dissuade his friend said at last, "Despite the way you have treated me I am your friend and I have always said you can rely on me whatever happens."

Richard clasped his hand. "I really appreciate this and am truly sorry for having not confided in you before. I have always valued our friendship as one of the best things in my life and now more than ever. If ever I can repay you or help you in any way you know I will do so. But Will, this must be kept secret, no word of it to anyone, not even Betty."

Will nodded. "I take it your family doesn't know."

"Nothing at all. They won't be pleased either. I wish it could have been otherwise and I need not have upset people. But I happen to have fallen in love with Debra

Crane and I cannot give her up no matter what it costs me. Love is a hard thing to fathom. My mother once told me that love brings more grief than joy. I don't believe that but fate is a hard master."

When Richard met Debra in their secret place as arranged on midsummer day, a day of blue skies and warm sunshine, he was in possession of the licence. "We can now marry at any time we like and in any church we choose," he said.

She heaved a sigh of relief and said contentedly, "So less than a month to my birthday."

"We now have to decide where we are going to marry," Richard reminded her. "It will be better if we keep away from Ormskirk, Upholland or Eccleston and I thought of Standish. It isn't too far but no-one knows us there."

Debra voiced her agreement and Richard continued, "I want you to be absolutely sure, Debra, that you don't mind not having a proper wedding with all the festivities, not having a bridal gown that all the girls would envy, your family and friends around you admiring you, scattering flowers and ribbons to the spectators and selling your bridal ale. Then merrymaking afterwards with music and dancing. I know how much a wedding day means to girls." (He called to mind his sister Mary and Betty Plumb.) "There would only be you and me."

"That would be enough. I shall make myself as beautiful as I can for *you* and that is all that matters."

He was moved beyond words and they were silent for a time, holding hands as they sat on the grass beneath the trees where clusters of wild violets nestled amongst the roots. "Let's plan the day then," he said at last. "I thought at first we could ride together but it would be best to ride to Standish separately. Can you make your way there?"

"I shall be twenty-one then and completely independent," she smiled.

"The quickest way is up Parbold hill but the easier way would be to follow the river to Appley Bridge." She nodded then said with a little frown puckering her brow, "One thing does worry me, darling, and that is that festivities for my birthday have been planned for the day before. There will be feasting and gifts and I shall feel such a hypocrite knowing I am running away the day after. My father is also pressing me to agree to an engagement with William Barton."

His face clouded over at her concern and he said, "We can leave it for a time if you like. The licence allows us to marry at any time."

She shook her head, "No, I don't want to wait any longer, we have waited two years. We have already wasted two years of our life together. If people wish to give me gifts then I will accept them gracefully and I will try to appease my father and William until my birthday is over."

They were both aware of the moral implications of their actions, neither enjoying the duplicity and weighing more heavily on Richard as he was no young boy but thirty years old and almost ten years older than Debra. But they had made their decision, a decision that had been forced upon them, and nothing was going to stop them now. They went their separate ways, Debra to pick up her pony where she had left it, Richard walking in a different direction, a little apprehensive but excited at the thought that when they next met they would be man and wife.

On the morning of the twenty-fourth of July Richard rode up Parbold hill on the horse he had hired. The mist was still hanging over the valley but the sun was already touching Dalton's hills on the other side and it promised to be a fine day. His suit was new – a grey wool jacket in the new longer length with large pockets and turned-back cuffs to show his shirt, and black woollen breeches tied below the knee. His shirt of crisp linen was also new and for the first time in his life he wore white stockings with his latchet shoes. His fair hair touched his shoulders beneath a broad-brimmed black felt hat with shallow crown circled by a band of woven braid. He rode slowly for the meeting time was noon and when he reached the brow of the hill he stopped to rest his horse after the hard climb and to gaze at the prospect spread out before him – the sun now bathing the undulating hills and the flat fields of Lathom spread out at the bottom of the hill. A silvery strip of light marked the sea where in the far distance could be traced the shadowy outline of the Welsh mountains. He rode past Wrightington Hall where much of his Catholic life was spent and wondered what the Dicconsons might think of his present actions, they would expect him to marry a Catholic girl. Debra wasn't a Catholic but she had accepted his faith and although not wanting to change her own he hoped that one day she might wish to do so especially as she had agreed that any children they might have would be baptised as Catholics.

He came into Langtree where the road changed direction to Standish and recalled how his family had lived there as weavers for several generations. It was when his grandfather, another Richard Webster, at the time of the civil war had married Mary Aspinwall from a weaving family on the Wrightington/Parbold border that he had gone to join his skills with theirs leaving older brothers to carry on the trade in Langtree. There were still many relatives living in Langtree but Richard had lost touch with them when his father went to Maryland and they had been forced to move to Dalton with his maternal grandmother. Distances were not easy in this part of Lancashire, especially without a horse. Also everyone had large families and as they married and multiplied there were just too many cousins and half-cousins to stay closely-connected. Those who shared the same employment tended to join forces, keeping trades in families and inter-marrying with other families in the same work. Richard was breaking the mould that had kept his family together for several generations.

Just before he came into Standish he passed Standish Hall, another Catholic hall with a secret chapel where the owner William Standish had been involved with the Dicconsons and others in the plot to reinstate King James for which they had almost forfeited their lives. He left the road to take the opportunity to see the Hall, following an avenue of beech trees to where a pleasant half-timbered building dating from the time of Queen Elizabeth was set on a grassy plateau with a fine prospect overlooking the valley of the river Douglas.

He judged it could not be very far from noon by the time he rode into Standish, the little town crowded with the morning's business. The church with its tower was set in the busy market place and he threaded his way through shoppers and traders, the air filled with chatter and vendors' cries. Debra was already there, seated on a stone bench near the lych-gate making a daisy chain.

"I could hardly ride through Appley Bridge with flowers in my hair but I wouldn't be a bride without them," she said, leaping up when she saw him and laughing with happiness. She put the daisy circlet on her shining brown hair and twirled in front of him. She was wearing a long-waisted bodice of deep green mockado over a kirtle of primrose-yellow linen with a wide hem embroidered with a trellis of green leaves. The back-laced bodice emphasized her trim waist and the bodice's low curving neckline showed the ruffles of her white shift beneath.

"I had a new gown for my birthday so I made sure it was green and yellow, green is the colour for weddings and green and yellow together signify joy and happiness," she said.

"Happy birthday," he kissed her, "and happy wedding day. You look so beautiful."

"And you are the handsomest man I know, I'm so proud that you are going to be my husband," she responded to his kiss.

"I have a present for you," he said, taking a ring from one of the deep pockets in his jacket. "I know that Protestants don't bother with wedding rings but we Catholics do and I wanted you to have one as a token of our marriage and my undying love for you. It is only silver but it is engraved." He placed it in her palm and she took it up and looked at it. "It says amor vincit omnia which is Latin for love conquers all."

"Do you know Latin?" she asked in surprise.

He shook his head, "No, I am no scholar. But I was born with the sound of Latin ringing in my ears and the sound of it has always been part of my life, all our prayers and masses are in Latin. You get to understand it instinctively and more than that it becomes a channel to God where the meaning of the words is less important than the emotion. I'm sorry if that seems too high-sounding," he said with an apologetic half-smile.

"No it doesn't. It's beautiful," she said. "And this ring is beautiful, the most wonderful present I have ever had. I love you so much."

He took it from her saying, "I will put it on your finger in the ceremony. It has been blessed by a priest so that makes our marriage sanctified by my own faith."

They were alone in the old stone church apart from the rector and the verger and clerk who were to act as witnesses and see the marriage recorded in the register. The sun filtering through the stained glass windows lit the gold cross on the altar and cast shifting patterns on the stone floor and on their rapt faces as they made their vows and he put the ring on her finger. Then they signed their names, Debra biting her lip in concentration and he watched her proudly as the achievement brought a smile to her face.

In the churchyard they kissed and hugged, oblivious to the attention of onlookers who saw them come from the church and surmising a wedding clapped and shouted their greetings.

Debra said contentedly, "Now I am really your wife."

"Not quite, Deb," he said smiling. "Let's go home."

They rode back down Parbold hill, walking their horses down the steepest part. At the bottom where the roads to Newburgh and Dalton diverged Richard said, "We are going to have to send your pony back, we cannot take anything of your father's without his consent."

"Yes I know. I shall be sorry to lose him, he has been with me since he was born." A shadow clouded her face momentarily and Richard said, "I'm sorry too, love, and if I can ever get you a horse I will."

"It doesn't matter, it's a small price to pay," she assured him, smiling again, "but how can we do it?"

A young farm labourer was coming towards them and Richard stopped him. "Will you take this pony back to Richard Crane's farm for us?" he asked, holding out his hand with some pennies.

The lad's face brightened and his acceptance was eagerly given.

"Don't be tempted to keep it, Master Crane is expecting it and won't be pleased if he doesn't get it," Richard warned. The lad gave his promise, obviously knowing something of the farmer's reputation but also considering the money and a ride on a horse sufficient incentive to do as he was asked. "There is also a message," Richard continued. "Tell him that Debra Webster is at home."

Debra rode pillion behind him for the rest of the way. When they reached his house he dismounted then lifted her down and still holding her in his arms he carried her over the threshold. He returned to tether the horse then led her immediately upstairs. The bedchamber was light and warm, the yellow walls catching the glow of the sun through the open casement, the bed inviting with new linen sheets, goose feather pillows (there were hundreds of geese on the huge mere) and the blue woven counterpane. He had never in all his life felt such unalloyed happiness. Richard Webster had achieved his heart's desire, Debra Crane was now his wife.

Chapter 11

1701–02

The night was long but they slept little, not only making love but lying entwined they talked about all the details of their lives before they met. Richard relayed to Debra the story of his life, not only the facts but his deepest feelings that he had never confessed to anyone before – fear, humiliation, exhaustion, despair. Sharing brought a lightness of being that he had never before experienced, as if a great load had been taken from him, and tied them together as closely as the physical ecstasy they discovered in a knot that was never to be broken.

"Do you think your father would ever have come back?" she asked gently.

He hesitated then replied, "I have to think so. So as not to lose faith."

They fell into an exhausted sleep at last, sated by passion and talk.

They rose early, ravenously hungry, and Debra made her first meal in her own house for her husband. She proudly laid the plates of ham and cheese with chunks of rye bread and a jug of small beer on the table and they sat opposite each other.

"I shall have to put my hair up now that I am a married woman," she said.

However she had no time to do so before the door of the workshop smashed open and the sound of booted feet could be heard on the flagged floor. Richard rose to open the door into the living room and Richard Crane strode in. His face was red with anger and his voice harsh as he bellowed, "So this is where you are!"

Debra rose from the table and though her face was pale her voice was strong and steady as she faced him saying, "I am of age now, father, and a married woman so I am no longer under your control."

Richard went to stand beside her, his hand in hers as he added, "I am aware this is not pleasing to you, sir, but we were married yesterday, legally by licence in the parish church of Standish as two mature adults past the age of consent."

Crane ignored him and continued to fix his gaze on Debra, "You Jezebel, you betrayer of your family and everything that I have planned and done for you. You have broken all the rules of decent society and religious observance. A secret marriage is an abomination. Marriage is a social contract, made publicly in the sight of family and community, and a marriage to a Papist beggars belief. Well let me tell you this, you are no longer a daughter of mine, you have cut yourself off completely from any consideration of mine and from all the rest of your family. To the Cranes it will be as if you no longer exist."

Debra stood proudly beside her new husband as she said steadily, "I know I should have informed you but you made it clear you would never accept my choice of husband. And he is my choice. We have done no wrong other than followed our hearts and I waited until I was of age and legally able to make my own decisions. And we will continue to have different faiths, I shall continue to follow my own religion, you need have no fear of that."

Her father laughed mockingly, "Do you really think that? Do you think the Papists will allow that? Your children will be forced to be Papists and I will never accept Papist grandchildren."

Richard intervened but knew that he could not deny this. He said, "I love Debra dearly and I swear to you as her father that I will love and care for her all my life. I will do all in my power to make her happy, I will work to give her everything she needs, I will keep her as safe as is humanly possible and would give my life for her if need be."

Crane still ignored him and said to his daughter, "You have chosen to be Goodwife Webster instead of Mistress Crane so now you have made your bed you can lie in it without any help from me."

A little smile tickled Debra's lips and she was tempted to reply that she liked very much the bed she had chosen to lie in but it was Richard who spoke.

"I do not expect any help from you, sir, that was never my intention when I asked Debra to marry me. I am a skilled craftsman and am able to support a wife and possible family with my own efforts, not with luxury but with love and care. We have no desire to be anything but independent."

"You could have had so much, you foolish girl," the farmer retorted. "I will have all your belongings sent over to you but from now on you are a stranger to us. You will not contact any of us, neither your mother nor your brothers and sisters, all who have been ordered to have no further communication with you."

He strode from the room without acknowledging his new son-in-law, slamming the door behind him and they could hear him bang shut the front door also as he left the house.

Both Richard and Debra had been expecting his arrival some time but they were still shocked and Debra sat down on a chair and began to cry. Richard was devastated and pulled her into his arms, his heart riven at what he had inflicted upon her. Her face was streaked with tears as she looked up at him but she said, "Darling, there will be times when I shall cry, because I am upset or hurt or disappointed, but you must never, ever, think that I am crying because I have any regrets. I have no regrets about becoming your wife and I never shall have. There is nothing more I want in the wide world, I love you to the ends of my being and I always will. Do you think I care about a few clothes and trinkets that I have left behind? Yes I am sorry that he says I can't see my mother and my brothers and sisters again but I have never been close to my mother and I'm sure that my sister Esther at least will find some occasion to see me. You are all my family now and any children we might have. I wasn't crying for any of this but because of you, because of how my father has not estimated your worth, degraded you even, not seen your merit as I see it. I feel ashamed of my father and it hurts me to see you so badly treated."

He stroked her hair gently. "My darling Debra, you mustn't cry for me, I am the happiest man in the world because I have your love. Let's forget farmer Crane. You are Debra Webster now. Let's enjoy the first day of our life together."

In the late afternoon they had another visitor. Will Taylor couldn't resist the temptation. His cheery greeting drew Richard into the workshop before he could come further. "Well how's married life? Is it worth it so far? How many times did you manage last night?"

"Don't pry," Richard retorted but he was laughing.

"I heard you had a visit from Dick Crane," Will said then.

Richard grimaced. "It wasn't pleasant," he admitted. "But how did you know?"

"Half of Dalton knows," replied Will.

Richard told him briefly what had occurred.

"Watch your back for a bit, he could be vengeful. He could blackguard you about. Trade might suffer for a time," his friend warned.

"I don't intend working a lot just at present, I want to spend time with Debra in these early days. It will be only a nine-day wonder, people will soon find other things to excite their interest. As for Crane, I don't think he will do anything to harm Debra even if he does nothing to help. Come through and meet her, you have never really known her."

Richard led Will through into the living room where his wife and his best friend weighed each other up with appreciation and some curiosity. Debra had coiled her hair in the nape of her neck and fastened it with a bone comb but paradoxically it made her look younger and Richard gazed on her with affection. She had a blue canvas apron over her kirtle and was mixing something in a bowl. She hastened to bring mugs of ale for the men and said eagerly to Will, "Richard is going to weave some linen which I shall dye and then needlework it and we are going to have curtains and cushions."

"Jesu, don't let Betty know," Will groaned. "She's just told me she's expecting another babe and I have no money for fripperies like cushions and curtains."

Debra gave him a black look and Richard laughed saying, "Now go home to your wife, Will, and leave me with mine."

As he led him to the door Will said to his friend, "I've never seen you so happy. Hope it continues for you."

"It will," Richard said.

The next hurdle was his mother and next day Richard took Debra to the cottage where Marie and Eddy lived. They walked arm in arm through Dalton and most people greeted them, some offering their best wishes on their marriage though they were aware of a great wave of curiosity. Eddy was out at work but Marie was washing clothes and looked up in surprise as they entered.

"Good day to you Ma, I would like you to meet my wife, Debra," Richard said.

Marie's face reflected the series of emotions convulsing her – astonishment, anger, unease, compounded by humiliation that she was wearing her shabbiest clothes with her hair escaping in tendrils from her rough linen coif in this first encounter with the wife she had so often urged her son to take, his young well-dressed wife. Debra had dressed plainly but there was no disguising that her gown was of the best wool and her upswept hair covered only by a small circle of lace-edged linen.

"You're married! When? Why wasn't I told anything? Did you think me unworthy to attend your marriage celebrations?" was her first response, tinged with bitterness.

"Don't fret, Ma, it was no such thing as you should well know," Richard spoke comfortingly. "We were married yesterday by special licence in a private ceremony with no-one there but Debra and me. Nobody knew, neither friends nor kin. Now greet Debra as my wife. Debra, this is my mother Marie Webster."

Debra held out her hand with a shy smile but Marie didn't take it and said to Richard, "Not by a priest then."

"The ring was blessed by a priest. But as I said it was a private ceremony by special licence. Debra is not a Catholic as you know," Richard said calmly.

"Why have you done this? You should have married a Catholic girl after waiting so long. You are out of your class and what is worse, out of your religion." There was no forgiveness and no welcome in Marie's voice.

Debra could see that Richard was losing his temper and put her hand on his arm. Then she took the hands that Marie resolutely refused to proffer and holding them in hers said earnestly, "I love your son dearly and I promise you, Marie, that I will do all in my power to make him happy, to care for him and to be the best wife it is possible to be. Apart from my religion you will have nothing to complain about in me as a wife and I assure you that although it is true that our faith takes different forms we share a faith in God that is the same in importance and sincerity."

Marie was still overwhelmed by disappointment but even she was not immune to Debra's serene face and natural charm and briefly returned the pressure on her hands though still unable to welcome her new daughter-in-law.

"You must be satisfied that I am no longer a bachelor," Richard said jokingly. But he knew that it was no use prolonging the visit and that he should give his mother time to get used to the idea. He would visit her alone soon and talk her into acceptance with Eddy present also. As a peace-offering he said, "I believe there's a mass at Mossborough on Sunday, I'll come for you and we will go together." He made their excuses of having much to do at home and they took their leave.

They were subdued as they walked home hand in hand. "I'm sorry that was no easier than with your father," Richard said.

"Don't worry. I know that your mother has had a hard life and I do understand how she feels. It is a pity that we don't have the approval of our families but we expected that. They may come round in time and I shall do my very best to prove to your mother that I am worthy of you and make her like me eventually," Debra said.

"Oh Debra, how could anyone not like you?" Richard said fervently. "In the meantime we have each other and that is all that matters isn't it."

"It's all that matters," she replied.

For a time they were a subject of curious attention and an item of gossip in the streets and alehouses. Reaction was mixed – disapproval for flouting the rules of society, awe at crossing Richard Crane, envy at Richard's good fortune and some censure from both Catholics and Protestants. Some of Richard's religious associates were cool but many people came to wish them blessings on their married life bringing with them small gifts of flowers, a few eggs or pears, home-baked biscuits, a jar of honey or strawberry preserve, a jug of elderflower cordial. As a weaver Richard had always been respected and those who were treated to Debra's ready smile and her gentle unassuming courtesy were compelled to respond with like warmth.

It was an idyllic summer that was to remain in their memory as they enjoyed the warm weather, grew to know each other intimately and spent time improving their little house. It wasn't very long before Debra realised she was expecting a baby and her cup of happiness was filled to the brim, "something we made together," she said.

Then in September came unexpected news from St. Germain, Louis XIV's royal chateau twenty miles from Paris where King James had been living in exile since he was deposed. The King had died of a fatal stroke. Although he had stipulated that he wanted only a simple funeral as a gentleman, King Louis had given him a royal burial as King James II of England.

Catholics mourned his passing, taking consolation from the fact that he had left a son and heir, Prince James Edward Stuart. Reports said he was well-educated, courteous, spoken well of. His father had loved him dearly and there was no doubt that he would take on the mantle of his father and pursue the Catholic cause. A determination to restore him to the English throne was still a driving force for English Catholics and was a talking point at all the secret meetings Richard attended but although he shared everything else with Debra this was something he kept to himself, chiefly because he did not want to worry her, especially at this time.

Debra thrived with childbearing. Her rounding body suited her as she let out the laces of her kirtles and bodices, her skin had a healthy glow, her brown hair shone glossy when she let it down at night and Richard looked at her with pride and affection and a growing excitement that he would soon be a father. He was determined to be a good father and give his children what he never had. The only cloud on their horizon was the continued repudiation of the Cranes. True to his promise, Dick Crane had had Debra's clothes and personal belongings delivered but no further contact had been made by any of the family.

"I thought my mother might have asked after me because she must surely have heard that I am expecting a baby," she said wistfully and Richard was moved by her disappointment. His mother was not much better and there was little converse between them apart from Sunday visits though Richard accompanied her to masses.

As Yuletide approached Debra had considered going to visit her parents but instinct warned her that her present condition, now all too obvious, might possibly inflame her father more. But they made many Yuletide visits to friends and Webster relatives, enjoying happy hours with Will and Betty, now close to her time with her fifth child, so that they could share their experiences. On the eve of Christmas Richard regretfully left Debra alone in bed and on a cold frosty night with the stars stamped clear on the heavens' dense black canopy made his way to Wrightington Hall for the customary midnight mass. As he made his solitary way there was a stillness in the silent wooded paths enveloping him in a feeling that heaven and earth were intermingling and he might expect to see angels above him in the night sky. Later as he knelt on the cold stones of the little secret chapel and let the familiar Latin words pour over and through him he wished desperately that Debra could be beside him on this occasion when the imminent birth of their own child made this nativity so special.

Afterwards on Christmas day his mother and Eddy came to share the Christmas dinner. Marie looked around the room with surprise and some longing. A log fire burnt in the grate making the stone walls of ox-blood glow with warmth. Festoons of holly, ivy and laurel had been twined around the hearth and the window where blue linen curtains were ready to draw when early darkness fell, and linen cushions decorated with crewel work made the hard wood of the settle and the two chairs more comfortable. Debra's face was rosy with the heat from the oven as, her swelling figure enveloped in a linen apron, she served them a pease pudding then proudly placed the roast pork on the table which Richard proceeded to carve in generous portions. Watching him, Marie could not help her thoughts winging back to the Christmas after Edward had left when she had had to cut up her cloak to make him a warm enough coat as they had made the long cold walk to Fairhurst Hall, fingers and feet freezing, carrying the baby Eddy beneath her shawl and trying desperately to keep warm. Although she could have wished another wife for him she knew he was happier than she had ever seen him and when Debra served her mince pies she had to nod her approval.

After Yuletide the time passed slowly as it always did in the winter months but Richard worked hard and Debra was content to sit quietly by the fire sewing, her concentration on making household linen now turned to shifts and caps for the baby. Richard had got Harry Moss the carpenter to make a crib and Debra was also working a coverlet whilst Betty was teaching her to knit a shawl.

Spring came at last and time for the child's birth drew near. But before they could celebrate Easter the whole country was disturbed by startling news. King William was dead. While out riding, his horse had stumbled on a mole hill and thrown the King to his death. He was only fifty-two years old. Devout Catholics considered the unusual event to be an Act of God. However any hope of King James's son, Prince James Edward Stuart, becoming the next monarch was dashed by Parliament passing an Act of Settlement that decreed no Catholic should ever again sit on the English throne. Because William and Mary had no children the crown passed to Mary's younger sister Anne who was crowned Queen. Catholics considered this a betrayal. Anne was half-sister to James Edward Stuart by King James's first wife but *he* was the legal heir to the Crown. They were determined not to meekly stand by and accept this but to continue to work for the restoration of their rightful king.

By the time Easter had been celebrated it was obvious there was not long to go before the birth of Richard and Debra's first child. Debra now found it difficult to move around, a pleasant lethargy had overtaken her and the child had stopped kicking and had settled down preparing for its entry into the world. Help for the birth had been requisitioned in the shape of Marie, Betty, now delivered of another son, Betty's mother and a neighbour of hers who had much experience of childbirth and had attended many confinements. Richard hastened to collect them as soon as Debra's pains began and they hustled her to bed. He felt completely at a loss. He wanted to comfort her in her distress but the women took over the house, bustling around to find cloths and boil water, relegating him to the weaving loom though the midwife, a large, red-faced vulgar dame, was prone to making jests about having to pay now for the pleasure they had earlier enjoyed. He tried to concentrate on his work but found it impossible to do so as Debra's cries grew stronger. He heard his mother scold her in what seemed to him an unsympathetic voice, "Stop crying Debra and save your energy for pushing. All of us have had several children and we are still alive." It was useless, he was breaking threads and spoiling the weave so he gave up and sat on a stool reciting all the prayers he knew, trying to calm his turbulent spirits and praying for the safety of his beloved wife in this perilous time for he knew that if anything went wrong there was little that could be done. The hours seemed endless. Betty came to give him drinks from time to time then made him something to eat at noon. "All's going well," she assured him, "we are nearly there." Afterwards they told him it had been a relatively quick birth for a first child but it had not seemed so at him. A piercing scream, a long pause then a baby's loud cry followed by laughter and cheers.

His mother came downstairs, a smile lighting her careworn features. "You have a son," she said. "He seems healthy enough to thrive." Then she added, "Debra did well. She'll be good at childbearing."

He ran upstairs two at a time. The women were still around the bed tidying Debra, and the child who was still bloody was being carried away to be washed by the midwife. "Can't you wait till you're called," she scolded him but his first desire was to see Debra and they made room for him. She was lying still, breathing deeply and her eyes were closed but she opened them when she heard him. They were shining with happiness and love. He stroked the damp dishevelled hair back from her forehead.

"Have you seen him?" she asked.

He shook his head. "I wanted to see you first."

Betty brought the child back wrapped in a blanket, put him in his mother's arms and left them quietly together.

"Thankyou for giving me a child," he said.

"Are you glad it's a boy?" she asked.

He shook his head. "It wouldn't have mattered to me. So long as you are safe and we have a child to share together."

"I'm glad I've given you a son," she said contentedly.

"I couldn't bear you to be in pain. Does this mean you won't want to have any more children?"

She laughed. A delighted, bubbling laugh that echoed round the bedchamber and lit her face with joy. "I want to give you lots of sons. It's women's work. But chiefly because I love you and it's something I can do for you."

When Betty returned to show Debra how to suckle her child she found them wrapped in an embrace with the child almost suffocated between them.

She tutted disapprovingly, "Go away now, Richard, Debra needs to rest. Go over to Will and wet the baby's head and leave us to finish our work."

With a last fond look at his wife, thinking her lovelier than ever with the babe in her arms, her serene face bathed in a glow of contentment that he could only assume was the aura of motherhood and brought to mind the Virgin and child, he went off to Will's house to accept his friend's relief and good wishes.

When he returned he found only his mother there. Marie had made them a meal but was determined to depart. He knew that although she said little she was happy to have another grandchild. As she grew older her life was becoming easier and happier with the settlement of her children, only Eddy now to find himself a wife. She took a fond look at the little boy before going on her way. He was lying in the crib beside the bed. The other bedchamber was still empty of furnishings but Richard had the incentive to complete it now that their family had increased.

"What are we going to call him?" Richard asked.

"Can we call him Richard?" Debra asked, her eyes wide and a little anxious. "I want him to have your name."

And your father's name too, he realised. It was common practice to give the first son the name of his grandfather. "Whatever you wish," he said.

In the days that followed, although neither of them mentioned it, they both hoped and half-expected that some word would come from the Cranes. But nothing happened even though Richard had written a note. Then when the child was two weeks old Esther Crane arrived at the door of the workshop, looking slightly bewildered and asking to see the baby. It was obvious she had been brought there because although she was sixteen she was childish for her age and rather slow. She had Debra's serene features but without any of her vivacity and her eyes always seemed slightly unfocussed while her movements were clumsy and unco-ordinated. The sisters were awkward with each other but Esther never said much and seemed happy when Debra let her hold the baby. "You are his aunt, Esther," she said, and the girl seemed pleased. No gift was offered but Richard and Debra surmised this would be granting too much, the Cranes had after all acknowledged the event. Esther had obviously been told to leave the house after a certain time and would no doubt be picked up at an arranged place.

The child had not yet been baptised. Richard had agreed with Debra for a Catholic baptism but they had to wait for the arrival of a priest to do so. It was decided that if the baby happened to ail or did not thrive then they would take him to be baptised at Upholland or Ormskirk, as was often done with sickly Catholic children if a priest could not be found in time. Little Richard Webster grew strong and eventually his father was able to take him to Wrightington Hall. Debra did not accompany him but this was not unusual as mothers did not generally attend the baptisms of their offsprings. Will and Betty were the sponsors.

The summer passed happily. Richard's trade had increased again and Debra found great pleasure rearing their little boy and attending to his every need. They walked out together whenever they could, proudly showing their little son to friends and acquaintances, even strangers, for a new baby was always a matter of interest to the village. Their little child, a product of their love, was the seal set on their happiness. It had been a wonderful year.

Chapter 12

1705–07

The following years did not continue their unalloyed happiness. Their little son Richard died when he was only a year old. He was beginning to talk and walk after Richard had first made a walking frame for him with instructions from the carpenter Sam Woodcock. Debra was inconsolable and cried for three days. Richard was desperate as he held her in his arms, not knowing how to comfort her. The loss of his son was as painful to him but this was exacerbated by his sorrow for Debra and his inability to do anything for her. She was the one who had borne the child and taken such delight in every stage of his development. "He was so beautiful and so clever, how could he be taken from us so cruelly?" she sobbed over and over again. Richard wanted to go alone to have him buried in Upholland churchyard, thinking to spare Debra more grief but she was adamant about accompanying him. "I brought him into the light and I want to see him go into the dark," she wept.

"Don't think that my darling, you must believe that he is not going into the dark but is already in the light of our Saviour's presence," Richard insisted, holding onto every thread of his Catholic faith. When he carried the little box down the steps of Upholland churchyard he could not help but be reminded of the time when, only a little boy himself, he had helped his Uncle Tom Swift carry the coffin of his brother Jamie. He had grieved then at the loss of his brother and playmate and been frightened by this unexpected threat to the stability of life. But only now could he understand the grief his mother must have felt, alone without his father to share the sorrow.

Debra was pregnant again but this time there was not the exhilaration she had shown before. She was sick and soon became weary, anxiety etched on her face. "I am frightened that we might lose another child," she confided to Richard. He tried to comfort her by reiterating constantly that all would be well. The birth of the child was not as easy as the first one had been and Debra ascribed it to anxiety. But the same people were there to help and eventually another boy was born on a day of spring showers and fitful sunshine. They named him Thomas which was a family name for both the Websters and the Cranes and the name of Debra's grandfather but Debra could not rid herself of anxiety, watching him carefully and worrying about every little ailment.

It was a difficult time for Catholics. The accession of Queen Anne in the place of William of Orange who had died without children did not lessen the determination of many Catholics to pursue the Jacobite cause. King James II might be dead but he had left a son and heir – Prince James Edward Stuart–whom they believed to be the rightful sovereign of Great Britain, not his half-sister Anne. The recent Act of Settlement decreeing that no Catholic should inherit the Crown had only increased their intention to work for his restitution. In Catholic Halls and houses he was prayed for and referred to as "King over the water." It became the custom to raise a toast to the sovereign by raising their glasses over a vessel filled with water. The significance did not go unnoted but there was no way anyone could be accused of treason.

There was a constant flow of Catholics to the palace of St. Germain where Hugh Dicconson as one of the tutors to Prince James Edward Stuart served as a link with west Lancashire. Messengers travelled constantly between St. Germain and Catholic centres in England with plans for an invasion by the prince for which King Louis had promised to supply a supporting army. The great Lancashire Catholic Halls of Stoneyhurst, Browsholme, Townley, Hoghton Tower together with the local Standish Hall and Wrightington Hall were actively involved.

All this was well-known in the secret circles of west Lancashire and most ordinary Catholics, including Richard, Will and their friends and associates were confused in their opinions. They all wanted to see a Catholic as king, they all believed that James Edward Stuart was the rightful king, but they were not happy about the involvement of England's enemy France. However they were not called upon to make a decision as to whether to fight or not because Government spies had a clear idea of what was being planned. Ever since the Reformation Catholic plots had always been infiltrated. The authorities pounced, not only on the ring-leaders but on *all* Catholics on the suspicion that they were actively working for the return of "the pretender" as James Edward Stuart was officially termed and penalties against them were renewed. As always, it was not possible for all Catholics to be identified for a variety of reasons but once again in 1705 recusant lists were drawn up of those who were known, helped by informers. The lists for the local villages contained many of the familiar recurrent names. But strangely enough the list for Dalton contained only five names, a fraction of the number on the previous list. Besides two paupers who were too poor to pay the fines and could not therefore be pursued there was only Richard, his mother Marie and his brother Edward. When he was commanded to appear before the magistrates at Wigan Richard was thoughtful. There was something very strange about this. Why not more of the Catholics in Dalton? Why was only his family being picked out? He had never been a militant activist. He attended masses and secret meetings and occasionally as a boy he had guided priests on their travels, most of the Catholic boys did so from time to time. His father had probably done more but Will Taylor had always been far more active than Richard.

The more he thought about it the more he became convinced that someone had a grudge against him. Someone had informed on him particularly and it hinted at an act of vengeance. He called to mind Will's warnings about Richard Crane's possible reactions. He was loath to voice his suspicions to Debra but she also was worried about the implications and finally said tentatively, "Do you think my father could have had a hand in it?"

Richard remained silent but he had harboured the same suspicions though was unwilling to believe that his father-in-law could go to such lengths to punish him.

However he replied, not too confidently, "No I don't. Even though he hates Papistry I do not for one moment think he would do anything to harm you, Deb."

"I think he might, Richard, much as I am trying not to believe it. He is very unforgiving. He hasn't exactly shown any kindness to me and I don't think he would refrain from hurting me in order to get at you. Who else could it be? Who else might have a grudge against you?"

"Perhaps it could be someone I have upset in some way, one of my customers, one of the agents," Richard suggested, trying valiantly to absolve his father-in-law from blame.

"Can you think of anyone?" Debra asked and when her husband shook his head she continued, "Everyone thinks highly of you as a weaver, love, you are always fair and just."

They were both worried and upset, especially Debra at the thought that her father could do them harm. When Will Taylor heard the news he was not slow to blame Richard Crane, reminding his friend of how he had warned him of such an eventuality.

The people on the Recusants Lists were called before the magistrates at Wigan and if they refused to take the oath of allegiance they were fined a sum of money. From long experience the authorities knew that persecution produced martyrs and a more effective punishment was to impoverish the culprits. The objective was to destroy the Catholic gentry by fining them so heavily that they would be unable to carry on their estates, a process that had begun in the Civil War by sequestration. But they didn't stop at the gentry. They knew that if they touched the pockets of honest working men and craftsmen then this would be an effective deterrent once they were unable to support their families. Also successive governments had come to rely on Catholic fines as a reliable source of finance for the national economy.

Debra waited anxiously for Richard to return from Wigan and as soon as he entered the living room she knew by his face that it was not good news.

"How much did they fine you?" she asked, her eyes wide with apprehension.

"Forty pounds."

She was unable to stifle the sudden intake of breath. " Oh God, how are we going to pay it?" she asked.

He threw his hat on the settle and sat down at the table. "I shall have to borrow it somehow and pay it back as I can. I shall have to pay it or they will put me in jail, especially as they let me off lightly, it should have been sixty pounds. They said Eddy and I can pay mother's share but they did fine Eddy twenty pounds and I shall have to help him pay that, he can't afford." He had been relieved that his brother, with his slower mind, had not realised their family had been specially targeted so had not pondered any further.

She came to sit beside him and put her arms around him. "Don't worry about it, we shall do it. I'll find ways to economise."

Debra was pregnant again and he held her close, feeling her body swollen with another child. He loved her so much and he had failed her. He had promised to care for her and give her the best he could. Now there would soon be another child to provide for. He had planned to buy her a new gown after the birth of the baby, she was still wearing the clothes that the Cranes had returned to her. He would have to work harder and all the extra money he earned would have to go to paying off the debt instead of improving their circumstances as he had intended. Paying off such a huge fine would take years and meant he could never expand his business, buy another loom, take on an assistant.

"I love you," she said. "More every day. Whatever happens it doesn't matter so long as I have you. Never think I have any regrets about your Catholic faith. It is what makes you as you are and I hate the cruelty and intolerance that believes it is right to punish those who follow their consciences. And I am ashamed and so unhappy that my father might be behind this attempt to ruin you. I have brought you trouble and I wanted to make you happy." Tears streamed down her face and he held her close. "My darling you have brought me more happiness than I ever dared hope for and I am sad that I cannot give you everything I promised."

"So long as we are together life can only be good, no matter what else is lacking," she said.

"Debra Webster, Debra Crane as was, I cannot believe how fortunate I am to have you as my wife, for you to love me as I love you. And I swear to you I will do everything in my power to be worthy of you."

The little room was filled with the aura of their love as they sat wrapped in each other's arms.

The birth of the child on a warm sunny day in July was accomplished safely. It was another son to join Thomas who was growing well. They named him John which was another family name for both the Websters and the Cranes.

"I think it would be wise for us to have him baptised in the parish church instead of privately by a priest, in view of the recent investigation and penalties against Catholics. To guard against more trouble I think we should take him to Upholland and have his birth inscribed in the registers," Richard said reluctantly though he knew Debra was pleased and this salved his conscience. Because the baptism was to be in the established church Debra wished that she might ask her elder brother John, now twenty-one years old, to be his sponsor. Richard thought he might not agree, they had only accidental encounters with the Cranes, but he helped her write a letter. Ever since their wedding he had been teaching her to read and write when they had much time in the evenings and she was now reasonably competent. To their surprise John Crane agreed though no other member of the family attended and he didn't stay for the celebratory meal afterwards.

The baby John was smaller than his other brothers had been and didn't seem as strong but he had all the summer to thrive and they forgot their financial problems as they enjoyed a renewal of happiness in having another child to join little Thomas in their house. Christmas was particularly happy in the fellowship of friends and family. Then a particularly severe winter struck and Richard was once again carrying a little coffin to the churchyard, trudging alone through the snow as Debra felt unable to go with him. Her grief was unsupportable.

When he returned exhausted, wet, and inconsolable she helped him change his clothes and served him hot broth and mulled ale. Then they sat together on the settle before the fire.

"Why are our children dying?" she asked. "Do you think we have angered God and he is punishing us?"

"How can we have angered Him, love?" Richard asked wearily, holding her in his arms.

"We have not kept His commandments. The Bible tells us 'Honour thy father and mother,' it is one of the ten commandments, and I have not done so."

Richard sighed. Then he said, "The Bible tells us also that the three chief virtues are faith, hope and caritas but that caritas, love, is the most important. All that we have done is through love." He stroked her hair gently. "You know it is common to lose children, the churchyards are full of them and all our family and friends have had their losses – my brother Jamie, your brother Peter and sister Elizabeth, Will and Betty's Jane."

"But we have lost two of ours. We have only Thomas now and I am so worried about him." She began to weep and Richard thought his heart would break. He had never suspected that love could bring such agony and remembered his mother's words that love brought more grief than joy.

It was a sad winter and Debra watched fearfully over Thomas but he continued to thrive and their little house was filled with his laughter, his tears and his babbled words. And by the spring Debra was expecting another child. The weak sunbeams and light spring showers, fields full of crocuses, wild violets and daffodils, lambs bleating in the fields, blossom on hawthorn and cherry trees with their own apple trees showing magnificent, raised her spirits to their old level. She was animated with excitement, her movements quick and light as she moved about the house busying herself, her face was full with healthy pink cheeks, her eyes and hair shone. Besides looking after Thomas who was becoming a handful with his boisterous ways she took to sewing baby clothes again. When Thomas was asleep she would take a chair to sit beside Richard in the workshop so that she could talk to him as they worked. She was also scrubbing out the other bedchamber and making curtains, filled with an inexplicable assurance that this new baby would live and grow up.

At the Easter mass service Richard, standing beside his mother and brother Eddy with Will and Betty and many other of their friends and relatives amongst the company, was filled with an assurance of new life after death and felt more hopeful than he had done for a long time. There was joy and anticipation in the air.

The child was another boy, strong and lusty and brought into the world comparatively easily as harvest time approached and the fields turned from green to gold and the trees began to shed their leaves. Neither of them wanted to give the new child the names of the sons they had lost so he was named James. James was a favourite name for Catholics especially as their hopes rested now on the young Prince James Edward Stuart and it was a show of defiance from Richard. But it was also the name of Richard's maternal grandfather and of Debra's younger brother so no ulterior motive could be suspected. This time he was baptised at Wrightington Hall without Debra but with Richard's brother Eddy as sponsor.

The little boy thrived and their household seemed complete with two growing sons. Richard was working as hard as he could to pay off the debt he had borrowed though it seemed to be decreasing slowly and he still hadn't managed to buy Debra her new gown. She said it didn't matter and worked at putting some embroidery on her old ones and altering them so that they looked different, making the sleeves of her bodices interchangeable and buying new laces from the haberdashers at the market. But Richard knew that if he was fined again he would find it difficult to cope and it could well be the ruin of him. As it was all his hard work could not be invested in improving their circumstances.

Further persecution became a possibility when suspicion against Catholics was revived by an attempted invasion by James Edward Stuart. He left France and with the assistance of a French fleet landed in Scotland as the beginning of a bid to take the English throne. However it was a short and ultimately disastrous attempt. The English navy were prepared and in readiness and the French were forced to return home together with the "Pretender." Though the escapade had alerted the English government again to the fact that Catholics were continuing to plot against the established monarchy and suspicion against them was intensified.

A short time later Richard was working at his loom while Debra was in the back garden playing with the children, happily in the early stages of another pregnancy. Suddenly he was surprised by one of Dick Crane's labourers entering the workshop and informing him that his master wished to see him. Richard was puzzled and somewhat alarmed but he gave his assent. Deciding that now was as good a time as any and not willing to be kept in suspense he went to tell Debra he was going on an errand and would be back in due course. She surmised he would be delivering an order and he did not want to enlighten her further until he knew what her father wanted with him. He was sure it could be nothing amicable and tried to control his anxious thoughts as he walked the road to Newburgh.

He called first at the large farmhouse, the first time he had been there. Debra's mother Sarah answered his knock but her careful acknowledgement and her impassive face told him nothing. Neither did she ask anything of her daughter. She merely informed him that the farmer was working in the first field and pointed the way.

Dick Crane was busy helping his labourers plant winter wheat and though he saw Richard he made no move to stop his work immediately but made him stand waiting. Then he shut the seed box and walked towards him with no welcoming smile on his face and Richard feared the worst. His face was hard and unrelenting and his voice harsh as he barked, "Enough is enough. Paying bloody fines to the government and children dying. How long will these latest ones last?"

Richard felt anger rising but he knew he could not deny the first accusation. However he retorted firmly to the second. "If you are implying that the loss of our two sons is through any neglect or insufficiency of mine then I strongly refute that. The children were loved and cared for with every provision it is possible to make. Children die often and unexpectedly as you yourself should know. Our grief was overwhelming but we have great hopes for Thomas and James and another child is on the way."

"I need to have great hopes for my grandsons and that does not include them being brought up as Papists as well as vast sums of money being squandered for a useless cause, a dying cause bolstered only by ignorance and superstition," Crane snapped. He paused then said, "Give up your Catholic religion and I will give you fifty acres of land, freehold land, now, and another fifty acres when I die, plus a farmhouse at Lathom rent-free. I will also get what remains of your fine cancelled."

Whatever Richard had been expecting it was nothing like this. He was astounded and felt that he could not be hearing aright. He had the sensation of being in the middle of a dream, the world swirling around him.

"Well," his father-in-law barked, "what do you say?"

"I.......I need time to think about it," Richard stammered.

The farmer looked taken aback. "I thought you would have jumped at the chance," he barked.

"Then you do not know me," Richard replied steadily.

"I know you to be proud and stubborn," was the retort. He stood scowling at his recalcitrant son-in-law then said, "I'll give you a day, no longer, then the proposition is off and won't be repeated. Let me know your decision by this time tomorrow."

He began work again with no expressions of farewell, leaving Richard as if a hole had opened beneath his feet.

On the way home Richard felt as if he were living through a dream. He walked the familiar road without taking any notice of his surroundings, he wasn't aware of others on the path, some of whom greeted him, he couldn't have said whether the weather was fine, cold or rainy. He couldn't take in what Dick Crane had said. He was being offered a new life as a farmer, a farmer of freehold land, a land-owner. His family, including his father, grandfather, his uncles and cousins had only worked other men's lands as poorly-paid labourers, and as a child he had picked stones from farmers' fields to earn a penny. Instead of sitting at a loom in a small room doing monotonous work for twelve hours a day he could be outside in the open air, granted in all weathers, but with freedom and variety. Included was a farm house, bigger than his own small dwelling and with no rent to pay and no insecurity of tenure. Also the huge crippling debt was to be lifted from his shoulders. But at what a price! He felt like Christ being tempted by the Devil, being offered the kingdoms of the world if he would renounce himself.

Although the life of a farmer, being his own master and paying others to labour for him with a substantial house in the bargain, was a great temptation he honestly felt that he could have resisted, albeit with longing and regret. His faith meant more to him than worldly goods and an easier life. But he didn't have only himself to consider. He had promised Debra to do everything in his power for her and there were children to think of. Thomas and James were growing up healthy and strong and she was expecting another child. Even with the loss of two sons he believed their family would steadily increase. Instead of being reared in a weaver's small cottage they would have the run of acres of land, animals, plentiful healthy food from their own produce, they would never be cold through shortage of fuel. More importantly their future would be assured. As things were their future would be as weavers, becoming apprenticed at an early age, inheriting his looms and perhaps his debts and more than likely having to supplement their income by working in the fields as labourers. He was proud of his own work and what he had achieved but he would like something better for his children. This was where the temptation lay. Not for himself but for them and his beloved Debra. If the offer had not been made then he would not have thought beyond the life they had. They were happy in their little home which he and Debra continued to improve even though it was not in their personal possession and he would continue to work hard so that he could support his growing family adequately and they could enjoy a few more comforts. But now the prize had been dangled before him and an alternative was being offered to him. To make the decision to stay where he was would be to willingly deprive his children of their future and they were half Cranes after all. Richard Crane wasn't thinking of him but of his grandsons who as Catholics would not be able to inherit his lands even if he wished it. A bonus would be the reconciliation of Debra with her family which he knew distressed her though she rarely made mention of it. All these considerations raced through his brain as temptation poked harder. But then came the sickening realisation of the price he would have to pay. To renounce his faith was to renounce part of himself, the part that held him together through all vicissitudes. It would be a betrayal of all his extended family and his long-time friends, martyrs who had withstood everything for their faith, the priests who had braved danger and death to minister to them and all the poor workers of his acquaintance who beggared themselves by paying fines because they would not compromise their beliefs. He had always insisted, to his mother, to Eddy, to Will, that he would never leave the faith, even at the beginning when they feared Debra might tempt him to do so. The tumult in his mind got worse.

As he neared home he decided he would reveal nothing to Debra even though he longed to share his anguish with her. He knew what she would say. "You must not let my father blackmail you, love. I am happy here and want nothing more as long as I am with you. Your faith is everything to you." But her expressive eyes in her lovely calm face would be saying something else.

No, he had to sort this out for himself. Whatever happened the responsibility had to be his alone.

He was quiet during supper and Debra noted though he made an effort to respond to her chatter. At last she said, "Are you worried about something? Did anything happen on your errand?"

"No, nothing at all, love," he forced himself to answer. "I'm tired, that's all. It was a long walk."

"Early bed then?" she queried, with a little smile on her face.

As they made love he realised again how much he loved her, she was everything to him and he would do all in his power to make her happy. Afterwards when she slept peacefully beside him he tossed and turned. She would never ask him to renounce his faith, she was willing to bear all the disadvantages but when he had asked this sacrifice of her he had not given sufficient thought to the children they would have, children whose inheritance lay with her family as much as his. This depriving them of one half of their inheritance was what he had not taken into consideration when everyone had tried to dissuade him from his marriage. As Catholics his sons would never be able to own land or inherit land and their inheritance lay with their mother's family as much as his. He owed it to Debra to do the best for the children she bore. He made his decision even though it tore him in two. He would sacrifice everything for her and not just for her but for the sons they shared. God had tempted him and found him wanting. But he had never believed in a cruel God even though the priests sometimes emphasized His vengeance. What if God was giving him this gift? He was accepting through love for others and love was the greatest virtue of all. This salve to his conscience was soon washed away. If he was being completely honest must he not admit that, deep down in his heart, he desired it for himself also – a place of his own, a landowner, a big step up in life from where he had started. He had always believed, been taught to believe since infancy, that the old faith was the true faith and all else heresy and now he was damning his eternal soul. It was not a comforting thought to try to sleep on.

Dick Crane had given him only a day to accept his offer and Richard knew he must return at once. Although he had made his decision he did not welcome having to humiliate himself. Luckily Debra had taken the children with her to visit Betty so he left the house without her knowing. He called first at the farmhouse and it was Sarah Crane again who answered the door. She was obviously expecting him for she led him into the parlour saying that her husband was at present eating his eleven o'clock dinner. With an unexpected show of humour she added, "He's generally in a good mood when he's had something to eat."

Although being invited to sit, Richard remained standing and looked around, his first time in Debra's home. The parlour was a long, comfortable, oak-beamed room of timber and red-painted plaster, filled with old shabby furniture on which lay games of Nine Men's Morris and Fox and Goose, fishing rods and a hunting horn. An embroidery frame stood in one corner, a livery cupboard against one wall had a selection of pewter, and a pottery jug filled with gillyflowers stood on a chest. There were two windows of small-paned glass framed by unbleached linen curtains. A wide brick hearth was surrounded by an oak mantlepiece on which stood a jar of tobacco and a selection of clay pipes together with some roughly-carved wooden animals.

"My sons made them when they were young." Richard had not heard Dick Crane enter. The farmer walked towards him and said merely, "Well?"

"I would like to accept your generous offer, sir," Richard said, feeling both ashamed and angry as a satisfied smile crossed Crane's face.

"Now it's up to you. Tomorrow you go to the magistrates at Wigan, sign the oath of allegiance and tell them to take you off the recusants list. Tell them I will vouch for you." Richard nodded his agreement, forcing himself to look his father-in-law in the face. "Afterwards I will see to all the arrangements for the transfer of land and you may take possession of the farmhouse. I know you are unfamiliar with farming so I will let you have one of my best men as your bailiff. My son John will also help you, it will be good training for him, and Debra is familiar with everything."

"Thank you. I will put my mind to study and you may have no doubt that I will work hard to learn everything I can," Richard promised.

Crane looked at him carefully. He was shrewd and although he had never accepted Richard he knew enough about him to recognise that he was hardworking. "But no going back on your word," he warned sternly. "No creeping off to secret masses, keeping missals and crucifixes hidden away. Catholics can neither own land nor inherit it as you well know and I'm not having land of mine taken away by the bloody government."

"I have given my word and I will keep it," Richard said stiffly.

Crane nodded then after a few more words of warning Richard was dismissed without further invitation to stay, the farmer only commanding him to return when he had fulfilled the instructions.

On the way back Richard felt empty of all feeling. He couldn't believe what he had done. But he must now keep the bargain. Debra was still out when he reached home so he didn't have to make any excuses especially as he would have to explain another absence to her for the morrow. He was still determined to keep the matter secret from her until it was finally accomplished. Some warning deep inside him alerted him to the possibility he might still change his mind before all could be finalised.

She was surprised when on the morrow he said he had a journey to make to Wigan.

"Why Wigan, is it something serious?" she asked, anxiety evident in her voice. "It isn't more trouble with the government?"

"No, love, just some routine business, nothing to worry about," he answered.

"I am worried because you haven't been yourself for a day or two. You will tell me if anything is wrong won't you, we have always shared everything. You aren't going to see a physician are you?"

He laughed then. "I am perfectly healthy and definitely not in need of a physician. No this only concerns business and I promise I will tell you everything when I return. I shall be as quick as I can."

"Get a lift there, it's a long walk, someone will surely be going. Or you should hire a horse," she said, holding onto his arm.

"I'll find a lift," he said, though he had no intention of doing so, wanting the long walk to calm his spirits and put his thoughts in order.

He took the path by the river Douglas. There was talk about making the river navigable between Wigan and the coast but so far nothing had been done though it would greatly benefit the people of the area. As he walked he prayed. The Latin prayers always calmed his spirits. There was nothing to stop him continuing with the prayers he had always said, spoken silently in his head, nor making silent worship to the God he had always known. He would subscribe to the law and make his statutory attendances at the parish church, but his private worship would remain the same in his heart and no-one would ever know what was not spoken. He was determined that the fact of becoming an Anglican parishioner would not change him though he would never do as some Catholics did when they were forced to attend the parish church, put cotton wool in their ears. That would be hypocrisy, it was still Divine worship. Neither could he bring himself to destroy his missal and Catholic artefacts but though he would never again keep them, everything would be given to his mother and brother Eddy.

He had formed his resolutions by the time he reached Wigan but his visit to the magistrates was one of the hardest things he had ever had to do. They were not sympathetic but gleeful as they rejoiced, "We are glad you have at last seen the error of your ways, Webster. No doubt this is the doing of your father-in-law Crane."

His hand shook as he signed the oath of allegiance to Queen Anne, his signature crooked and unsteady, praying silently that James Edward Stuart would forgive him. From this time on he must accept Anne as queen and renounce all hopes for a Catholic king in the "Pretender." His mind travelled back to when as a small boy he had asked his mother what the oath of allegiance was and when she had explained it to him he had said, "Will I have to sign it one day?" and she had replied, "I hope you never will."

As he walked home, needing the two hours solitude to calm his emotions, he wondered if he would ever be free of guilt. He would have to bear that guilt in order to give his children the life he had never had, and an inheritance. But at the cost of depriving them of the true faith. He tried to console himself with the possibility that one day in the future there might be a reconciliation of the two faiths when they would worship in unity again and all persecution of Catholics would end.

When he reached home Debra was waiting anxiously. He smiled encouragingly at her and said, "Come and sit here beside me because I have a lot to tell you." Then he told her the whole story from beginning to end. Her face changed from amazement to anxiety to compassion but she said nothing through the long account. Then at last she turned towards him with tears streaming down her face.

"You once said you would give your life for me. Today you have done so, haven't you?"

Chapter 13

1708–12

It was not an easy time. When word got out, and news was disseminated quickly (with a speed that was often astonishing) in a small community where there was little enough of interest, Richard found himself the object of much criticism. Catholics shunned him, feeling that he had betrayed them, even his closest friends keeping out of his way. Will and Betty were out when he called on them. Gossip amongst Protestants tended to centre on the opinion that he had married Debra Crane in the first place in order to benefit from the superior assets of her family. This animosity was an added burden on his own troubled mind.

The worst experience he had to endure was the confrontation with his mother. As soon as he could he went to the cottage and he found her alone, putting a patch on one of Eddy's work shirts and squinting at the stitches, her eyesight not so sharp. She welcomed him warmly, glad to put aside her mending, and they talked generally, she asking about her grandsons and he wanting to know about Eddy's seemingly serious courtship. But he was on edge, only making talk until he could find an opportunity to come to the heart of the matter. Finally he told her what had happened. Marie did not storm and shout, long years of hardship had formed a hard shell around her emotions. She sat silently, her careworn hands clasped in her lap, her eyes devoid of expression, just staring into nothing as if she hadn't heard what he had said. She was silent so long that Richard, sitting uncomfortably opposite her, didn't know whether to speak further and indeed what to say. He felt like running out of the house as he had done when a boy and she had been angry with him.

At last she said, "Is this true? You have left the faith?" her voice so low that he could barely hear. He didn't answer and she said, "You have broken my heart, Dickie," (using his childhood name), "you of all people, the one I relied on. You have broken my heart more than your father ever did."

Richard felt as if his own heart was cracking in two. All his life he had cared for her, supported her, tried to take his father's place. He had done the job all too well. He had broken her heart like his father had done before him. He sat miserably and there was anger now in his mother's voice as she said, "This is all Debra Crane's fault. I told you in the first place that you should not have her, she was not for you. I always knew she would tempt you away from the faith."

"It isn't Debra's fault, you mustn't blame her," he insisted but he knew that indirectly it was true, he had done it for her as well as their children. In order to keep his promise to one of the women he loved he had broken the heart of the other. "Debra would never have asked that of me, she was content with my faith. It is for my sons' inheritance, they are half Cranes after all and as things stand they could never inherit what is rightfully theirs. I have an obligation to do my best for them surely you can understand that, Ma. I have to ensure that when I am no longer here they will not sink back into poverty such as we knew."

"You have sold your soul and betrayed your family and friends for worldly gain." His mother was intransigent. "All the hardship we have tolerated, the sacrifices we have made to keep the true faith alive. All the martyrs who have suffered unspeakable tortures without breaking, no matter how great the temptations have been. All we common folk who have paid money we couldn't afford. You have betrayed them all by your actions. All for a piece of land and a bigger house. Our blessed Lord said, 'Be thou faithful into death and I will give thee a crown of life.' A crown in heaven, not a piece of land. I hope you get no joy from what you have done."

"Ma, that is the cruellest thing you could say to me." He was devastated but Marie's lips were set in a hard line.

"Will you tell Eddy?" he asked.

"No. You can tell him yourself." She stood up and opened the door. She remained there holding the door open and he was forced to leave. He turned to say something more, to plead for her forgiveness, to wait for some farewell, but she had slammed the door in his face.

He couldn't wait to get home to Debra's love and understanding, she was the only one who understood him, who understood the sacrifice he had made and at what cost. He ran part of the way and only when he entered the living room and saw her calmly mixing dough in a bowl while the children played contentedly on the mat with a felt ball did his heart cease its painful hammering. A sense of normality enveloped him and he took her in his arms ignoring the flour on her hands.

"Look at your jacket," she admonished him, and he felt her swollen stomach against him with its promise of another child. Then she saw his face and understood what must have happened. She put the bowl aside and washed her hands then came to sit beside him on the settle. She didn't say anything but leant against him, putting her hand in his and he knew that she shared his grief and lifted the load and that was all that mattered.

The difficulties of the next few weeks were submerged in all the arrangements that had to be made. There were visits with Richard Crane to a lawyer in Ormskirk to settle land transfers and sign deeds. Then he had to find someone to buy his loom and stocks then finally to surrender the lease of the weavers' cottage. A happy event to lighten all this unexpected activity was a safe delivery for Debra of another boy who seemed strong and healthy. They called him William after Debra's paternal grandfather and his friend. He now had three sons to inherit.

A family event in which he could not participate was the marriage of his brother Eddy to Mary Rigby, one of the daughters of a Wrightington blacksmith. He could not attend the secret Catholic marriage at Wrightington Hall and was not invited to the celebrations afterwards so had to be content with sending his good wishes. Mary Rigby was to move in with Eddy so at least he was confident that his mother would be well cared for. But it grieved him that in reconciling Debra's family he had alienated his own.

One attempt at reconciliation he was determined to make and as soon as he had some time he made his way to Will Taylor's house. Betty opened the door, the newest baby on her hip and no friendly smile on her face.

THE YEW AND THE ROSE

"Is Will at home?" he asked.

"He's in the workshop but he doesn't want to see you," she replied curtly.

"Please ask him. It's important, Betty," he pleaded and she reluctantly went back into the house, leaving him standing at the door.

A short time later Will appeared and they stood looking at each other.

"I need to talk to you, Will, don't deny me," Richard said. "Can I come in?"

"The weavers are working on the looms and Betty is busy in the living room," Will replied. He hesitated then said, "Let's go in the yard." He led the way round the back of the house and unfastened the wicket gate into the patch of garden. There was nowhere to sit so they stood.

"I know you are angry with me, Will, and I'm sorry you don't agree with what I've done but for me that is no reason to break up a friendship that has tied us together since we were young boys. We have worked and played together for twenty-five years, shared so much, both happy times and sad. You are the best friend I have ever had and I don't want to lose you. Can't we over-ride what has happened? My circumstances may have changed but I haven't. Will you at least give me the chance to explain?" Will shrugged but remained silent so Richard began to put into words his reasons, a lengthy speech which Will didn't interrupt and from the expression on his face Richard could not tell what he was thinking. He finally concluded, "My feelings haven't changed, I shall always be a Catholic in my heart. But I have three sons now, three sons who are half Cranes and with a just right to their grandfather's inheritance."

"I can see that," Will acknowledged, "but you shouldn't have got entangled with the Cranes in the first place, I warned you against it."

Richard sighed. "Be honest, Will, you have inherited what you have from your grandfather. I was ever only a serving apprentice with nothing of my own but you knew the business would be yours one day and a furnished house with it. George left you a thriving business which is something you can leave to your sons." Will acknowledged this with a nod and Richard took advantage of this by saying, "Can we still be friends, my life would be poorer without you. I want to call our new son William. He will be baptised in the parish church so I know you won't want to be godfather but I would like him to have your name as a token of our long friendship."

Will was struggling with his emotions and Richard could see this and began reminiscing of all the times they had spent together since they had first been introduced as new apprentices when they were ten years old – learning a trade together, playing truant, chasing girls, going to the festivals and the races, drinking in the taverns.

Finally Will broke and took his hand and clasped it. "How about a drink in the Millstone on Sunday night? I don't suppose we shall see as much of each other when you move to Lathom."

"Sounds good to me," Richard smiled. "I'll see you there. But Lathom isn't the end of the world you know, only the next parish. I do hope you will visit us, your children will enjoy a farm and whenever we need linen I shall come to you."

Reconciliation with his friend cheered him enormously. The year was passing and things were now moving ahead. The cottage with its large loom and space for another one together with a stock of yarn was soon snapped up by two sons of the weaver James Heys who wanted to set up on their own and were delighted with the well-kept property.

When the time finally came for them to leave the house both Richard and Debra did so regretfully. It had been their first home and they had known great happiness there. They had first made love in the little bed-chamber on their wedding night and although they had also experienced grief with the loss of their two children it had been a haven of content, small and without luxuries but full of homely touches, evidence of Debra's loving care. For Richard it had been the first place of his own. When he had seen the farmhouse at Lathom it seemed old and shabby and he doubted he would ever feel at home there.

It was an old building of seasoned timber with browning plaster between the closely-set timbers with a huge chimney stack and a steep-pitched roof of thatch, its irregular shape evidence of enlargement over the years. Beside it stood a stable and cow byre with chicken runs and pigsty. A recessed oak door within an archway of clay bricks led into a flagged passageway where a stone bench and iron frame was for the shedding of muddy boots. On one side of the passage a door led into a spacious living room while the door on the other side was the entrance to a large dining kitchen. Along the back of the house was a larder and dairy. The living room had a long low window of tiny glass panes, an ingle-nook fireplace lined with brick and surrounded by a roughly-carved oak mantle, and an oak staircase leading to the upper floor. The kitchen had a wide brick fireplace stacked with blackened cooking pots with an oven beside. The floors in both rooms were flagged and the roof supported by heavy oak beams from which hung iron hooks. The staircase from the living room led to three interconnecting bedchambers, from one of which a ladder led to an attic in the eaves. It was sparsely furnished with a couple of chairs and some joint stools in the living room, an extensive beechwood table with benches in the kitchen which was also supplied with shelves and alcoves for storage. Upstairs there was a truckle bed and an ancient iron-banded chest. Their own few pieces of furniture would fit easily while Richard reckoned he could afford to buy anything further with the money he had received from the sale of his loom and yarn.

At the moment it had a spare unwelcoming aspect but Richard knew that Debra would soon transform it with her loving care. She looked around eagerly and he knew she was already planning in her mind how she could add the little touches of her own creation to make it a home. "Our cushions and curtains will make it look a lot different," she said contentedly and his heart warmed at the eager expression on her face. His own attention was focussed on the expanse of land surrounding the farmhouse, the orchard and then fields of wheat, barley, oats and beans, in actual fact not much for a prosperous farmer but to him a kingdom.

Lathom had none of Dalton's hills and dells. It was almost entirely flat, stretching over an area of six miles up to Ormskirk but there were copses of woodland and the River Tawd and the Ellen brook flowed into the river Douglas which was its northern boundary. It was dominated by the ruins of Lathom House, Lord Derby's great medieval fortress which was slighted in the civil war by the Roundheads. The ruins stretched over some fifteen acres, giving an indication of the size and grandeur of this regal edifice. What had not been completely destroyed by Lord Derby's enemies had been further reduced over the last fifty years by locals taking stone for their own building projects. It was still owned by the Stanleys but they had never had enough money to restore it having spent all their time and resources after the war trying to recover the land they had lost, though unable to regain more than half of what they had, and they now resided at Knowsley Hall several miles away. So the majestic ruins stood as a grim reminder of the terrible conflict, still within living memory, and an exciting playground for children.

Richard and Debra now began a life of great content. Debra was in her natural element in the farmhouse and with the duties of a farmer's wife, having helped her mother for so many years. The three boys -Thomas, James and William—were growing up strong and healthy. Richard put his mind and body to learning about farming. Dick Crane had lent him one of his most experienced workers Luke Moorcroft to supervise, and Debra's elder brother John to help and guide him. Richard learnt quickly as he had done with weaving because he was hard-working, interested and motivated. He never hesitated to ask his father-in-law for advice and Dick Crane was always willing to give it. Although never liking each other they maintained a civil relationship that was adequate for their needs. Richard loved being in the open air all day after having spent twenty-five years in a weaving workshop though he soon came to realise how labour intensive the work was with little free time, especially from spring to autumn. Sundays and festivals were no longer a holiday. If Will came over to see him on a Sunday he would be working in the fields, sowing, planting, hoeing, scything, ploughing with men to help as needed, and the friends would have to talk there, there was no time for a drink in the tavern until darkness fell. During most of the spring and summer festivals Debra would have to leave him working and take the boys in the company of friends or with her mother and Esther. The rare occasions when he could accompany his family were times of great excitement. Esther loved helping to look after the children and her childish ways fitted in with theirs. And Debra was happy to be back on good terms with her family though in deference to Richard she only spent time with them when he was working. But during family celebrations the extended Crane family treated him courteously, acceptance by Dick Crane was justification enough and now the practice of farming bound them together especially as they began to realise how committed and hardworking he was.

The only cloud on the horizon was his mother's unforgiveness. She never welcomed him and when he took her gifts – eggs, butter, a capon – she would never accept them. "I don't want anything that has been gained by apostasy," she said. "I would rather be poor." Richard would occasionally take the boys to visit her on special days like Easter and Christmas and she would be polite enough to them but she never showed any warmth and in the end he had to accept defeat. Another blow to her was the death of her little grandson, Eddy's first-born whom he had named Edward. Richard's condolences went unacknowledged.

It was only a few weeks after she had attended the Easter mass service at Mossborough Hall in the spring of 1712, even though Eddy said she had barely the strength to do so, that she died. She was fifty-seven years old. Richard provided the horse and cart to take the coffin to Upholland church on the twenty-sixth day of April, a day of April showers and sun. Debra didn't go with him as she was carrying another child and the bumping of the cart over the rough roads was not considered wise at this early stage. She kissed him tenderly as he set out, knowing it would be a hard time for him and wishing she could be beside him. Eddy and his wife Mary had decided to walk by themselves and although disappointed Richard knew it was not a particularly long walk from their home in Dalton. His sister Mary and her husband Benet and their three children made their own way from Skelmersdale. Leaving the horse and cart on Church street, Richard was joined by Eddy to help him carry the coffin down the steps to the churchyard, it was surprisingly light but Marie had always been thin and towards the end she was little more than skin and bone.

"She'd just had enough and your leaving the faith was the last straw for her," Eddy said.

Richard felt an unbearable sadness as they laid her in the ground. Marie Webster had not made sixty years but her life had been hard. He had tried to do as much for her as he could but he felt that he had finally added to her burdens. "She never forgave me," he said to his brother.

"You can hardly blame her," Eddy said unsympathetically but his sister Mary laid her hand on his arm. "She always loved you, Richard. I'm sure that in her heart she never stopped loving you. I think she loved you best."

Richard's sorrow continued for a long time but as the seasons of the year passed the child in Debra's womb grew, visible presence of a new life after death. The harvest had been safely gathered in and Richard was at home to welcome into the world his first daughter.

"I'm so glad to have a little girl," Debra said joyfully. She had wanted to give Richard sons but she had borne five boys and was now delighted to have a daughter to dress and indulge with feminine interests. Dick Crane suggested they call the child Anne after the Queen, a positive declaration of their loyalty to the Crown.

"She will be called Mary," Richard said. It was the custom in Catholic families to name the first daughter after the Virgin but it was also general custom to name a child after their grandparents. His mother's name had been Mary and the child would take her place in the family. The child brought him hope, a new life after a death.

It was a happy Christmas. Richard was now forty-two years old. Seated in his own house after a year of productive and fulfilling labour with his family around him, three healthy boys and a little daughter, he felt that he had done what he could for them and they would have something better in their childhood than he had had. The farmhouse, made comfortable and beautified by Debra's work, the beams hung with holly, ivy and laurel and they had even found mistletoe, breathed out a rich strong scent. The table was spread with good wholesome food, for some of the animals had to be killed off as they wouldn't have enough fodder for the winter, and Debra had made wheatbread, butter and cream as well as the usual Yuletide delicacies. Thomas, James, and William were playing on the rug before the log fire with some farm animals he had got one of the carpenters' apprentices to carve for them while Mary slept peacefully in her cradle, her face rosy and content with the suckling she had just received from her mother. Richard believed that Debra grew more beautiful with motherhood and farm living, her serene face with a healthy glow beneath the thick coils of her chestnut hair, a little plumper with her full breasts straining against the laces of her gown. He had got Robert Fairclough the tailor to make a new gown for her from a fine piece of blue linen that he had bought from Will and which he had then taken to the print shop in Ormskirk to have a pattern of green leaves block-printed onto it, a new fashion that had finally travelled north from London. He thought back to the Christmas after his father left and the nadir of their poverty and was glad his children would have something better. But he was always aware of what it had cost him, and the loss of his Catholic worship with the reassuring familiarity of the rituals never ceased to trouble him. Just as he had to face the fact that in reconciling Debra and their children to her family he had to alienate his own, he was forced to acknowledge that in trying to give them a better life materially he had robbed them of their Catholic faith which also should have been their birthright.

Chapter 14

1715–24

Though Richard had renounced his Catholic faith, his work schedule released him from the necessity to often attend the parish churches, there always being something to do on the farm on Sundays and feast days, though Debra took the children. Since signing the oath of allegiance the children had been baptised in the Anglican church, either Ormskirk parish church or Douglas chapel which was nearer but there was not always a clergyman in attendance there. However because of Will's continuing friendship he was always aware of developments in the Catholic circle and the Jacobites had not given up hope. Queen Anne died in 1714 and though she had borne seventeen children none had lived and she left no heir. Catholic hopes were renewed for King James's son, James Edward Stuart whom Jacobites called King James III. However the Act of Settlement decreed that no Catholic should ever wear the crown of England. Consequently the succession passed to a distant cousin, the German prince George of Hanover who was crowned King George I even though he spoke no English. This did not seem right to those calling themselves Jacobites. By the time George of

Hanover landed in England the Jacobites were already planning an invasion by their King James III. Once again the Catholic gentry of Lancashire played a prominent part and meetings were held secretly in inns and taverns sympathetic to the cause. A favourite ditty bandied around, said to be written by a Lancashire man and blatantly ambiguous, was -

> "God bless the King, I mean our faith's Defender,
> God bless, no harm in blessing, the Pretender,
> But who Pretender is and who is King,
> God bless us all, that's quite another thing."

From past experience Richard guessed what would be happening and Will let slip some covert remarks. He knew he had to distance himself from his old friends and buried himself in work on the farm, making excuses to keep away from Will and increasing his rare attendances at Ormskirk church. But he couldn't help feeling fearful for what his former friends might be up to.

The secret rebellion however needed time in preparing and it was the following year before plans were completed. The first rising took place in Scotland where the Earl of Mar raised an army of Stuart supporters. However as they began their march south they were relying on the Jacobites of Lancashire who had promised to join them with a force of at least 20,000 men. When the Scots army with white cockades in their hats reached Lancaster a service was held in St. Mary's Priory church. They then proceeded to Preston where a proclamation was issued that *"George Elector of Brunswick has usurped and taken upon himself the title of King of these realms and James the Third by reason of the right of the first-born son and the laws of this land did immediately after his father's decease become our only and lawful liege."* Many of the local gentry joined the army at Preston and the town resounded with cries of *"God save the King."* All this was well known in Ormskirk and Standish and the villages inbetween and people waited with bated breath to see what would happen, Protestants and Catholics taking opposing sides. Richard felt that Dick Crane was keeping a close eye on him and though he would never break his given word he couldn't help thinking that if the Jacobite army was successful it might change his destiny again. After the first day's fighting the Jacobites were victorious but on the next day they were forced to surrender to prevent themselves from being hacked to pieces by the superior government forces. The rebellion was over.

More than fifteen hundred Jacobite prisoners were taken, many of them local. The officers were taken to inns in Preston, the rank and file incarcerated in Lancaster castle. In the new year they were brought to trial at Liverpool. Those who weren't sentenced to be executed were sent as slaves to the West Indies, Liverpool merchants taking advantage of the trade and one of them transporting over six hundred himself. The leaders of the rebellion were taken to London to be tried for treason where their appearance raised an outcry of patriotism from the spectators who cried, *"No Popish Pretender. Down with the rebels. Long live King George."* Some, like the Earl of Derwentwater, were executed, some of the Lancashire leaders were given lengthy prison sentences and heavily fined. Out of the ordinary soldiers seven were hanged at Wigan, one of them a weaver.

This event naturally created much local interest. Many people made their way to Wigan to watch the spectacle, some to exult at the downfall of Papist traitors, sympathetic Catholics to grieve at the fate of their brave militants. Will Taylor was one of them and a day or two later he made his way to Richard's farm. Still upset he gave a graphic account to Richard, bitterly condemning those who had laughed and jeered at the victims. Richard refrained from making comment but put his hand on his friend's shoulder in understanding.

"Do you think this is the end for Catholics?" he dared ask.

But Will shook his head. "No I don't. It's a setback, I grant you, but we won't give up. King James is only young, he will marry and have sons to inherit his cause."

The Cranes thought otherwise and Dick Crane was openly jubilant. "Aren't you glad you aren't part of this fiasco?" he asked his son-in-law and Richard was forced to admit to himself that he was relieved he would not share the recriminations that would inevitably result.

However it was a happy year for them as another son was born, he now had four sons to ensure a livelihood for.

"Let's call him Richard again," Debra said, "I want one of our sons to have your name." They wondered if they might be tempting fate but he appeared strong and healthy. For a time it brought to mind the loss of their first-born but Dick Crane was pleased by the decision. He had four grandsons now to inherit the land he had given to Richard and justified his action. Debra thrived with her growing family, she loved having the children around her and was proud to have given her husband four sons while the rearing of her little girl was a delight.

Richard was becoming increasingly familiar with the complexities of farming. The years followed the pattern of farming life dictated by the seasons, seed time, lambing, ploughing, reaping, threshing with some respite in winter when there was little to do but hedging and ditching. This however was the time for doing repairs, to the farmhouse and to the tools and implements and to ensuring that the horses and such animals that were kept through the winter did not starve. The looked-for festivals corresponded with the seasons, Easter, May Day, Whitsun, Harvest, Yuletide. Richard worked long hours but he had always done so and he loved being out in the open air, even in the worst weather. He employed labourers depending on the time of the year and what work had to be done but much of it he did himself and he knew every yard of his land and what had to be done with it. The early months of the year were for ploughing, hard slow work for the ground had to be ploughed three times before it was ready for the next crop and then heavily manured. Springtime was for sowing, best before the rain, harrowing best after it had rained, everything needed much organisation. Heavy clods of earth had to be broken up first then the seed scattered by hand, evenly so that none was wasted, and this was skilful work. Afterwards the harrow with its wooden prongs made sure the seeds were lightly covered by the earth. By early summer weeds and thistles were rife and boys were needed to help weed, while any cattle had to be watched so they didn't stray and hedges and fences well kept. June was a busy month for those who kept sheep and July for haymaking, long hours when help again was needed from occasional labourers, often those whose work was also weaving, and they had to be provided with food and drink. The corn harvest followed immediately after and as well as working from dawn till dusk there was the fear of storms that could ruin everything so that when the weather was fine the work was non-stop. The farmer himself had to watch his workers closely to ensure the corn was cut cleanly and tied securely into sheaves. Then the fields were full of carters with heavy loads being taken to the barns. Afterwards the harvesters had to be rewarded with food and drink and entertainment and the farmers were only too glad to do this once they could see their harvest safely gathered in.

Debra had been born and reared on a farm so the organisation of the farmhouse came naturally to her. Besides looking after her growing family she saw to the dairy, (the making of cheese and butter), the baking of bread, brewing, cooking their own meat, preserving and salting, looking after the poultry, the orchard, the herb garden with its usefulness both for cooking and for medicines. She had a young maid to help, who cost only a small wage and her meals, and Richard's labourers to do the heavy work, so that it left her some time to do needlework and make scented potions, usually in the evenings. Her sister Esther sometimes came to help her with the children. She liked to make her weekly visits to Ormskirk market to buy what they could not produce themselves and now she had a horse again she could pay visits to her mother and her many relatives. She was well-known in the area and approved for her kindly manner and her generosity. It was a typical life for a farmer's wife and Debra embraced it joyfully, her greatest satisfaction coming from making Richard's life as comfortable as she could. Their happiest times were when they could be alone together in the evenings, talking or reading a little. Richard had bought books on husbandry and one day in the booksellers in Ormskirk he had seen a book by Thomas Culpeper, whose Herbal had been one of George Taylor's precious books, entitled 'A Directory for midwives'. Written for all women it covered not only the subject of birth itself but married life, the rearing of children, health and diet, and he had bought it for Debra who was slowly working her way through it. Sometimes they would just sit companionably together by the fire in winter or in the orchard on summer nights when work was done, knowing that as soon as they wished they could escape to their bedchamber.

Richard loved watching his sons grow and knowing they had a life that he could never have dreamt of as a child. As they grew older they helped in the fields scaring birds which they tried to hit with their slings and picking stones which were then used to build walls. But it was play for them, seeing who could hit a bird or pick the biggest stones, they could stop when they wanted and it was their own land. They were not having to work for a penny a day under supervision on someone else's land as their father had done. They were fond of their grandfather and it was a regular cry, "We're off to Grandpa's farm. He lets us ride on the plough horses." They were unaffected by Richard Crane's harsh manner and when he shouted at them they only laughed. Despite his brusqueness he had an affection for them.

"He's much more tolerant of them than he ever was to us," Debra laughed but she was glad of it, glad that he liked his grandsons for the inheritance he had bequeathed to Richard had in reality been for them.

Will Taylor and Betty sometimes came to visit but they didn't see each other so often as Richard had little free time. Will didn't envy his friend's good fortune so much when he saw how hard he had to work.

"I would rather have my Sundays off and free time to go to festivals. Weaving might be tedious but it isn't really hard work and I can stop when I like," he said.

Betty was envious of the larger farmhouse and the more comfortable furnishings that Debra created but said, "How can you bear to live with all these horrible smells surrounding you," wrinkling her nose at the all-pervading stink of pigs, horses, cattle, hens and manure. She preferred her neat little garden patch behind their house to the often muddy farmyard with its collection of farm tools, wheelbarrows and clucking hens. But they always went home with a generous selection of farm produce.

Debra was expecting another child as she usually did every two years or so, as was normal when women were suckling their infants. It was another girl and she was glad as Mary was now five years old and out of babyhood. She was named Ellen and was baptised at Douglas chapel on a warm day in August when the harvest was being gathered in. She was followed at Christmas two years later by another son who was taken to be christened at Douglas chapel on a snowy day in Yuletide. They decided to give him the name John again after their second son who had died in that sad period of their lives almost fifteen years ago. But by Easter the second little John had died to the great sorrow of all the family. It was the first time the children had faced death personally and they were devastated at the loss of their little brother. Their sad parents had to explain to them how they themselves had lost brothers and sisters when they were young and they must believe that John had gone to Heaven together with the two elder brothers they had never known.

As well as the loss of his son Richard suffered another family tragedy that year by the death of his brother Edward. He was only forty-two years old but he had never been strong and their mother had always thought she might lose him as a child. The tragedy was more poignant in that Edward's wife Mary was expecting another child and their son James was born two months after his father's death. Richard was sad that his brother had never reconciled himself to his leaving the Catholic faith and their relationship had been cool and he vowed he would do what he could for his widow and her little child.

His own son John's place in the family was later taken by another child, another girl to Debra's delight and whom Richard was determined should be given her name. Mary who was ten years old was delighted to have two little sisters to look after, boasting to her four brothers that there were now three girls to challenge their superiority and they might soon be equalled. In her devotion to her baby sisters she reminded Richard of his own sister Mary when she was a child. His sister seemed happy with her husband and her own growing family and periodically Richard would send her gifts from the farm.

Then came the second tragedy to disturb what had become a happy comfortable existence as the following April one year old Debra died.

"We had been doing so well," her mother wept. Now the last two of their children had died, both at the joyful time of Easter, whereas the preceding five had all lived and were growing up strong and healthy. The eldest boys were now attending school in Parbold. A philanthropic yeoman called Richard Durning had left money for the building of a school when he died in 1693 as well as other behests to the poor and for a preaching minister to service Douglas chapel.

"April is a cruel month," Richard said. His mother had died in April and his little brother James as well as their latest son and daughter. It seemed particularly ironic that when they had survived harsh winters they should be struck down when spring burgeoned with promise of new life.

Debra was inconsolable. "She was becoming a real little person with her own special ways. It wouldn't be quite so bad if she had died at birth, before I had time to know her and love her and now I miss her so much."

However life went on and after mourning their loss they had to acknowledge that it was part of the pattern of life that was hard and often difficult to understand. Many of their friends and neighbours lost children, Will and Betty had now lost two, there were so many diseases that were fatal when the children had not yet built up strength to withstand them. Ellen was still only five years old and her mother watched over her anxiously, helped by the loving care of her sister Mary.

Another death touched the family personally when Debra's sister Esther died. She was thirty-seven years old. She had been such a help in looking after the Webster children and they were sad at the loss of their gentle kindly aunt who had often joined their company at the farm. Debra was particularly affected by the loss of her only sister who had never been quite as others were and had never married. She had never been a companion but her quiet presence had been taken for granted in the Crane family and they were all fond of her. For the first time Richard realised how important Dick Crane had thought it for Debra to make a good marriage as she was his only marriageable daughter. Her father did not survive her long. A short time later Richard Crane was dead having suffered a seizure while working. The loss of this powerful irascible man was incalculable to all his family and the great number of people who attended the large funeral was a testimony to the respect he had gained. By his death Richard increased his land holdings as his father-in-law had promised and though most of his inheritance was passed to his two sons John and James Richard found his land doubled in size. His widow Sarah was now bereft after losing both her husband and her daughter Esther whose care for both had provided the sole purpose of her life. Richard and Debra offered her a home with them but she chose to live with her elder son John who was now married and would take over their farmhouse. She herself would only live for another three years.

Debra was expecting another child and was filled with foreboding. "There have been so many deaths recently," she said anxiously to Richard.

"It's because we are all getting older, love. It happens sometimes that deaths seem to come in a crowd. Look how many of us are still alive, you have two brothers with growing families and I have a sister. We have four healthy sons and two daughters, we have good friends and you have a lot of cousins."

"I'm afraid this time."

Richard held her close. He knew women were usually afraid when the time drew near for their confinement, it was a dangerous time and a high proportion of women died. He was always afraid for Debra but he tried never to let his fears show and spoke reassuringly to her, "All will be well you'll see. You are strong and healthy and have always borne your children safely. You are anxious because there have been so many losses lately but I'm sure there will be no more deaths just now."

"But I have never been afraid before and that frightens me," she whispered, holding onto him. "I don't want to leave you. I mustn't leave you with the children."

He was desperately afraid but he soothed her, "You won't leave me darling, we are too closely glued together. Recent events have made you anxious but it is needless, you must believe that. It will soon be over."

It was a hot summer after several wet ones and Debra felt the heat intensely. The birth was scheduled for August. There were fevers about and people were worried. In July Ellen died just before her seventh birthday. The shock hit the family like a thunderbolt and they were all distraught. One moment their little sister was running about, always happy and playful though a little wary of her boisterous older brothers and reliant on her elder sister, and the next minute she was tossing and turning on her bed while her mother soaked her with cold cloths and her siblings tiptoed about fearfully. A physician was brought speedily but there was nothing he could do and for Richard it brought to mind the unexpected death of his brother James in similar circumstances. She died with Debra holding her in her arms and her mother's grief was terrible to watch as Richard tried to do what he could for his shocked and frightened children. They all went with their father to take the small coffin to Ormskirk church while Debra wept at home, comforted by her brother John's wife. Everyone thought grief would bring on her labour as she cried over and over again, "I thought she was safely grown. She had a character of her own, how could she die now. It would have been her seventh birthday soon and we were planning a special treat for her." The loss of another child increased her apprehension about the forthcoming birth and when Richard returned from the sad little funeral he found her lying on the bed weeping. He had never seen her like this before, she was always so calm, always so hopeful, always busy.

"We have lost our last three children. What is happening to us?" she cried desperately to Richard. "I carry them for nine months with all the discomfort, I suffer all the pain of bringing them into the world, I grow to love them so much and then they are taken away from me."

Richard was filled with despair as he didn't know how to comfort her. "I don't know why, darling. I don't carry them or bear them but believe me I suffer with you. I would do anything in my power to spare you this grief. We must pray that all will be well and put a brave face on so that the children will not be more troubled than they already are."

The death of Ellen left a big gap in their lives because as the youngest they had all indulged her. Thomas was now nearly eighteen with James sixteen and William fourteen, all of them working full time now with their father on the farm. Mary was twelve and learning the skills of housewifery while Richard at ten attended the school in Parbold.

THE YEW AND THE ROSE

It was harvest time, the busiest time of the year for a farmer and Richard was away in the fields when Debra began her labour, a labour that was short and trouble-free. As she rid herself of the child and heard its first cry she experienced a wave of exultation that swept away all her fears and apprehensions. She was alive, feeling on top of the world and the child was a girl with a strong pair of lungs.

"Such a healthy little maid, she'll turn your household upside down," the midwife-neighbour cried with satisfaction.

When Richard was brought from the fields he found Debra smiling and happy. She didn't look as if she had given birth to their twelfth child. For the hundredth time he thought how amazing she was. She was strong, a farmer's daughter who had been reared on fresh air and healthy food. But more than that, she was strong in mind and spirit, a characteristic he had recognised when he first met her. She had borne twelve children, half of whom had died, but to him she was as beautiful at forty-five years old as the day he first saw her. Her rich brown hair hung loose over her shoulders and her serene face was aglow with happiness, tiny lines crinkling around her laughing hazel eyes.

"Take hold of her," she said, handing him the swaddled bundle.

"You know Deb, I'm too old for this. I'm well past fifty," he said.

"Then you should stop making love to me," she said smiling mischievously.

"Easier to stop breathing," he replied smiling back at her. They had been married for twenty-five years and the years had drawn them closer together through the vicissitudes of joy and grief, they were as one, they understood each other instinctively, their thoughts coalesced without need for explanation.

"But I'll be an old man when she's growing up," he said regretfully.

If she does grow up was the thought passing through their minds but they dismissed it in the joy of having a new life that was a product of their love.

"Then you'll have had a lot of experience." She looked at him fondly. He was stouter, his hair grey at the temples and his face ruddy with spending all his time out of doors but he was still the handsomest man she had ever known.

"Don't you think she's beautiful?" she asked.

"Yes she is." The little face was smooth without puckers and wrinkles, a fuzz of fair down on her head. She opened her eyes and looked at him. Debra had told him that newborn infants couldn't focus but she kept her eyes seemingly on his face.

He laughed. "She's weighing me up to see if I'm good enough for her."

He was middle-aged yet he felt he had a lot to give her – a comfortable home, a loving family, enough money to ensure she was well fed and clothed, a respectable place in local society.

"What shall we call her?" he asked. "Do you want to give her Ellen's name, she's come to take her place."

"No, nobody could take Ellen's place, she was a person in her own right and I want to remember her as such. This baby is her own little self. And I don't want to tempt fate. Can we call her Sarah after my mother?" Debra asked. Sarah Crane had died the year before. But Debra felt convinced that this child would live and grow up and an exhilarating happiness overcame her. Richard looked at her lovingly and shared her confidence for the future.

Sarah she was to be named. She would be their last child.

Epilogue

October 1744

Sarah Webster stood before the altar in the little medieval stone chapel by the side of the river Douglas near Parbold. With a long history of intermittent worship it sat on a slight rise surrounded by green gently-undulating hills which could be seen through the leaded window behind the altar with its simple wooden cross. It was a chilly October afternoon but Sarah was warm with happiness and excitement and her apple-green wedding gown festooned with yellow satin bows was of the softest finest wool. Her shining chestnut hair flowing around her shoulders and falling almost to her waist had a garland of interweaving green and yellow ribbons for there weren't many flowers still blooming in October. She thought her heart would burst with joy. She was twenty-one years old and marrying the man she loved, Robert Halliwell a husbandman farming land in Parbold. Her father would have liked him, been pleased with her choice for the Halliwells were a large farming family in the area. If only he could have been here to see her married.

But her eldest brother Thomas was there in his place. He was forty years old now and head of the family and

Sarah had lived with him and his wife and family in the farmhouse. All her brothers were married with families of their own. She turned to look at them, all handsome and dressed in their Sunday best – Thomas, James, William and Richard (Tom, Jamie, Will and Dickie to her), all farming land in Newburgh, Lathom and Dalton. Only her sister Mary was absent, at home in Bickerstaffe where she lived with her husband Jervis Smith, a farmer's son, because she was near her time with her third child. The little church was full and she was surrounded by family and friends, some of the Websters, her Crane relatives, and the Halliwells who were accepting her into their midst.

Sarah turned to smile at her brothers and they looked at her with affection. This little sister of theirs whom they had always known as "the little un" had their mother's shining brown hair, wide hazel eyes, an expression of gentle calm that could easily break into laughter. She was a constant reminder of their mother.

Debra had died when Sarah was fourteen. All the remaining six of her children had gathered in their parents' bedchamber in the farm to bid her farewell, clinging to each other for support and trying not to cry so as not to distress her for she lay calm and sleepy with the draught of poppy juice, her face with an expression of serenity as she managed a smile for them, assuring them of her love. Then their father had ushered them outside and closed the door. As they clustered together on the other side of the door they could hear him weeping. "Don't leave me, Deb. Please don't leave me." They had been married for nearly forty years.

He had been unable to exist without her. In less than a year he had died and they laid him beside her in

Ormskirk churchyard. He was sixty-nine years old. He had died a respected farmer, well-known in the countryside of Lathom, Newburgh and Dalton and appreciated for his hard work, his kindness and his generosity to those less fortunate. And not least a good father to his children. How she had loved him and how he had adored her, she suspected she was his favourite, his last child. She thought of him now and wished he could have been here with her mother, his beloved Debra, beside him on the day the last of their children married.

Sarah felt a touch on her arm and turned to look at Robert Halliwell with a smile. How handsome he was and how she loved him as much as she knew he loved her. He took her hand and they made their vows. It was a marriage that was pleasing to all and she knew they would be happy together in the farmhouse in Parbold. Parbold was where her father had begun his life but he had given them a better start in life than he had had. His life had begun in poverty and loss but he had given her a happy comfortable upbringing and the means to make a good marriage. In a year she would give Robert a son to join with the children of her brothers and sisters, grandchildren her father and mother would not know but a new beginning, a new generation.

Marie's petition to the magistrates at Wigan, dated October 1678

To ye Right Worpll his Maties Justices of the
peace and Quorum at ye Quarter Sessions of the
peace held at Wigan the 14th day of October 1678.
The humble petition of Mary Webster wife of Edward
Webster of Parbold and her ffower children
Humbly sheweth.

That yor petrs husband Edward Webster haueing
left her and fower smale children and gone to Mary
land not leaueing yor petr and her children
any thing to Mainteine themselues who
are Ready to Starue for want of Releife

May it therfore please yor good Worpps
to Order yor petr and her ffower children
some Speedy Releife and yor petr as in duty
bound will euer pray &c.

The Removal order from Lathom to Dalton of John Webster and Thomas Swift on the orders of Robert Crane, dated 1671.

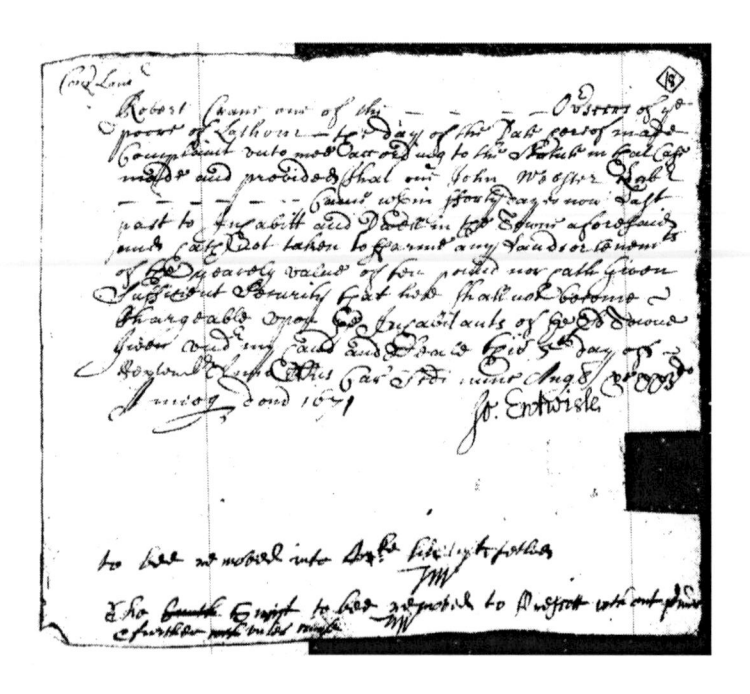

My grandfather William Webster,
a kind, religious, handsome man
who was part of my childhood
was the great-great-great-great-grandson
of Richard and Debra.

Author's note

It has taken me twenty-five years to write this book. I have spent hours and hours trailing through the church registers of Upholland, Ormskirk, Eccleston, Croston, Standish, Lathom chapel and Douglas chapel as well as official records and magistrates' proceedings in Preston records office, the Recusants lists, maritime records, American records of the early settlers and a journey to St. Mary's city in Maryland U.S.A.

The substance and main narrative of the book is true.

However it is a history of 350 years ago and some things are impossible to verify.

It is impossible to find Catholic baptisms and marriages which took place privately in Catholic Halls with secret chapels and for which no records are extant. Therefore these dates have to be surmised from other sources. Also there are large gaps in Anglican church registers, notably Ormskirk and Upholland, just when I needed them. Some of these are a result of the Civil War when records were either not kept or were destroyed. Lathom chapel and Douglas chapel were not in use all the time.

There is no record of births or marriages of many of Richard Webster's family who were Catholics but other records can provide enough information to make an educated guess. There is no record of a birth for Debra Crane, though there is for many of her family, and this most probably occurred in a gap in Ormskirk registers and therefore can provide a clue.

The only children documented in the family of Richard and Debra are John (2), Debra, Ellen, Richard and Sarah. However from the closeness of the known births and the fact that Debra was still having children when she had turned 40 I reckon they must have had 10–12 children during their long marriage. On information from the next generation I have guessed at Thomas, James and William. All these are family names of both the Websters and the Cranes. It is also inconceivable that Richard should not have called a daughter Mary, after his mother as was custom and also as a Catholic. There is a Mary Webster of the right age and place who marries a local man Jervis Smith in 1734. Other children as well as two Johns, Debra and Ellen (whose deaths are documented) probably died, infant mortality being high as church registers show.

There is no record of when Edward Webster died in Maryland but it must have been before the end of his time of service to Mark Cordea because his name does not appear in the land registers of Maryland colonists which it would have done and by 1705 his wife is calling herself a widow.

There is no definite proof that the John Turner who shared a passage with Edward Webster on the 'Nathaniel' bound for Boston from Barbados was a member of the Catholic weaving Turner family from Parbold but I think it highly likely.

It is impossible to discover where Richard Webster served his apprenticeship as a weaver but he would definitely have done so. The Taylors were a weaving family in Dalton and slightly related to the Aspinwalls in Richard's family so I chose them.

Will Taylor is my invention but Richard would certainly have had a friend who was a weaver and a Catholic.

I am not certain when Richard changed his religion and although I prefer the earlier date as I have given it, it could have been later, perhaps after the failed Jacobite rebellion of 1715, but he was definitely not a Catholic by 1717. There is no proof that Crane was behind it but I think it likely, he would have been concerned for his grandsons who as Catholics would not have been able to inherit his lands.

I have spent years building up a picture of the inhabitants of Parbold, Dalton, Upholland, Lathom, Newburgh, Wrightington, Skelmersdale and the surrounding areas at this time, making myself familiar with the families and their inter-relationships and also their occupations which are sometimes noted in the church registers and in the recusants lists. Consequently the surnames, the places of residence and the occupations are taken from contemporary records.

Christian names are more difficult to identify.
In the first place there was a very small selection of names in use. Masculine names were limited to John

(most popular), Thomas, Richard, Edward, James, Henry, George and Robert with the occasional Nicholas, Roger, Peter and Brian. Other names were a novelty. Mary, Elizabeth, Anne, Ellen, and Margaret dominate the girls' names. Less common are Dorothy, Alice, Katherine, Cecily, Jane and Isobel. In Protestant families are found Sarah, Esther, Susanna, Judith and one would expect the similar Debra though I only found one other instance of the name.

Secondly, families used the same names over and over again. A child was usually called first after its grandparents then its parents, then after other members of the family or even close friends. When a child died another child was given the same name. Hence constant repetition. When you consider that every family had an average of ten children, in three generations there would be hundreds of people all closely related and all sharing a small pool of names. Catholic girls were always called Mary with Anne as second favourite though the names were not restricted to Catholics.

Because names run in families it is possible to identify various family groups. Identification of family groups is also helped by occupations because most people worked together in families. The children of artisans and craftsmen followed them, agricultural labourers rarely bettered themselves. Every trade is represented in the area at this time because the villages were self-supporting though the majority worked on the land with also a high proportion of weavers. However despite having other jobs many people also spent time working on the land to supplement their income and this sometimes makes identification difficult as for example you can find someone with the same name classed as a labourer in one record and a tanner in another.

When places of residence are given it is a great help in identifying people with the same name, Upholland registers often give residence as does Eccleston. People at this time did not generally move about, there were strict laws governing residence. However because of the uncertainties of boundaries in this area Dalton is sometimes given as Upholland and vice versa, Parbold and Wrightington are interchangeable while Ormskirk often only differentiates between the town itself and 'the parish' which could mean Lathom, Newburgh, Burscough, Bickerstaffe and Skelmersdale. Also a particular problem in this area is that people used 3–4 parish churches and 2 chapels, whichever was most convenient at a time, and you find members of the same family being baptised, married or buried in different churches which confuses the fact of residence.

So bearing in mind the small number of Christian names in use and their constant repetition it is not easy to be absolutely sure of Christian names and I have sometimes had to make guesses and even invent names on the pattern of names popular within a family. It is not certain, though likely, that Marie's mother was Ellen, that the child who died was called James, that Edward's brother was Thomas, and that Debra's mother was Sarah, it could have been Esther.

The background of the story is authentically portrayed as for many years I have been a social and political historian of the 17th century. Lancashire was the most Catholic county in England and west Lancashire the most Catholic area within the county. Parbold, Mawdesley and Wrightington had more Catholics than anywhere else in England. They were actively involved in Catholic plots and in Jacobite resistance and I wanted to portray what these national events would have meant to ordinary working people.

The lives of the poor and the ordinary working people of the 17th century are scantily documented. Apart from church registers the only time they come to be worthy of notice is when they are in trouble with the authorities. However social histories of the period give general information on living and working conditions. A unique document is the diary of Roger Lowe, a young Ashton shop-keeper living at the same time as Richard Webster, which gives an insight into the type of pleasures and leisure activities that were available for working people. Because my imagination feels at home in the 17th century I use a lot of simple common sense to recreate how they must have done things and how they felt, enriched by many years playing an active role in historical re-enactments of life at this time.

The seasons of the year and festivals of the church were much more important than they are today and provided most of the recreation for working people. They are well documented in books of folklore and country festivals and in the contemporary poems of Robert Herrick. Living in Italy in a quiet valley that has changed little over the centuries, where contadini have worked on the land for generations, where the church festivals and the progression of the seasons mark the year, where their recollections tell of a life similar to the 17th century, gives me an insight into a world long past in England.

The geography is one of the most difficult aspects of the 17th century to imagine today before the M6, the railway, the canal and the quarries cut up the peaceful landscape, before Wrightington Hall became a famous hospital and Skelmersdale an overflow for Liverpool. Skelmersdale with its Viking origin was a quiet little hamlet set in pleasant countryside, the river Douglas was the only waterway, Appley Bridge not much more than a bridge across the river, Upholland an ancient little village surrounded by farms, Dalton a place of woods, streams, rolling hills without Ashurst's beacon and a golf course. But even today Dalton, Lathom and the upper reaches of Parbold are still characterised by tranquil dales and wooded glens, wide vistas and rich farmland. I am familiar with the area, it is my home ground and I have spent much time exploring the paths and trackways they would have known and estimating how long it would have taken them to walk from one place to another, using not our modern roads but their intimate knowledge of a landscape then unspoilt.

That a lot of working people at this time could read and write is a fact. Literacy increased dramatically during the 17th century when Grammar schools were established in most of the towns. Working people would not normally be eligible for these but there were little schools and dame schools even in villages. Adam Martindale had a school in Upholland church during the civil war and from his own account we know that village children attended, and Richard Durning established one in Parbold later in the century which is still in existence. Catholics had their own tutors, often priests working undercover, and lessons were usually open to the local Catholic children as a way of teaching them Catholic doctrine. Working people were probably only semi-literate because if they did attend a school it would only be sporadically when they were not needed for other things, in fact Adam Martindale makes this complaint. But most of them could at least write their name as witnessed by the church registers and other documents. Marie Webster signed her petition to the magistrates at Wigan and Edward Webster witnessed a will in Barbados. People were taught to read first then to write afterwards so this presupposes they could make an attempt at reading, even with difficulty. Unfortunately this asset did not continue into the next two centuries and we have to get to the 20th century before working people went to school again and learnt to read and write.

Because there was no standardised speech at this time everyone spoke with local accents, including the gentry and the nobility. When a 'yokel' in a novel speaks in a broad country accent it is acceptable to write the dialogue phonetically to emphasize its peculiarity. But everyone in this book would have spoken with broad Lancashire accents, including the Dicconsons, Standishes and Lord Derby. If I had written phonetically it would have been understood only by a few people and then with difficulty so in the interests of comprehension I have written standard English which is not how it would have sounded at the time.

Lightning Source UK Ltd.
Milton Keynes UK
UKOW02f1100281016
286316UK00001B/3/P